"Then die!" shouted Magua. . . .

Twigs crackled under his feet and logs tripped him, but that was all fun and exciting. It led him on, and he walked further to where the light was dimmer, and trees crouched nearer and nearer, and holes looked like ugly mouths on either side.

At the same instant he spoke, he violently hurled his tomahawk at her. The axe cleaved the air in front of Heyward, and, cutting some of the flowing ringlets of Alice's hair, quivered in the tree above her head.

The sight maddened Duncan to desperation. Collecting all his energies in one effort he snapped the twigs that bound him and rushed upon another savage, who was preparing, with a more deliberate aim, to repeat the blow. They grappled and fell to the earth together. Heyward was unable to get a firm hold on the naked body of his adversary. The Huron glided from his grasp and rose with one knee on his chest, pressing him down with the weight of a giant. Duncan saw the knife gleaming in the warrior's hand above him. . . .

A Note about *The Last of the Mohicans*

For 150 years after the first colonists came to North America from France and England, these two countries struggled with each other for control of the New World. The French and Indian War was the last major clash in this struggle. The conflict is called the French and Indian War because the French enlisted the aid of the Huron Indians to fight the British. This conflict lasted nine years, ending in 1763 with France giving Canada to England. Much of the war was fought in the wilderness around Lake George (Lake Horican) and Lake Champlain in what is now the state of New York. The fighting that took place in this region was the fiercest and most savage of the war.

The fighting was made all the more difficult because the armies had to travel through wilderness just to get to the enemy. Large armies would go into this mountainous region, often returning in skeleton bands. The few remaining soldiers would be exhausted and discouraged by the loss of so many of their companions.

The British eventually won the war. But the outcome of the war was not at all clear in 1757, when this story takes place. A few months before the story begins, a large British army had been disgracefully defeated by a handful of French and Indians. This defeat left a large part of the frontier unprotected from attacks by the French. It also left the British settlers with almost no protection against the Native Americans who threatened them. Fears of these threats became magnified in the imaginations of the colonists so that it seemed as if every gust of wind from the forest carried the terrifying yells of "savages."

JAMES FENIMORE COOPER

THE LAST OF THE
MOHICANS

CANADA
NEW YORK

LAKE
CHAMPLAIN

FORT
WILLIAM
HENRY ■

LAKE
HORICAN

THE
PROVINCE
OF
NEW YORK
1757

HUDSON RIVER

NEW YORK CITY ■

Edited, and with an Afterword,
by Bill Blauvelt

TP THE TOWNSEND LIBRARY

THE LAST OF THE MOHICANS

TP THE TOWNSEND LIBRARY

For more titles in the Townsend Library,
visit our website: **www.townsendpress.com**

Townsend Press, Inc.
1038 Industrial Drive
West Berlin, New Jersey 08091

ISBN 1-59194-032-X

Library of Congress Control Number:
2004105872

TABLE OF CONTENTS

AFTERWORD

CHAPTER I

Late one summer afternoon in 1757, General Webb received disturbing intelligence. He was told that Montcalm, a French general, had been seen moving south on Lake Horicon with an army as "numerous as the leaves on the trees." The Indian runner who brought this information also brought a request from Colonel Munro, the British commander of Fort William Henry on Lake Horican. Munro had only a small number of soldiers at Fort William Henry and could not possibly hope to stop the large French army that was advancing with Montcalm. He urgently requested that General Webb send him a large number of reinforcements—3,000 or more if possible.

At Fort Edward, on the banks of the Hudson River, General Webb had more than 5,000 men at his command. Fort William Henry lay fifteen miles to the north. Webb knew that he could get reinforcements to Munro in a day's time.

Shortly after General Webb received the request, he issued orders that a detachment of 1,500 men was to depart at dawn for Fort William Henry. Soon the noises of the troops preparing to march the next morning filled the air, covering the bubbling sounds of the Hudson River. The less experienced soldiers rushed anxiously about while the more experienced soldiers appeared calm as they got ready. But their eyes showed that they did not look forward to the dreaded warfare of the wilderness. As darkness settled over the area, the sounds of preparation faded. The trees cast their deep shadows over the rippling waters of the river. Soon the camp was as silent as the deep forest that surrounded it.

Just as day began to reveal the shaggy outlines of the tall pines by the river, the rattling echoes of the warning drums broke the silence of the night. The heavy sleep of the army was broken. In an instant the whole camp was in motion. Every soldier in the encampment was hurrying back and forth. Some were preparing to march into the wilderness toward Fort William Henry. Those not going were rushing to witness the departure of their comrades and to share in the excitement of the hour.

Before the rays of the sun softened the gray light of morning, the column of 1,500 soldiers, along with the horse-drawn wagons carrying their equipment, began its march. The drums rolled, and the fifes played. Many of the soldiers had not been in battle before. But their fears and uncertainties were masked in the show of high military bearing. Those who remained behind watched with admiration as the column was swallowed up by the dark forest.

Tranquility settled over the camp again. But in front of General Webb's quarters, there were signs of preparation for another, much smaller departure. Six horses waited patiently in front of the cabin. One of the horses was an impressive military steed belonging to an officer.

A small group of soldiers, having nothing better to do, stood at a distance admiring the horses. One man in this group seemed different from the rest. He was not a soldier. He wore a sky-blue coat and close-fitting yellow trousers. He wore a spur on one of his boots. His physical appearance made him look awkward – his head was large but his shoulders narrow, his arms long and dangling but his hands small and almost delicate. He wore a hat with the brim turned up in three places. It gave his good-natured face a sense of dignity and trust.

This oddly dressed man was also different from the rest of the group in that he did not keep his distance while admiring the horses. He walked boldly to the officer's horse. After examining it, he exclaimed, "I have seen a lot of horses, both in England and here in the Colonies, but I've never seen a horse like this before. He reminds me of the Biblical verse: 'He paws in the valley, and rejoices in his strength.... He smells the battle far off, the thunder of the captains, and the shouting.'   This horse would seem to be descended from that horse described in the Bible, wouldn't you say?"

Receiving no reply, he turned and found himself face to face with a silent figure. It was the "Indian runner" who had brought the news of the French army the afternoon before. There was something frightening in his silent appearance. He had a knife and a tomahawk. His eyes glistened like fiery stars amid lowering clouds. But there was also an air of neglect about him. The colors of his war paint had blended in dark confusion about his fierce face, making him look even more savage.

The two men looked at each other silently. Then their attention was drawn to the door of General Webb's cabin. From the door a young officer and two young women emerged, along with the general.

The General turned to the young officer and said, "Major Heyward, make sure that these two women get safely to their father. Colonel Munro is expecting them before nightfall."

"I will, Sir," replied Heyward.

Duncan Heyward then proceeded to help

Alice, the younger of the two women, onto her horse. As she mounted, the morning breeze blew her green veil aside. This revealed a glimpse of her dazzling complexion, her golden hair, and her bright blue eyes. She gave Heyward a lively smile that lit up her face like the gentle glow of the morning sun that hung low above the trees.

Heyward then turned to help Cora, the other young woman, onto her horse. Cora was four or five years older than her sister. She was graceful and of the same exquisite proportions as Alice. Because of her greater maturity and sense of modesty, Cora was careful not to let the breeze brush her veil aside.

Mounting his military steed, Heyward saluted General Webb. The three then turned their horses toward the northern entrance to the encampment and proceeded at a slow pace. Three soldiers on horseback accompanied them. As the small group approached the camp entrance, the Indian runner glided past them on foot to lead the way along the military road ahead. His swift and silent movements startled the two young women. Alice let out a slight gasp. Cora made no sound. But in the moment of surprise, her veil fell open. Her face showed a look of pity, admiration, and horror as her dark eye followed the easy motions of the Indian runner. Cora's hair was shining and black, like the feathers of a raven. Her complexion, darker than that of her sister, appeared charged with rich blood. Her face was flawlessly regular, dignified, and extremely beautiful. Before replacing her veil, she smiled to herself, revealing teeth whiter than the purest ivory. She bowed her head and rode on in silence, seemingly lost in her own thoughts.

CHAPTER 2

As Cora rode on in silent thought, Alice quickly recovered from her surprise. She turned to Major Heyward and asked playfully, "Is it common so see such silent, frightening creatures in the woods? Or did you arrange that special entertainment for us?"

"That is an Indian runner employed by the army," Heyward replied. "He has volunteered to guide us to the lake by a secret path that will get us there sooner than if we were to follow the army on the main trail."

"I don't like him, Duncan," Alice said with a shiver of fear. "How are you sure you can trust him?"

"I know him, Alice. He can be trusted. Even though he is a Huron, he has served our friends the Mohawks. I have heard that some strange twist of events brought him into contact with your father. I understand that your father had to deal with him severely. But I forget the details. What is important is that he is now our friend."

"If he was once my father's enemy, I like him even less!" exclaimed Alice, becoming even more anxious. "Speak to him, Duncan, so that I can hear his voice. I know it is foolish, but I believe I can tell a lot by a man's voice."

"It would be a waste of breath for me to speak to him. He may understand English, but he pretends to be ignorant of it and would not condescend to speak it. But look, he is stopping. We must be approaching the secret path that we are to take."

The Indian stood pointing into the thick bushes that fringed the military road. Looking where he pointed, they saw a narrow and blind path, barely wide enough to admit one person at a time.

"This is the trail," said the young Heyward. "Don't be afraid."

"What do you think, Cora?" asked Alice. "Even though it would be tiresome to follow the troops on the main trail, wouldn't we feel safer?"

Heyward replied, "You don't understand the ways of the savages, Alice. The greater danger lies in following the troops. If our enemies are in the area, they will be watching the soldiers. They would know the route the army is taking. Our route was decided less than an hour ago, so the enemy would have no way of knowing it."

"Should we distrust the man just because his manners are not our manners and only because his skin is dark?" asked Cora coldly.

Alice hesitated no longer. Giving her horse a smart cut of the whip, she was the first to push aside the branches of the bushes and follow the runner along the dark and tangled pathway. The Major looked at Cora with admiration for her courage and good sense. He then pushed the branches aside for her so that she might enter the thicket.

The three soldiers who had accompanied them this far continued on the main trail, following the column. Heyward said that the runner had suggested this. If there happened to be any Hurons in the area, it would be less obvious that the Major and the two sisters had taken the secret trail if only three horses used it.

The three followed the Indian runner through the thick underbrush until they emerged beneath the high arches of the forest trees. Here they were able to move at a fast, easy pace behind the trotting Indian. He guided them deeper into the cool darkness of the woods.

Just as Heyward turned to speak to Cora, he was stopped by the distant sound of hoofs clattering over the trail behind them. The whole party came to a halt to see who was overtaking them.

In a few moments, they saw an awkward man in a blue coat and yellow trousers, riding as fast as he could on the uneven path. To an experienced horseman like Heyward, the approaching rider looked ridiculous. He alternately rose up tall in the stirrups and shrank low to the horse's neck as he straightened and bent his long, skinny legs. The movement was emphasized by the bright colors of his clothing. The action of the single spur that he used to urge the horse to move faster caused one side of the animal to appear to move faster than the other. Another horse, a young one, raced behind this wild rider and his mare. The foal was desperately trying to keep up with its mother.

Had Heyward not been so concerned with the safety of the two sisters, he would have laughed out loud at the approaching horseman. As it was, his frown relaxed and his lips curled into a slight smile. "I hope you are not bringing bad news," he called out as the rider came near.

"Not at all," gasped the stranger, fanning himself vigorously with his hat. "I understand that you are riding to Fort William Henry. I am going there, too. I thought it would be pleasant to travel together."

"If you are going to the fort, you've taken the wrong road," Heyward said, coldly. "The trail is a half a mile behind you."

"I'd rather not travel with the army. I want to maintain my professional relationship with the soldiers I instruct. Therefore, I decided it would be pleasant to travel with you three," the stranger said with a self-satisfied air.

Heyward could not decide whether to show his anger toward the intrusive stranger or laugh in his face. "Do you instruct the soldiers in the art of warfare or what?" he demanded sharply.

The stranger looked at Heyward for a moment. Then, in a tone of solemn humility, he replied, "Oh, no, sir. I am David Gamut and I know nothing of such intellectual efforts as those. I merely practice the glorious art of giving the Lord thanks through the singing of psalms."

"Oh, Duncan," said Alice, "take that frown off your face. Let him join us and sing us a song if he wishes." Then, in a quieter voice, she added, "Besides, it may be helpful to have another friend with us if we run into danger along the path."

"Alice, how can you believe that I would take you on this path if I thought there were any danger to you or your sister?"

"I trust you, Duncan. But let Mr. Gamut come with us. His songs may entertain us," Alice said persuasively. She looked into the Major's eyes for a long moment, and he returned her look. Then he turned his horse and the four of them continued on the forest path behind their Indian guide.

"I am glad you have joined us, Mr. Gamut," Alice said. "If you were to sing a song, it would help pass the time."

"I should be delighted to," Gamut replied. "And rest assured that my songs give spiritual enlightenment. I wouldn't dream of letting a secular song cross my lips. All of my songs are drawn from this book, the finest collection of Biblical songs in the English language." And with that, he produced from his pocket a copy of *The Psalms, Hymns, and Spiritual Songs of the Old and New Testaments*.

Opening the book, he selected a song. He then produced a pitch pipe from another pocket and sounded a note. He enthusiastically launched into the song in a nasal voice. As he sang, he kept time by mechanically raising and lowering his hand as if he were conducting a whole choir—although he was, in fact, the only person singing.

As Mr. Gamut sailed into the second verse, the Indian guide muttered a few words in broken English to Heyward. The Major then turned in his saddle and said to Alice, "Though we are not in danger, it would be wise for us to travel through this wilderness as quietly as possible. I am sorry to spoil your fun, Alice, but I must ask

that this gentleman postpone his chant until a more appropriate time."

"Oh, Duncan," Alice said, "you are such a spoilsport! You have no appreciation for the finer things in life!"

Annoyed by her remark, Heyward replied sharply, "I know only that the safety of you and your sister is worth far more to me than a whole orchestra of Handel's music." Heyward turned his head quickly toward the thicket beside the path, thinking he saw something there. He then looked suspiciously at their native guide who continued on the path ahead of them. After a moment, he smiled to himself. He had mistaken some shining berries in the bushes for the glistening eyeballs of a prowling savage.

But the Major had not been mistaken. Shortly after the four riders and their guide had passed, the branches of the bushes were cautiously pushed aside. A fierce human face peered out at the group as it rode away. A gleam of joy shot across the darkly painted face of the inhabitant of the forest as he watched his intended victims being led deeper into the dark woods.

CHAPTER 3

The unsuspecting Heyward and his companions continued deeper into the dangerous forest. A few miles west, two men sat by the bank of rapid stream. They appeared to be waiting for someone as they relaxed in the shade under the vast canopy of trees. The intense heat of the early August sun became less fierce as the afternoon drew on. The sound of the stream and the low voices of the men were the only sounds that interrupted the drowsy stillness of the forest. They were speaking in the native language of the Lenape Indians.

One of the men sat on the end of a log. His close-shaved head had one tuft of hair in the middle. A single eagle's feather hung over his left shoulder. His red skin was decorated with black and white war paint. A scalping knife and tomahawk were tucked into his wampum belt, and a short rifle rested against his knee. He had the strong build and serious look of a mature warrior. This was Chingachgook, a Mohican chief.

The other man was Natty Bumppo. Although he was a white man, his skin had the ruddy complexion of an outdoorsman. He was dressed in a forest-green hunting shirt and buckskin leggings. On his feet were decorated Indian moccasins and on his head he wore a summer cap made of animal skins. At his waist he had a knife in his wampum belt. Close to him, leaning against a tree, was his long hunter's rifle, the weapon he called Killdeer. The eyes of the hunter were constantly moving as if looking for game to shot or, possibly, watching for the approach of some lurking enemy. His Indian friends had named him Hawkeye. In spite of this, his face had an expression of open honesty.

"Even your traditions are not so different from mine," Hawkeye said. "Long before my ancestors arrived here, your ancestors came from the west and fought those who inhabited this land before you. Mine came from across the ocean and took the land from you."

"My ancestors fought against other red men. Is there no difference, Hawkeye, between the stone-headed arrow of the warrior, and the leaden bullet with which you kill?" asked Chingachgook.

"I am no scholar," replied the white man, "but it seems to me that a rifle in the hands of my grandfathers was no more dangerous than a hickory bow and flint-head arrow was in the hands of a skilled Indian warrior."

"You have been told the story by your white fathers," Chingachgook said, coldly waving his hand. "What have your elders said?"

"Even though I am white and my worst enemy on earth is a Huron, I am not a prejudiced man. My people have many ways which, as an honest man, I can't approve of. It is one of their customs to write in books what they have done and seen. In books, it is possible to hide the truth and to ignore misdeeds that occurred in the past. As a result, a man may never hear of the wrongs done by his fathers, nor feel a pride in working to make up for them. But every story has its two sides; so I ask you, Chingachgook, what happened, according to the traditions of the red men, when our fathers first met?"

A short silence followed, during which the dignified Indian sat mute; then he solemnly began his brief tale. "This is what my fathers have said and what the Mohicans have done. We came from the west, over great plains where the buffaloes live, until we reached the big river, which you call the Mississippi. There we fought the Alligewi, till the ground was red with their blood. We then continued east until we reached the great salt water from which the sun rises. We met no other tribes in this journey, so we said that this country between the great river and the ocean would be ours. The Hurons followed in our tracks and tried to take our land from us, but we drove them into the woods toward the land of winter, the land you call Canada."

The Indian paused for a moment. As he continued, his low voice betrayed deep emotion. "My fathers had made peace with the red men around them. Then, Hawkeye, then we were one people, and we were happy. The great salt water gave us its fish, the wood its deer, and the air its birds. We took wives who bore us children; we worshipped the Great Spirit; and we kept the Hurons in the woods to the north, beyond the sound of our songs of triumph."

"I have heard all this and believe it," said the white man; "but this happened long before the English came to this land."

Chingachgook nodded. "The first pale faces who came among us spoke no English. The Dutch landed and gave my people the firewater; they drank until the heavens and the earth seemed to meet, and they foolishly thought they had found the Great Spirit. Then my people parted with their land. Foot by foot, they were driven back from the shores."

"Do you know anything of your own family at that time?" asked Hawkeye. "Judging by your gifts as a man, your fathers must have been brave warriors, and wise men at the council-fire."

"My tribe is the grandfather of nations, but I am an unmixed man. The blood of chiefs is in my veins. Because my fathers were driven from their land, I, that am a chief and a Sagamore, have never visited their graves. All of my family departed, each in his turn, to the land of spirits. I am on the hilltop and must go down into the valley; and when my son Uncas follows me to the land of the Great Spirit, there will no longer be any of the blood of the Sagamores, for my boy is the last of the Mohicans."

"Uncas is here," said another voice, from behind the two men. "Who speaks to Uncas?"

At this sudden interruption, the white man loosened his knife in his sheath with one hand while his other hand reached toward his rifle. The Indian sat composed and did not even turn his head at the unexpected sounds.

At the next instant, a youthful warrior passed between them with a noiseless step and seated himself on the bank of the rapid stream. After a few moments, Chingachgook turned his eyes slowly toward his son, and demanded:

"Do the Maquas dare to leave the print of their moccasins in these woods?"

"I have been on the Huron's trail," replied the young Indian, "and know that they number as many as the fingers of my two hands; but they lie hidden like cowards."

"They are spying for the French general,

Montcalm," Hawkeye said. "He sends his Huron spies into our midst so he can find out what plans the British have."

Chingachgook looked toward the setting sun. Then he replied, "They shall be driven like deer from the bushes. Let us eat tonight, Hawkeye, and show the deceitful Maquas that we are men tomorrow."

"To fight them we must find them. And to eat we must find game," the white man said. Then, eyeing the foliage a short distance off, he continued, "There is a pair of the biggest antlers I have seen this season, moving the bushes below the hill. Now, Uncas, I will bet my rifle against a foot of wampum that I can shoot that buck between the eyes."

"That's not possible!" the young Indian said. "All except the tips of his horns are hidden by the bushes."

"He's a boy!" Hawkeye said to Chingachgook, shaking his head. "Does he think that when a hunter sees a part of an animal, he can't tell where the rest of it should be!"

Taking aim with Killdeer, he was about to prove his skill as a hunter, when the warrior reached up and pushed the long rifle aside.

"Hawkeye! Do you want to fight the Maquas not?"

"You are right, my wise friend," the white man said, putting down his rifle. Then he

turned to the young Indian and continued, "I must let you use your arrow to kill the buck, Uncas, or we will bring the thieving Hurons out of the woods to feast on our kill."

Uncas threw himself on the ground and approached the animal with wary movements. When within a few yards of the bushes, he fitted an arrow to his bow. The antlers behind the foliage moved, as if the deer scented an enemy in the evening air. The cord of the bow twanged, and a white streak glanced into the bushes. The wounded buck plunged from the cover to the very feet of his enemy. Gracefully avoiding the horns of the infuriated animal, Uncas darted to his side and passed his knife across the throat. As the buck bounded to the edge of the river, it collapsed, its blood turning the waters red.

"It was done with great skill!" exclaimed the scout with a laugh. He was about to continue complimenting the youth when Chingachgook gestured him to silence. The Indian then bent his body forward until his ear nearly touched the earth.

"I hear the sounds of feet," he said. "The horses of white men are coming." Raising himself with dignity and resuming his seat on the log, he continued, "Hawkeye, they are your brothers; you speak to them."

After listening for a moment Bumppo replied, "I don't hear the sounds of man or beast. I am a pretty good woodsman, but I'll never be able to match your skill, my friend."

He listened again for a moment and then said, "Ha! There goes something like the cracking of a dry stick—now I hear the bushes move—yes, yes, there is a trampling that I mistook for the waterfalls. They are close now. God keep them from the Hurons!"

CHAPTER 4

The words were scarcely out of Hawkeye's mouth when the first of the riders came into view. The stranger was riding a mare and leading a foal. Hawkeye was on his guard because it was surprising to find travelers so deep in the forest at any time of day, but even more so as the gloom of evening fell across the wilderness. Holding Killdeer, he took a step toward the stranger.

"Who comes?" demanded the scout, throwing his rifle carelessly across his left arm, and keeping the forefinger of his right hand on the trigger. "Who comes here, among the beasts and dangers of the wilderness?"

"Believers in religion, and friends to the law and to the King of England," replied the tall skinny stranger. "David Gamut, singing master, at your service, sir. We have journeyed since sunrise in this forest. We are hungry and tired."

"Then you are lost," interrupted the hunter, "and don't know whether to turn to the right or the left."

"We are," said the rider. "Do you know how far it is to the British fort William Henry?"

"Hoot!" shouted the scout with a laugh. He immediately checked his laughter because of the risk of being overheard by any lurking enemies. "You are as much off the scent as a hound would be if the Lake Horican lay between him and the deer! But why on earth would you want to go to Fort William Henry, man? Likely as not, that fort will be under attack by General Montcalm and his French troops before you know it. If you have business with the British army, you should follow the river down to Fort Edward and speak with General Webb."

Before the stranger could reply, another horseman appeared from the bushes and stopped on the pathway in front of Natty Bumppo.

"How far, then, are we from Fort Edward?" demanded the new arrival. "We left there this morning and we are headed for Fort William Henry at the head of Lake Horican."

"How in tarnation did you miss the main road? Are you blind, man?" the scout chuckled.

"We saw the main road," replied Heyward, for that is who this stranger was. "But we were being led along a secret shorter path by an

Indian guide and he has gotten us totally lost."

"An Indian lost in the woods!" Hawkeye said, shaking his head in doubt. "It seems strange that an Indian should be lost between Lake Horican and the bend in the river. Is he a Mohawk?"

"He was not born a Mohawk," replied Heyward, "but he was adopted by that tribe. He is a Huron by birth."

Chingachgook and Uncas gave an exclamation of disgust when they heard this information.

"A Huron!" repeated Hawkeye, shaking his head in open distrust. "Those of that tribe are as dishonest as the day is long. I am amazed you haven't fallen in with more of the enemy."

"But I told you, our guide is now a Mohawk, and he serves the British army as a friend," the Major emphasized with some annoyance.

"And I tell you that he who is born a Mingo will die a Mingo," responded the scout. "A Huron! And one who has joined the Mohawks! No, give me a Lenape for honesty as well as skill as a warrior."

"Enough of this," said Heyward, impatiently. "I wish not to inquire into the character of a man that I know, and who is a stranger to you. You have not yet answered my question; how far are we from the main army at Fort Edward?"

"It seems that may depend on who your guide is," Hawkeye countered.

"I don't want to argue with you, friend," Heyward said, curbing his impatience and speaking in a gentler voice. "If you will lead me to Fort Edward, I will pay you for your trouble."

"How will I know that I am not guiding one of General Montcalm's French spies to the fort? Not everyone who speaks English is a loyal subject of the King."

"If you are a scout for the British army, then you must know of the Sixtieth Regiment," Heyward said. "Do you know who is in command of the companies of the Sixtieth stationed at Fort William Henry?"

"I have heard that a wealthy young gentleman has been given that position. They say he is pretty young to hold such a rank but that he is a knowledgeable soldier and a gallant gentleman."

"I am Major Heyward, the man you have heard of. Whether or not you believe I am qualified for the command, I clearly am not the enemy."

The scout looked at Heyward in surprise. Then, in a tone still doubtful, though less confident than before, he said, "I have heard a party was to leave the Fort Edward this morning and head for Lake Horican?"

"That is correct; but, on the advice of the Indian I mentioned, I preferred to take the shorter route rather than the main road."

"And he deceived you, and then deserted?" asked Hawkeye.

"I don't believe he deceived me," Heyward answered. "And he has not deserted me for he is behind me in the shadows."

"I'd like to have a look at him. If he is a true Huron, I'll know him by his dishonest look and by his paint." And with that, the scout stepped past Heyward. He then brushed past David Gamut's mare and the foal that was quietly feeding at her side. After shoving aside the bushes and advancing a few steps, he discovered two young women. Alice and Cora Munro were nervously waiting. Behind them the Indian runner, Magua, leaned against a tree. Hawkeye studied the runner for a moment. Magua continued leaning against the tree but with a look so dark and savage that it would have frightened a lesser man than the scout.

A few moments later he returned to Heyward. "A Mingo is a Mingo, and neither the Mohawks nor any other tribe can change him," he announced. Then he went on, "If we were alone I could take you to Fort Edward myself in less than an hour. But with the women it would be impossible."

"Why is it not possible?" asked the Major.

"They may be tired, but they are able to ride a few more miles."

"It is impossible," the scout repeated. "I wouldn't walk a mile in these woods after dark with that runner of yours. The forest is full of Hurons, and your mongrel Mohawk knows where they are. I wouldn't trust him as my traveling companion."

"Do you think so?" asked Heyward. Then leaning forward in the saddle and dropping his voice to a whisper, he continued, "I have to admit, I have had my own suspicions but I have kept them to myself for the sake of the women. Because I began to doubt him, no longer trusted him to lead us, and I made him follow us, as you see."

"I knew he was one of those cheats as soon as I laid eyes on him! If I were to go back to him, the cunning varmint would suspect something and dash off into the woods like a frightened deer." the scout replied. "The thief is leaning against that sugar sapling you can see above the bushes. His right leg is in line with the tree trunk." He tapped his rifle. "I can take him from where I stand with a single shot in the thigh. That would put an end to his tramping about the woods for at least a month."

"It will not do. He may be innocent, and I don't like that plan. We must think of some other scheme—and yet, I have much reason to believe the rascal has deceived me."

The hunter, who had already abandoned the idea of maiming the runner, thought for a moment. Then he gestured to his two red companions and they stepped close to him. Speaking quietly in the Lenape language, he explained the situation of the enemy who stood hidden from view. After a moment, Chingachgook and Uncas laid aside their rifles and disappeared silently into the bushes on either side of the path.

The hunter then turned back to Heyward and said, "Now, go back to that varmint and talk with him to distract him. These Mohicans will take him without breaking his paint. Go and talk openly to the miscreant. Act like you believe he is the truest friend you have on earth."

Heyward realized that his own over-confidence had put the young women he was to protect into a dangerous situation. The sun had already disappeared. The growing darkness reminded the young Major that night was when the savage and violent acts of vengeance occurred in the forest. His worry convinced him he must carry out the scout's plan. As Heyward turned to go talk with the Indian runner, Hawkeye launched into a loud conversation with the singing master.

Riding past Alice and Cora toward the tree where the Indian runner slouched, the Major said a few words of encouragement to them. He was relieved to find that they had no suspicion that their current difficulties were anything more than an accident.

Heyward attempted to assume an air of relaxed confidence as he approached the sullen runner. "You can see, Magua, that night is closing in around us but we are no nearer Fort William Henry than when we left Fort Edward at sunrise. We have lost the path. But, fortunately, we have come across a hunter who is familiar with the deer paths and byways of the woods. He promises to lead us to a place where we may rest in safety until morning."

The Indian riveted his glowing eyes on Heyward as he asked, in imperfect English, "Is he alone?"

"Alone?" Heyward answered with hesitation. He was not used to deception and was not convincing. "Oh, not alone, surely, Magua, for we are here too."

"Then Sly Fox will go," the runner replied, "and the pale faces will see none but their own color."

"Go? Who is Sly Fox?" Heyward asked, desperate not to fail in his mission.

"It's the name given to me by my fathers in Canada," Magua answered. "Colonel Munro expects me at Fort William Henry."

"And what will you tell the chief of Fort

William Henry happened to his daughters? Will you dare tell the hot-blooded Scotsman that his children are left without a guide, even though you promised to be one?"

"Munro has a loud voice and long arms," Sly Fox said, "but he cannot reach me in the woods."

"But what will the Mohawks say? They will call Sly Fox an old woman who is not to be trusted with the work of a man."

"Sly Fox knows the path to the great lakes, and he can find the bones of his ancestors," the runner replied.

"Enough, Magua," Heyward said. "Are we not friends? Why should there be bitter words between us? Munro has promised you a reward for your services, and I will also give you one. We have a few moments to rest. Let us not waste them arguing. When the young women are refreshed, we will proceed."

"The pale faces make themselves dogs to their women," muttered the Indian, in his native language.

"What do you say, Sly Fox?"

"Sly Fox says it is good." With that Magua sat down on the ground. He pulled a leftover bit of some former meal from his wallet and, after cautiously looking around, began to eat.

"Good," Heyward continued. "Sly Fox will have the strength and sight to find the path in the morning." He paused, for sounds like the snapping of a dried stick and the rustling of leaves rose from the nearby bushes. He recollected himself instantly and went on, "We must be moving before the sun is in the sky. Otherwise, General Montcalm and his troops may cut us off from Fort William Henry."

Magua's hand dropped from his mouth to his side. His eyes were fastened on the ground but his ears were listening carefully to the sounds in the bushes.

Heyward, watching the Indian closely, carelessly removed one of his feet from the stirrup and slid his hand closer to his holster. Then he hesitated, unsure of what to do next.

Sly Fox cautiously raised himself to his feet. His movement was so slow and guarded that he did not make the slightest noise.

The Major felt that he must act now or Magua would escape before the Mohicans in the bushes could get him. Throwing his leg over the saddle, he dismounted, determined to advance and seize his treacherous companion. In order to prevent unnecessary alarm, he still preserved an air of calmness and friendship.

"Sly Fox does not eat," he said, using the name the Indian seemed to find most flattering. "Your corn seems dry. Let me look at it. Maybe I can find something in my own provisions that you would prefer."

Magua held out his food wallet. As Heyward reached out and touched it, the Indian did not move. But when he felt the white man's fingers begin to close about his arm, he struck the hand aside and, uttering a piercing cry, ducked past the soldier. In a single bound he plunged into the opposite thicket. At the next instant Chingachgook appeared from the bushes, looking like a ghost in his paint, and glided across the path in swift pursuit. Next followed the shout of Uncas. Then the woods were lighted by a sudden flash that was accompanied by the sharp report of the hunter's rifle.

CHAPTER 5

The suddenness of Magua's flight, the wild cries of his pursuers, and the sound of the gunshot froze Heyward in his tracks for a few moments. Then, remembering the importance of keeping Sly Fox from escaping, he came to his senses. He dashed the bushes aside and pressed forward to help in the chase. But before he had gone a hundred yards, he met the three foresters already returning from their unsuccessful pursuit.

"Why give up so soon!" he exclaimed. "The scoundrel must be hidden somewhere nearby and we can catch him yet. We are not safe while he is free."

"Would you send a cloud to chase the wind?" replied the disappointed scout. "I heard the imp brushing over dry leaves like a black snake. Then I caught a glimpse of him over by that pine tree. I shot at him, but I should have known better. Look at the blood on these sumac leaves."

"It's the blood of Sly Fox! He's hurt and may not be able to go far," Heyward said.

"I only nicked him," Hawkeye replied. "When a rifle bullet hits an animal that way, it has the same effect as your spurs have on a horse: it quickens the motion and puts life into the flesh instead of taking it away. Only when a bullet cuts a ragged hole does it stop the motion."

"But we are four able bodies against one wounded man!" the Major argued.

"Don't you value your life?" the scout interrupted. "Yonder red devil would draw you into an ambush by his comrades before you'd chased him half a mile. It was a mistake for me to fire my rifle under the circumstances. I should have known better—but it was a natural temptation. Come, friends, we must leave this area and we must do it in such a way as to throw the cunning Mingo off our track. If we don't, our scalps will be drying in the wind by this time tomorrow.

This grisly prospect reminded Heyward of his charge to keep Alice and Cora safe. As he attempted to look around through the thickening gloom beneath the leafy arches of the forest he felt as if the women would soon be at the mercy of those barbarous enemies. His imagination took hold of him. In the deceptive light he thought each waving bush or branch of a fallen tree was a moving human form. Twenty times he was certain that he saw the horrid faces of savages peering from their hiding places.

"Don't desert me, for God's sake!" he said, feeling utterly helpless. "Stay and help me protect these innocent young women. I will pay you whatever you ask!"

Hawkeye and the two Mohicans were in the midst of a hushed discussion as Heyward approached them. They spoke in the Lenape language, but it was evident to the young soldier that they were discussing some action concerning the welfare of the travelers. Impatient to get the women out of danger, Heyward was about to offer a more specific reward for their help.

At that moment, the Hawkeye turned aside from the other two and said, in English, "Uncas is right! We cannot leave these harmless women to their fate. It is worth the price of revealing a secret hiding place to protect them. And there is no time to lose."

"How can anybody think otherwise? Didn't I just offer—"

"Offer your prayers to Him who can help us avoid the sneaky devils in these woods," Hawkeye interrupted calmly, "but skip your offers of money. Neither of us may live long enough to have any use for it. My two friends and I will do whatever we can to protect these women from the dangers of this wilderness.

First, you must promise us two things or you will bring harm on us as well as on yourself and the women."

"Name them."

"The one is that all of you must remain absolutely quiet no matter what happens. The other is that you must keep secret the place we will hide you. You can never tell another living being."

"I promise that I and the others will meet these conditions."

"Then follow me immediately. We are losing minutes that are as precious as the heart's blood is to a wounded deer. Get the women and meet me at the edge of the river."

Heyward returned to the place where Alice and Cora waited. He quickly and quietly explained the conditions he had agreed to. Although the young women felt the terror of their situation, they braced their nerves for whatever lay ahead. They dismounted from their horses and followed Heyward silently and swiftly to the water's edge. There the scout waited for them with the singing master.

"We need to get rid of these horses," muttered Hawkeye. "It would be a waste of time to cut their throats and dump them in the river. If we leave them here, the Mingoes will know that we can't be very far away."

He was interrupted by a noise in the bushes.

"What's that!"

"The colt of the singing master," Chingach-gook said.

"That colt must die before he gives us all away," the scout said. He grabbed for the young horse's mane but the playful creature moved beyond his reach. "Uncas, your arrows!"

"Wait!" exclaimed David Gamut loudly. "Spare that innocent foal! It is a gentle creature that would not hurt anyone."

"If you speak again, singing master, I will leave you here at the mercy of the Maquas! Draw your arrow, Uncas. The first shot must count."

The arrow found its mark. The wounded foal reared on its hind legs, then plunged forward to its knees. Chingachgook grabbed hold of the struggling horse and force it toward the water. Then he passed his knife quickly across its throat and dashed the horse into the river. There the creature glided away, gasping audibly for breath as life drained from it.

This cruel but necessary deed drove home the seriousness of the situation to the travelers. The two sisters clung close together, shuddering. Heyward stood, gun in hand, anxiously peering into the shadows of the forest. David Gamut stood in stunned silence, looking downstream as the foal slipped into the darkness.

Chingachgook and Uncas took the bridles

of the frightened and reluctant horses and led them into the bed of the river. A little ways from shore they turned upstream and in a moment had disappeared into the shadows.

In the meantime, the scout pulled out a canoe that was hidden under the branches of some bushes that hung over the water. He silently motioned for the women to get in. With fearful glances toward the dark barrier of the forest behind them, they obeyed.

As soon as Cora and Alice were seated, the scout directed Heyward to take hold of one side of the canoe. The two men then walked the craft with its precious cargo upstream. The dejected owner of the dead foal followed behind them in the water.

They continued this way some distance upstream. Hawkeye knew the river well and kept them in shallow water, at the same time avoiding sharp rocks. From time to time he would stop and listen for any sounds of approaching enemies. Satisfied that there was no immediate danger, he would then continue to lead the travelers toward the distant roar of a waterfall further upstream.

Heyward looked warily into the darkness on either side of the river as he helped push the canoe against the current. At one point his eye became riveted on a cluster of black objects in a spot where the high bank cast an unusually deep shadow on the waters. He silently pointed the place out to Hawkeye.

"It's all right," said the scout. "That is the place where Chingachgook and Uncas have hidden the horses. They have done well. The water hides their trail and the deep shadows will keep them from being observed by anyone on the shore. They will be safe there for the night."

They continued upstream a few more minutes, the roar of the falls increasing with every step. Presently, Hawkeye brought the canoe to a halt. Immediately ahead of them, the river was confined between high, cragged rocks topped with tall trees. Above the fantastic limbs and ragged tree tops a few stars were visible. Behind them lay the broad river with its curving banks. In front of them, extending toward the night sky, seemed to be only the raging waterfall. The water thundered down into caverns, sending sullen, hollow sounds into the night air. The wild beauty of the solitary spot made the sisters almost forget their desperate situation.

The scout signaled for Heyward and Gamut to get into the forward end of the canoe and he got into the back. Then, placing his pole against a rock, he gave a powerful shove. The frail vessel shot directly into the turbulent water just below the crashing falls. The canoe bounced on the swift current. It seemed as though it would capsize at any moment and throw its five occupants

into the deep, swirling waters. Twenty times the passengers thought the whirling eddies were sweeping them to destruction, when the master hand of their pilot would steady the course of the canoe and bring them ever closer to the torrent cascading from above. Just as it seemed as if they were about to be swept into the vortex at the foot of the falls, the canoe floated, stationary, at the side of a low, flat rock.

"Where are we? And what happens next?" Heyward demanded over the roar of the falls.

"You are at the foot of Glenn's Falls," the scout replied. "The four of you are to get out of the canoe and onto that rock before we capsize and all get swept down the river."

The passengers were glad to follow these directions. Once the four were standing on the rock, the scout continued, "I'll be back shortly. I am going back out under the falls to bring up the Mohicans and the venison we were about to eat when you appeared. There is no point in saving our scalps if we starve to death in the process."

And with that, he whirled the canoe about and disappeared through the crashing falls. The travelers waited in helpless ignorance. They were afraid to even move for fear a false step would send them into one of the deep and roaring caverns that were on every side of them.

In a few moments, however, the canoe shot

back into the quiet eddy behind the falls, carrying Chingachgook, Uncas, and the scout. In another moment, it came to rest next to the flat rock.

"Well, now we have a safe hiding place and food," Heyward said cheerfully. "Did you see any signs of our enemies? Have they followed us?"

"I trust not," Hawkeye replied. "I didn't see any signs of them. However, the horses did cower when I passed them, as if they scented wolves. A wolf is likely to hover around a place where Indians kill a deer, hoping to eat the remains. So they may be out there."

"Maybe the wolves have been attracted by the deer you killed, or maybe by the dead colt," Heyward suggested.

At the mention of the dead horse, the singing teacher sighed and murmured to himself, "Ah, my poor horse, Miriam! Your foal was destined to become food for wolves."

"The death of the colt hangs heavy on his heart," the scout noted. Then, in response to Heyward, he went on, "It may be as you say. Therefore, we should cut out steaks from this deer and let the carcass float downstream. Otherwise, we will have a pack of howling wolves along the cliffs above us, jealous of every mouthful we swallow. And the Hurons are quick enough to understand the reason a wolf would be howling near these falls."

Hawkeye then moved silently past the group of travelers, followed by the two Mohicans. Then the three of them seemed to vanish, one after the other, against the dark face of a large rock that sat a few feet back from the water's edge.

CHAPTER 6

Heyward and the two young women felt uneasy when the scout and the two Mohicans seemed to disappear into the darkness. The rumors of treachery and savage attacks on whites by Indians frequently circulated at Fort Edward and these now gripped their minds. Although the scout had given them no reason to fear him, the travelers still felt unsure of this strange white man and his two red companions. Could they trust them?

David Gamut, meanwhile, sat on a projection of rock, softly sighing over the death of the foal. Next they heard smothered voices, as if men were calling to each other in the bowels of the earth. Then a light shone from the place where the scout had disappeared. It revealed the much-prized and secret place that the scout had alluded to.

Toward the far end of a narrow, deep cavern sat the scout, holding a blazing torch. The strong glare of the flame fell on the scout's sturdy, weather-beaten countenance and gave him an air of romantic wildness. Uncas stood nearby, appearing dignified and unrestrained. His dark, glancing, fearless eyes were both terrible and calm. His finely proportioned and noble head was shaved except for the generous scalping tuft of hair that grew from the top. This was the first opportunity for Duncan and his companions to get a good look at either of the Mohicans. All three of them felt relieved as they looked on the proud and determined features of the young warrior. This could not possibly be someone who would use his rich natural gifts for treachery.

"I could sleep in peace," Alice said, "with a warrior of such noble appearance standing guard. Surely, Duncan, those cruel murders we have heard of could not be carried out by a man such as this!"

"I agree with you, Alice," he answered. "One would not expect a man who looks like this to be capable of deception. However, we must also be careful not to deceive ourselves. One must be careful not to judge by appearances alone. Even so, let us hope that this Mohican will not disappoint us, but rather will prove to be the brave and constant friend that his looks suggest he is."

"Now Major Heyward speaks as Major Heyward should," said Cora. "Who can look at this creature of nature and remember just the color of his skin?"

At that moment, their discussion was interrupted by the scout calling to them to come into the cave. As they entered, he said, "The fire is showing too brightly and may lead the Mingoes to us and our scalps. Uncas, pull the blanket across the opening."

As Uncas drew the blanket across the opening, the roar of the waterfall became like the rumbling of distant thunder.

"Are we completely safe in this cavern?" Heyward demanded. "Is there any danger of surprise? After all, a single armed man at the entrance would have us at his mercy."

A ghost-like figure appeared from the darkness behind Hawkeye. The figure seized the torch from the scout's hand and held it toward the far end of the cave. Alice gave a faint shriek and even Cora stood up quickly in response to this sudden appearance. But Heyward calmed them, assuring them it was only Chingachgook. The Mohican chief then lifted a blanket at the far end of the cavern, revealing a second entrance. Stepping out of the second entrance, he showed them a deep, narrow chasm that was open to the sky; beyond that lay another cave.

"Such old foxes as Chingachgook and myself are not often caught in a burrow with only one opening," Hawkeye said, laughing.

"You can easily see what a deceptive spot it is. In places the water has worn the limestone away, digging out deep hollows for itself. The falls, once smooth, no longer have shape or consistency. Here, the water flows around both sides of us."

"Then we are on an island!" Duncan exclaimed.

"Yes, sir. And, if it were daylight, it would be worth your while to step out onto the top of this rock and admire the beauty and the perversity of these untamed falls. The water tumbles as it pleases, following no rules at all. The whole design of the river seems to be confused at this point. It's as if the water is unwilling to leave the wilderness and go to the ocean. But down below the falls, it smoothes out again and flows on steadily toward the sea."

Heyward and the sisters were cheered by the assurance of the security of their hiding place, even though they felt less comfortable with the wild beauty that so captured the imagination of Hawkeye.

While he had been speaking, the scout had been preparing their supper. The food was exceedingly refreshing to the weary group. Throughout the meal, Uncas was attentive to the young women, trying to make them as comfortable as possible. Although he appeared to treat the two women with equal attention, a close observer would have noted that when he served Cora, his eye lingered on her rich, radiant countenance. Occasionally, he spoke to the women in imperfect English but with a voice so mild and musical that it caused both women to look at him with admiration and astonishment.

Meanwhile, the seriousness of Chingachgook seemed immovable. He had seated himself within the circle of light from the fire. Throughout the meal, his face wore a quiet, unemotional stare. By contrast, the roving eye of the scout seldom rested. Although he ate and drank with an appetite that no sense of danger could disturb, his vigilance never deserted him. Twenty times he would freeze with the food close to his lips as though he listened to some distant and distrusted sound. But these momentary pauses would quickly pass before the travelers noticed his uneasiness.

As they were finishing the supper, Hawkeye pulled a small keg from beneath a cover of leaves. Turning to the singing master, he said, "Come friend. Try a little of this; it will wash away all thoughts of the colt. I drink to our better friendship, hoping that a little horseflesh won't come between us. What is your name?"

"Gamut—David Gamut," the singing master said as he prepared to wash down his sorrows with some of the woodsman's flavorful brew.

"A very good name, I dare say. My name is

Natty Bumppo, though I prefer the name Hawkeye, given to me by my Indian companions. I admire names—particularly the Indian names because they ring so true. What an Indian calls himself, he generally is. I don't mean that Chingachgook, which means Great Snake, is really a snake; but he understands the windings and turnings of human nature, and is silent, and strikes his enemies when they least expect him. But what is your line of work?"

"I am a singing master," Gamut replied.

"You might be better employed. Can you handle a rifle?"

"Praise be God, I have never had occasion to use murderous implements!" Gamut responded.

"Perhaps you can use a compass and mark down the rivers and mountains of the wilderness on paper so that others who follow can find them?"

"I do not."

"Your long legs look as if you could make a long path seem short! Maybe you sometimes carry messages for General Webb?"

"Never; I follow no other than my own high calling, which is instruction in sacred music!"

"A strange calling" muttered Hawkeye with an inward laugh, "to go through life, like a cat-bird, mocking all the ups and downs that may happen to come out of other men's throats. Well, my friend, I suppose it is your gift and mustn't be denied any more than if it were shooting or something else. Let us hear what you can do. It will be a pleasant way to say good-night, for it's time for these ladies to get some rest."

"With joyful pleasure I will be happy to lead us in a song," Gamut said, adjusting his iron-rimmed spectacles. "I can think of nothing more fitting than to offer up evening praise after a day of such trials as we have had." He then pulled out his little book of hymns and, offering it to Alice, continued, "I hope the young lady will again join me."

Alice blushed and looked at Heyward. He gave her a nod of encouragement.

"All right," she said.

The singing master then played a note on his pitch pipe and began to sing, methodically raising and lowering his right hand to keep time. The voices of David and Alice filled every corner of the cave with the sweet and solemn music. The Mohicans riveted their eyes on the rocks and listened with an attention that seemed to turn them into stone. As the song began, the scout had listened with an expression of cold indifference. But as the piece progressed, his features relaxed as his iron nature subdued. The song carried him back to memories of his boyhood and soon his roving eyes began to moisten. Before the hymn had ended, scalding tears were rolling down his weathered cheeks.

The singers were dwelling on the final cord of the hymn when an unearthly cry rose from outside the cave. The sound penetrated the recesses of the cavern and the inmost hearts of those in it. Stillness followed the horrid interruption.

"What is it?" murmured Alice after a moment of suspense.

"What is it?" Heyward repeated in a louder voice.

Neither Hawkeye nor the Mohawks made any reply. They listened as if expecting the sound would be repeated. After a few moments, they spoke together earnestly, in the Lenape language. Then Uncas cautiously left the cavern.

After the young warrior had left, Hawkeye said, "I cannot tell you what it is for none of us has ever heard such a sound before. I had not believed, after ranging the woods for more than thirty years, that man or beast could make a sound I could not recognize. I was wrong."

"Then it wasn't the shout of warriors trying to intimidate their enemies?" Cora asked. She showed a calmness unfamiliar to her agitated sister.

"No. Once you've heard the war-whoop, you can never mistake it for anything else. This was some other sort of inhuman sound," the scout answered. A moment later, Uncas re-entered the cave. Speaking in the Lenape language to the young chief, he asked, "What do you see? Does our fire shine through the blankets?"

After a short answer, Hawkeye shook his head with discontent and said to the sisters, "He sees nothing outside. Our firelight is not visible. Go into the other cave and try to get some sleep. You'll find sassafras branches there that will make a good enough bed. We must be under way long before sunrise and get to Fort Edward while the Mingoes are still taking their morning nap."

Cora stood up before the more timid Alice. Before going into the other cave, however, she whispered to Duncan asking him to go with them. As Duncan picked up a torch from the dying embers of the fire, they saw the scout with his face resting on his hands. His manner showed how deeply he brooded on the unaccountable interruption of a few minutes before.

Duncan lighted the way to the other cave. Once the three were alone, Alice said, "Stay with us, Duncan. We cannot sleep in such a place with that horrible cry still ringing in our ears."

"First, let's make sure your fortress is secure," he replied. He approached the further end of the cavern, to an opening that was, like the others, covered with blankets. Pushing the blankets aside he saw one arm of the river flowed swiftly below him. It formed an effective natural defense, he believed, against any danger.

Replacing the blanket, he turned back to the sisters and said, "Nature has made an impenetrable barrier on this side. And good and true men are on guard in the outer cave. There is no reason not to follow the woodsman's advice and get some sleep. I am sure Cora will agree with me in saying that you must both get some rest."

"I agree with you, Heyward, but I do not believe I will be able to sleep," Cora replied. "Even if we had not heard that mysterious noise, I am not sure I would be able to sleep. How can our father not feel great anxiety not knowing where we are in this wilderness, surrounded by so many perils?"

"He is a soldier and knows how to estimate the chances of the woods."

"He is a father and cannot deny his concern for his children," Cora answered. "I may have pushed too hard for him to let us join him at Fort William Henry. But I wanted to prove to him that his children were faithful to him even if the army wasn't giving him the troops he needed in that isolated outpost."

"When he heard you had arrived at Fort Edward," Heyward said kindly, "there was a powerful struggle in his heart between fear and love. But it had been so long since he last saw the two of you that love quickly won. He told me that it was the spirit of his noble-minded Cora that was leading you to him."

"And didn't he say anything about me, Duncan?" Alice demanded with jealous affection. "Surely, he wouldn't forget his little Alice?"

"That would be impossible," Heyward replied. "He spoke loving of you and called you by a thousand endearing names. Once, indeed, he even said—"

Duncan ceased speaking. While his eyes were riveted on those of Alice, the same horrid cry as before filled the air, cutting off his words. A long, breathless moment of silence followed, during which the three looked at one another in fearful expectation of hearing the sound repeated. Moments later, the blanket at the entrance was slowly raised. There stood the scout. The firmness of his expression was beginning to give way. All his cunning and experience might be of no use against this mystery that seemed to threaten danger.

CHAPTER 7

"We cannot neglect this warning any longer," Hawkeye said. "The Mohicans and I will keep watch for the night on the rocks above us. I imagine the Major will want to join us."

"Is the danger that close?" asked Cora.

"Only the creature that makes such an unearthly sound can answer that," the scout replied. "If it was just a regular war cry, it would be a battle we can all understand and manage. But this shriek suggests some other kind of warfare."

"If all of our reasons for fear, my friend, come just from supernatural causes, we have little reason to be alarmed," Cora said calmly. "Are you sure that our enemies have not come up with some new and ingenious way to strike terror into our hearts?"

"Lady," returned the scout solemnly, "I have listened to all the sounds of the woods for thirty years. But neither the Mohicans nor I can explain the cry just heard. We, therefore, believe it is a sign we must pay attention to."

"Be it a sign of peace or a sign of war," Heyward said, picking up his pistols, "we must investigate it. Lead the way, my friend. I will follow you."

As they stepped from the cave, the whole party instantly felt refreshed by invigorating air that played around the swirling waters of the falls. In their hiding place, the roar of the falls had seemed like thunder rumbling beyond distant hills. Here the roar seemed alive and energetic. The moon had risen but the rock where they stood was still in shadow. The eyes of each individual strained to see some signs of life along the shores.

"There is nothing to be seen but the gloom and quiet of a lovely evening," whispered Duncan.

"Listen!" interrupted Alice.

The caution was unnecessary. Once more the same horrible sound arose, as if from the bed of the river. It echoed through the dark forest in dying cadences.

"Can any of you name the source of such a cry?" demanded Hawkeye. "If so, speak up. For myself, I would say it is not of this earth."

"I can tell you what it is," said Duncan. "In the cavern it was too muffled for me to recognize, but now I recognize it full well, having heard it often on the battlefield. It is the horrid shriek of a horse either in pain or in terror. My horse is either being attacked by a pack of wolves or else sees the danger close by and cannot escape it."

"I must take your word for it," said the scout, "because I am little skilled in horses. The wolves must be hovering on the bank above the horses and the terrified creatures are calling on man to help them." He then switched to the Lenape language. "Uncas, drop down the river in the canoe and drive the wolves away before they find a way to get to the horses. Otherwise, we will find ourselves without horses in the morning when we need them."

Uncas was climbing down to the water when the howls of wolves were heard. At first they came from the riverbank but then they faded into the forest. Uncas stopped his descent and rejoined the others on the rock. The scout and the two Mohicans held another of their low, earnest conferences.

"Something frightened the wolves off," said Hawkeye to his two companions, "and I suspect it was the Mingoes." Then, turning to the others, he continued in English, "I have been like a hunter who had lost his way, but now I have found the path again. We must be alert and protect the women. Seat yourselves in the shadow of that tree and let us wait and watch for what comes our way. Keep silent. If you must speak, make sure it is in a whisper."

It was evident that the scout's momentary uncertainty had vanished with the explanation of the mystery that his experience could not solve. He was ready to meet the realities of their situation with decisive energy.

Hawkeye, Chingachgook, and Uncas took up hidden positions where they could command a full view of both banks of the river. Heyward had Cora and Alice settle themselves at the bottom of the open chasm between the two caves where they could sleep and would be protected. He stationed himself in the rocks at the top of the chasm, where he could communicate with them without having to raise his voice. David Gamut, meanwhile, imitated the woodsmen and hid himself in the shadows where he could see both sides of the river.

The hours passed without interruption. The moon drifted across the sky. Gradually, David and then Duncan drifted into the unconsciousness of sleep. But Hawkeye and the Mohicans remained vigilant protectors, watching the dark margins of the trees along the shorelines with constantly roving eyes. Finally, after the moon had set, a pale streak above the treetops at the bend in the river announced the approach of day.

Hawkeye crawled along the rock and shook Duncan from his heavy slumber. "It is time to go," he said. "Wake the gentle ones, and be ready to get into the canoe when I bring it to the landing place."

"Has the night been quiet?" Heyward asked. "I believe sleep got the better of my vigilance."

"All has been as still as midnight. Be silent, but be quick."

Duncan, by now fully awake, moved to the chasm where the sisters were sleeping. "Cora! Alice!" he whispered. "It is time for us to be under way."

The answer he received was unexpected. Alice gave a loud shriek, and Cora leaped to her feet in bewildered horror.

They had responded, not to his words, but to the tumult of yells and cries that had arisen before he had finished speaking. The terrifying noise drove the currents of his own blood back into fountains of his heart. It was as if the demons of hell had taken possession of the air around them and were venting their savage dispositions in barbarous sounds.

David Gamut leaped to his feet in the midst of this infernal din, covering his ears with his hands and exclaiming, "Has hell broken loose, that man should utter sounds like these!"

The bright flashes and quick reports of a dozen rifles, from both banks of the river, followed immediately. They left the unfortunate singing master senseless on the rock where he had been quietly slumbering a moment before. This brought a shout of savage triumph from the riverbanks. The Mohicans boldly returned the intimidating yell of their enemies. There was a rapid exchange of gunfire between the two sides. But both sides were too skilled at concealing themselves for any of the bullets to find their mark.

Duncan listened with intense anxiety for the sounds of the canoe. He believed flight was their only hope at this point. The canoe was nowhere to be seen on the dark water. Just as he began to wonder if they had been cruelly deserted by their scout, a stream of flame streaked out from the rock beneath them. Immediately, there was a fierce yell blended with a shriek of agony. The messenger of death sent from the fatal weapon of Hawkeye had found its victim. At the death of one of their party, the enemy instantly withdrew and gradually the place became as still as before the sudden tumult.

In the quiet Duncan sprang to the body of Gamut and carried it back to the shelter of the narrow chasm where the sisters had spent the night. By the time he arrived the rest of the party was gathered there as well.

"It was madness for him to stand up on a bare rock in view of the raging savages. I am amazed that he has escaped with his life," Hawkeye observed.

"He isn't dead?" asked Cora, her voice struggling to maintain its firmness.

"No, no! He has life in his heart yet. And after he has slept for a while he will come to himself. Carry him into the outer cavern, Uncas. The longer his nap lasts the better it will be for him."

"Do you expect the Hurons will attack again?" Heyward asked the scout.

"Do I believe a hungry wolf will satisfy his craving with a mouthful! They have lost a man, and so have fallen back for the moment. But they will be back with new tricks to get our scalps. Our best hope," he continued, with just a shade of anxiety passing across his face, "will be to stay here until Colonel Munro can send out a party to rescue us. I hope he sends it soon!"

"You know, Cora, your father's concern for you and his experience in this wilderness gives us reason to hope," Duncan said. "You and Alice come into the cave where you will be safe and where you can take care of the singing master."

The two sisters followed him into the outer cave, where David was beginning to show signs of returning consciousness.

As the young major turned to leave the cave, Cora called him back. "Remember, Duncan, how important your safety is to our safety. You are very dear to all of the Munro family."

"Your kind assurance gives me strength," replied Heyward, his eyes involuntarily wandering past Cora to Alice. "But our task will be easy. It is merely to keep these bloodhounds at bay for a few hours."

Without waiting for a reply, he tore himself from the presence of the sisters and rejoined the scout and his two companions in the little chasm.

"I tell you, Uncas," the scout was saying, "you are using too much powder in your rifle and the kick throws your aim off. You'll have better luck bringing down a Mingo if you use less powder. Come friends. Let us go back to our hiding places on the rock. There's no telling when or where the Maquas will strike next."

Chingachgook and Uncas returned to their hiding places in the fissures in the rocks, where they could see the approaches to the foot of the falls. Hawkeye and Duncan darted to a thicket in the center of the little island. Here they hid themselves as best they could. Above them was a bare, rounded rock. On each side of it, the water flowed and plunged into the abysses below. By now, day had dawned, and the watchers were able to see a little ways into the gloomy woods that lined the river.

A long and anxious watch followed, but without any evidence of a new attack. Duncan began to hope that they had effectively repulsed the enemy in the earlier battle. He suggested this to Hawkeye, who gave an incredulous shake of the head.

"You don't know the nature of a Maqua if you think he is so easily beaten back without a scalp!" he answered. "There must have been at least forty of them this morning. And they know how many of us there are. Hey! Look up there, where the water breaks over the rocks. If I don't miss my guess, the risky devils have swum down from above and have arrived at the head of the island. Look sharp, man! or your scalp will be off your head before you know it."

Heyward raised his head cautiously from the cover. He saw that Hawkeye was right—a party of their bloodthirsty foes had ventured into the current and swum down to the head of the island in order to gain ready access to their intended victims.

As Hawkeye finished speaking, four human heads could be seen peering above a few logs of driftwood that had lodged on the naked rocks above. At the next moment, a fifth form was seen floating over the green edge of the fall, a little to the side of the island. The savage struggled powerfully to reach the safety of the island. He was stretching out an arm to reach the grasp of his companions when the whirling current caught him. He appeared to rise into the air with his arms uplifted and terror in his eyes. Then he fell, with a sudden plunge, into the deep and yawning abyss over which he hovered. A single, wild, despairing shriek rose from the cavern, and all was hushed again as the grave.

Duncan felt the impulse to rush to the edge of the abyss to see what had happened to his luckless enemy, but the iron grasp of the immovable scout held him where he was.

"Would you bring certain death on us by telling the Mingoes where we are hiding?" demanded Hawkeye sternly. "That's one less devil we have to shoot and be glad, for we are low on ammunition. Freshen the charge in your pistols, for the damp air of the falls can cause them to misfire. Be ready for a close struggle."

He then gave a shrill whistle which was answered by a whistle from the rocks where the Mohicans stood guard. Duncan caught a glimpse of heads above the scattered driftwood above them. A moment later he heard a low, rustling sound behind him. He turned to see Uncas creeping up beside them. The young chief took his position with caution and undisturbed coolness. To Heyward this was a moment of feverish and impatient suspense; but the scout remained calm and unmoving.

After a moment they heard an expressive "Hisst" from Uncas.

"I see them, Uncas, I see them!" continued Hawkeye. "They are gathering for the rush or else they would keep their heads down. Well, let them," he added, checking his rifle.

At that moment the woods were filled with

another burst of cries, and at the signal four savages sprang from the cover of the driftwood. Heyward felt a burning desire to rush forward to meet them, so intense was the delirious anxiety of the moment; but he was restrained by the deliberate examples of the scout and Uncas.

Their foes approached with long bounds, uttering the wildest yells. When they were within fifty feet, the rifle of Hawkeye slowly rose among the shrubs and poured out its fatal contents. The foremost Indian bounded like a striken deer and fell headlong among the clefts of the island.

"Now, Uncas!" cried the scout, drawing his long knife, while his quick eyes began to flash, "take the last of the screeching imps."

Uncas fired and the savage at the back of the remaining foes fell. Two enemies remained to be overcome. Heyward had given one of his pistols to Hawkeye, and together they rushed toward their foes; they discharged their weapons at the same instant, and both failed to fire.

"Worthless, just like I said!" muttered the scout, whirling the despised pistol over the falls with bitter disdain. "Come on, you bloody minded hell-hounds! You meet a man face to face!"

The words were barely uttered when he encountered a savage of gigantic stature, of the fiercest expression. At the same moment,

Duncan found himself engaged with the other, in a similar contest of hand to hand combat.

With ready skill, Hawkeye and his antagonist each grasped that uplifted arm of the other which held the dangerous knife. For nearly a minute they stood looking one another in the eye, and gradually exerting the power of their muscles for the mastery. At length, the toughened sinews of the white man prevailed over the limbs of the native. The arm of the latter slowly gave way before the increasing force of the scout, who, suddenly wresting his armed hand from the grasp of the foe, drove the sharp weapon through his naked chest to the heart.

In the meantime, Heyward had been caught in a more deadly struggle. His slight sword snapped in the first encounter with his foe. He now could depend only on his physical strength to defend himself. Although he was strong, he had met an enemy every way his equal. Luckily, he soon managed to disarm his adversary, whose knife fell on the rock at their feet. Now it became a fierce contest to determine who should hurl the other over the edge of the rocks into a cavern of the raging falls. Every successive struggle brought them nearer to the verge, where the final and conquering effort must be made. Each of the combatants threw all his energies into that effort. Both tottered on the brink of the precipice. Heyward felt the grasp of the other at his throat. The savage gave a grim smile as he pulled the white man toward the same grisly fate he was about to suffer. The young major felt his body slowly yielding to the resistless power of the hand that grasped his throat, and he experienced the passing agony of the moment in all its horrors.

At that instant of extreme danger, a dark hand and shining knife appeared before him; the Huron released his hold, as the blood flowed freely from around the severed tendons of his wrist. And as Duncan was drawn backward by the saving hand of Uncas, his eyes still were riveted on the fierce and disappointed face of his foe, who fell sullenly and disappointed down the irrecoverable precipice.

"Get under cover!" cried Hawkeye. "Get under cover! The work is only half done!"

The young Mohican gave a shout of triumph, and followed by Duncan, he again sought the friendly shelter of the rocks and shrubs.

CHAPTER 8

The scout's warning was not a moment too soon. During the struggle that had just occured on the island, the Hurons along the shores had remained silent. Those enemies who were in the woods had held their fire to avoid shooting the warriors who were on the island. As soon as the Indian who had been struggling with Duncan fell to his death, a fierce and savage yell arose from the forest. It was followed by the swift flashes of the rifles, which sent their leaden messengers across the rock in volleys.

Chingachgook, who had maintained his post throughout the fray, steadily returned fire into the woods. Though the rock, the trees, and the shrubs were cut and torn in a hundred places around the besieged party on the island, David Gamut was still the only one wounded, thanks to their well-chosen cover.

"Let them waste their powder," said the deliberate scout, while bullet after bullet whizzed by the place where he securely lay. "Uncas, lad, you waste the lead by overcharging the rifle; a kicking rifle never carries a true bullet. Your shots go high and the life lies low in a Mingo."

A quiet smile lighted the proud features of the young Mohican, betraying his knowledge of the English language as well as his understanding of the teasing advice of the scout, but he made no reply.

"I cannot permit you to accuse Uncas of lack of judgment or of skill," said Duncan. "He saved my life, and he has made in me a friend who will never forget the debt I owe him."

Uncas partly raised his body, and offered his hand to the grasp of Heyward. In reaction to this declaration of friendship between Uncas and Duncan, Hawkeye said solemnly, "Life is an obligation which friends often owe each other in the wilderness. He has stood between me and death five different times; three times from the Mingoes, once in crossing Lake Horican, and—"

"That bullet was better aimed than most!" exclaimed Duncan, involuntarily shrinking from a shot which struck the rock at his side with a smart rebound.

Hawkeye examined the shapeless piece of metal and shook his head, saying, "That shot didn't fall from the sky."

Uncas pointed his rifle toward the heavens,

directing the eyes of his companions to a tree, where the mystery was immediately explained. A ragged oak grew on the right bank of the river, nearly opposite to their position. Among the topmost leaves a savage was nestled, partly concealed by the trunk of the tree, and partly exposed, as though looking down upon them to determine the results his treacherous aim.

"These devils will scale heaven to get us," said Hawkeye, raising his long rifle; "keep him in your sights, Uncas, while I get him into the sights of old Killdeer here."

Uncas and the scout took aim, each of them taking a different side of the trunk that hid the enemy. At the scout's word, the rifles flashed and the leaves and bark of the oak flew into the air and were scattered by the wind. But the Indian answered their assault by a taunting laugh. He then sent down another bullet in return, that struck the cap of Hawkeye from his head. Once more the savage yells burst out of the woods, and the leaden hail whistled above the heads of the besieged, to keep them in a place where they might become easy victims for the warrior in the tree.

"We must fix this," said the scout, glancing about him anxiously. "Uncas, call your father up here to our position."

Before Hawkeye had reloaded his rifle, they were joined by Chingachgook. Hawkeye and the Mohicans conversed earnestly together for a few moments. Then each quietly took his post, in order to execute the plan they had speedily devised.

The three waited patiently for a clear shot. Meanwhile, the warrior in the tree continued to take ineffectual shots at them. Heyward's clothes made him especially conspicuous and they were repeatedly cut by the bullets from above. But he was hit only once, and that was just a slight wound to his arm.

Emboldened by the patient watchfulness of his enemies, the Huron in the tree attempted to improve his position to get better aim. The quick eyes of the Mohicans caught the dark line of his lower limbs incautiously exposed through the thin foliage, a few inches from the trunk of the tree. Their rifles fired at the same moment. Sinking down on his wounded leg, part of the body of the savage came into view. Hawkeye seized the advantage and discharged his fatal weapon into the top of the oak. The dangerous rifle fell from its commanding position among the leaves. After a few moments of vain struggling, the form of the savage was seen swinging in the wind, while he still grasped a ragged branch of the tree with hands clenched in desperation.

"Have pity on the man and finish him off," cried Duncan, turning away his eyes in horror from the spectacle of the wounded man dangling high above the river.

"I won't waste another shot," exclaimed Hawkeye. "His death is certain and we don't have any powder to spare. Indian fights sometimes last for days. It's their scalps or ours!"

From that moment the yells and the shots in the forest once more ceased. All eyes, those of friends as well as enemies, became fixed on the hopeless condition of the wretch who was dangling between heaven and earth. The body swayed with the breeze, and though no murmur or groan escaped the victim, the anguish of his cold despair could not be missed.

At length one hand of the Huron lost its hold, and dropped exhausted to his side. Then the savage was seen for a fleeting instant, grasping wildly at the empty air. That same moment, flame shot from the rifle of Hawkeye. The limbs of the victim trembled and contracted and the head fell to the chest. The body parted the foaming waters which closed over it in their ceaseless velocity. Every trace of the warrior was lost forever.

There was no shout of triumph on the island. The four faces—two red, two white—gazed at each other in silent horror. After some moments of silence, Hawkeye shook his head and said, "It was my last charge of gunpowder and my last bullet. That was a rash act. What did it matter if he struck the rock living or dead. Feeling would soon be over either way. Uncas, go down to the canoe and bring up the horn of gunpowder. It is all we have left and we'll need every bit of it if I know the Mingoes."

The young Mohican glided down through the rocks and disappeared from sight. A moment later the three who remained heard a loud exclamation from Uncas. The three were too overcome with apprehension about the cause of Uncas' cry to think of their own safety. Instantly, they jumped up and rushed down the pass to the chasm. They moved with such speed that the scattered fire from their enemies passed harmlessly by. The cry had also brought Alice, Cora, and David from the cavern. At a single glance all of them understood the disaster that had upset the usually placid Uncas.

At a short distance from the rock, their canoe was floating across the eddy, toward the swift current of the river. Its movement made evident that someone who was hidden from their view was directing it.

"Too late, too late!" Hawkeye exclaimed. "The thieving Maqua has already reached the rapids."

A few seconds later, the adventurous Huron raised his head above the shelter of the canoe. He waved his hand, and gave forth the shout of success. His cry was answered by yells and taunting laughter from the woods.

"Well may you laugh, you children of the devil!" said the scout, seating himself on a projection of the rock, and allowing Killdeer to fall neglected at his feet. "Our guns are useless now."

"What is to be done?" demanded Duncan. "What will become of us?"

Hawkeye made no other reply than to pass his finger around his scalp in such a way that none in the group could miss his meaning.

"Surely, our situation isn't that desperate!" the young major exclaimed. "We can defend ourselves from the Hurons in these caves."

"With what?" coolly demanded the scout. "The arrows of Uncas will not be enough to stop their rifles. You are young and that makes it all the harder to die. But let us remember we are men and will show these foes how to act when the final hour has come."

Duncan turned toward Chingachgook. What he saw confirmed Hawkeye's words. The Mohican chief, placing himself in a dignified posture on another fragment of the rock, had already laid aside his knife and tomahawk. He then took the eagle's plume from his head and smoothed the solitary tuft of hair in readiness to perform its last and revolting office. His face was composed, though thoughtful, while his dark, gleaming eyes were gradually losing the fierceness of the combat.

"The situation cannot be so hopeless!" said Duncan. "At this very moment help may be at hand. I see no enemies! They have tired of the struggle in which they have so little to gain!"

"It may be a minute, or it may be an hour, before the wily serpents steal upon us," said Hawkeye; "but come they will, and in such a way as will leave us no hope. Chingachgook, my brother, we have fought our last battle together. The Maquas will triumph in our deaths, but I will die without bitterness in my heart."

"Why die at all!" said Cora, stepping forward. "Escape through the woods. We owe you too much already. Don't stay here and die with us. Get away while you still can!"

"You don't know the Hurons if you think we could get past them in the woods," Hawkeye returned. Then he added, "However, the downstream current would quickly sweep us beyond the reach of their rifles."

"Then try the river. Why stay here and add to the number of the victims?"

"Why?" repeated the scout proudly. "Because it is better for a man to die at peace with himself than to live haunted by a guilty conscience! What could we say to your father when he asked us where and how we left his children?"

"Tell him that you came from them with a message to come and rescue them," returned Cora, "and that the Hurons are carrying them into the northern wilds; but that by quick action they might be rescued. And tell him that, if he should arrive too late, you have brought him a message of our love for him."

A few moments of silence followed while Hawkeye considered Cora's words. Finally he said, "There is reason in her words! Chingachgook! Uncas! hear you the talk of the dark-eyed woman?" And he repeated her words to them in their own language.

Chingachgook listened with a grave look. Then, after a moment's hesitation, he said in English, "Good!" He pick up his knife and his tomahawk from the rock. The warrior moved silently to the edge of the rock which was most concealed from the banks of the river. Here he paused a moment, then dropped into the water, and sank from before the eyes of the others.

"Wisdom is sometimes given to the young as well as to the old," the scout said to Cora. "They may spare your life for a while. If you are captured and led into the woods, leave a trail. Break the twigs on the bushes as you pass, and make the marks of your trail as broad as you can. Count on having a friend following you. Though I leave you now, I will not desert you."

He gave Cora an affectionate shake of the hand, lifted his rifle, and after regarding it a moment with melancholy concern, laid it carefully aside, and descended to the place where Chingachgook had just disappeared. For an instant he hung suspended by the rock, and looking about him, he added bitterly, "If the powder had held out, this disgrace could never have come to pass." Then, loosening his hold, the water closed above his head, and he also became lost to view.

Cora turned to Uncas, who stood leaning against the rock. After waiting a short time, she pointed to the water and said, "Your friends have not been seen. By now they must be safely ashore. Is it not time for you to follow?"

"Uncas will stay," the young Mohican calmly answered.

"If they find you here, there is less chance the Hurons will release us. Go, generous young man," Cora said, lowering her eyes under the gaze of the Mohican. "Go to my father, as I have said. Tell him to trust you with the means to buy the freedom of his daughters. Go! It is my wish and my prayer that you will go."

The settled, calm look of the young chief changed to an expression of gloom, but he no longer hesitated. With a noiseless step he crossed the rock and dropped into the troubled stream. Those he left behind watched until they caught a glimpse of his head emerging for air, far down the current. Then he sank again beneath the surface and was seen no more.

After a last look at Uncas, Cora turned and, with a quivering lip, said to Heyward, "I have heard of your skill in the water, too, Duncan. Follow the wise example set by these faithful friends."

"I have vowed to protect you and your sister. Do you believe that I would ignore that vow? Do you think so little of me?" said the young man, smiling mournfully, but with bitterness.

"I know that you are a man bound by your word," she answered, "but this is a moment when every duty should be equally considered. You can be of no further service to us here, but your precious life may be of service to others. The worst that will come to us is death, and none of us can know when that will come."

Duncan's eye fell wistfully on the beautiful form of Alice, who was clinging to his arm with the dependency of an infant. After a moment he said, "There are evils worse than death. But if there is someone here who will die for you, you may be spared such evils."

Cora turned and, taking her sister by the arm, led the nearly insensible Alice after her into the deepest recess of the inner cavern.

CHAPTER 9

There was a sudden and almost magical change from the chaos of the combat to the stillness that now reigned around Heyward. It acted on his heated imagination like some exciting dream. It was hard to believe that, just moments before, they had been engaged in violent struggle with the Hurons. In the silence the young major listened for any sounds that might tell him what had become of the scout and the two Mohicans. Had their attempted escape been successful or not? Their fate remained a mystery to him.

Similarly, every effort to detect the least evidence of the approach of their hidden enemies was as fruitless as the inquiry after his late companions. The horrible sounds of the battle that had so recently echoed through the forest were gone. All that could be heard now was the rush of the waters in the sweetness of nature. The wooded banks of the river seemed to have resumed their tranquility. A fishhawk, which had been a distant spectator of the battle, now swooped from his high and ragged perch atop a dead pine and soared in wide sweeps above his prey. As the forest seemed to be returning to normal, Duncan began to feel a glimmer of hope.

"There is no sign of the Hurons," he said to David. "We should go into the cavern to wait and trust the rest to Providence."

David was still bewildered from the effects of the stunning blow he received early in the battle. In his confusion he asked, "Is not the air yet filled with shrieks and cries, as though the departed spirits of the damned—"

"Not now," interrupted the impatient Heyward. "The cries have ceased. Everything but the water is still and at peace."

The major took the arm of the unsteady singing master and led him into the narrow mouth of the cave. After settling the gentle man near the sisters, Duncan set about concealing the entrance with branches. Next he arranged the blanket over the branches so that it darkened their hiding place.

As he finished, Heyward turned to the sisters. Alice trembled in Cora's arms. "Cora, your courage and clear thinking a few moments ago have helped to give us all hope. You did well to urge our three companions to attempt to escape and bring help. How can we now dry the tears that your sister weeps?"

"I am calmer, Duncan," said Alice, forcing an appearance of composure through her tears, "much calmer, now. Surely, in this hidden spot we are safe. And we will hope that help will come from those generous men who have already risked so much for us."

"Now does our gentle Alice speak like a daughter of the brave Colonel Munro!" said Heyward, pausing to press her hand as he moved past her. He seated himself in the center of the cavern, his hand convulsively clenching his remaining pistol. "The Hurons, if they come, will not get to us as easily as they may think," he muttered more to himself than to the other three.

A deep, a long, and almost breathless silence followed. The fresh air of the morning had penetrated the cave, and its influence was gradually felt on the spirits of the foursome. As minute after minute passed, the feeling of hope was gradually gaining hold of each heart.

A gleam of light from the opening crossed David Gamut's wan face, and fell on the pages of his little book of songs. He was busy leafing through the book, as if searching for some song that fitted their mood. At length, his work paid off. "The Isle of Wight," he announced. Then he drew a long, sweet note from his pitch pipe.

"May not this prove dangerous?" asked Cora, glancing her dark eye at Major Heyward.

"Poor fellow! His voice is too feeble to be heard above the noise of the falls," Heyward answered. "Let him indulge his passions. It may help all of our spirits."

"Isle of Wight!" repeated David. "It is a fine tune with solemn words! Let it be sung with proper respect!" After a moment of silence, the voice of the singer gradually filled the cavern with its gentle tones.

At the sounds, Alice unconsciously dried her tears, and bent her melting eyes on the pale features of Gamut, with an expression of delight. As Cora listened, an approving smile played on her lips. As the song continued, Heyward's stern gaze relaxed as he turned his eyes from the entrance of the cave to the gentle singer.

David's soft voice was filling the cave with long and full tones when a savage yell burst into the air. The song stopped instantly, as if the singing master's voice had been choked by his heart blocking the passage of his throat.

"We are lost!" Alice exclaimed, throwing herself into Cora's arms.

"Not yet, not yet," returned the undaunted Heyward. "The sound came from the center of the island. The Hurons must have found their dead companions. They haven't discovered us yet. There is still hope."

A second yell soon followed the first, then a rush of voices was heard pouring down the island, from its upper end. The voices reached the bare rock above the caverns, where, after a shout of savage triumph, the air continued full of horrible cries and screams.

The sounds quickly spread around the captives in every direction. In the midst of this uproar, a triumphant yell was raised within a few yards of the hidden entrance to the cave. Heyward abandoned every hope, believing it was the signal that they were discovered. Then he heard the voices collect near the spot where Hawkeye had reluctantly abandoned his rifle. A burst of voices shouted simultaneously, "Long Rifle!" causing the woods to echo the name.

On hearing this, Heyward now realized for the first time who the scout was. He knew that Long Rifle was the name the French enemies had given to a celebrated hunter and scout who helped the English troops.

"Long Rifle! Long Rifle!" passed from mouth to mouth, until the whole band appeared to be collected around a trophy which would seem to announce the death of its formidable owner. The sounds that followed made it clear to Heyward that the invaders were about to search for the body of scout in the crevices between the rocks.

"Now," he whispered to the trembling sisters, "now is the moment of uncertainty! If they overlook our hiding place, we are still safe! In any case, we now know that our friends have escaped. In two short hours we may hope for help from General Webb."

There were now a few minutes of fearful stillness. Heyward knew that the Hurons were searching for the body. More than once he heard their footsteps as they brushed past the branches that covered the entrance to their refuge. At one point, the branches moved enough that a corner of the blanket came loose. Cora folded Alice in her arms in agony, and Duncan sprang to his feet. At that moment, a shout was heard as the searchers discovered the outer of the two caves.

The inner passages to the two caves were so close to each other, that Duncan believed they could no longer escape discovery. He placed himself between the entrance and his three companions in preparation for the terrible confrontation. Moving close to the entrance, he put his face to the place where the corner of the blanket had fallen away. Here he could peer out through the piled branches that protected them from detection. In the chasm between the two caves stood an Indian who appeared to be directing the actions of the Indians searching the outer cave.

One of the warriors appeared with several branches in his arms. The leaves were stained with the blood of the wounded singing master. He showed the chief the bloodstains and said,

"Long Rifle!" Then, with a cry of satisfaction, he threw the branches onto the pile that Heyward was peering through, blocking his view.

The added security of these extra branches, placed there unwittingly by the warrior, gave the major a sense of relief. The Indians now could be heard leaving the cavern and rushing back up the island to the bodies of their fallen comrades. Duncan once more breathed freely.

"They are gone, Cora!" he whispered. "Alice, we are saved! Thank heaven we have been delivered from the grasp of so merciless an enemy!"

"We must give thanks for our salvation," Alice said, rising from Cora's protective embrace.

The eyes of the youthful Alice were radiant with the glow of grateful feelings. But as her lips began to move to pour out her prayer of thanks, they appeared to become frozen. The rosiness in her cheeks was replaced with the paleness of death; her soft and melting eyes grew hard and contracted with horror.

Heyward followed the line of her stare to the second opening of the cave, at the river end. There, peering just above the ledge that formed the threshold of the open outlet of the cavern, was the malignant, fierce, and savage face of Subtle Fox.

The Indian was straining to see into the dark interior of the cave. Then the sudden gleam of exultation and brutal triumph shot across the features of the savage. Heyward knew they had been discovered.

In that instant of horrible recognition, Duncan forgot everything but the impulses of his hot blood. He leveled his pistol and fired. The report of the weapon made the cavern bellow like an eruption from a volcano. When the smoke it vomited had been driven away by the current of air from the ravine, there was no sign of the Fox. Rushing to the opening, Heyward caught a glimpse of his dark figure disappearing around a low and narrow ledge.

Among the Hurons farther up the island a frightful stillness followed the explosion they had just heard from within the rock. But when Subtle Fox raised his voice in a long and intelligible whoop, it was answered by a spontaneous yell from the mouth of every Indian within hearing of the sound.

The clamorous noises again rushed down the island. Before Duncan had time to recover from the shock, his feeble barrier of brush was scattered to the winds. The cavern was entered at both ends, and he and his companions were dragged from their shelter and into the daylight, where they stood surrounded by the whole band of the triumphant Hurons.

CHAPTER 10

The instant he overcame the shock of what had happened, Duncan began to observe the appearance and actions of their captors. While some of the warriors stood guard over the four prisoners, others made a thorough search of their hiding place. Unable to discover any new victim, these searchers approached Heyward, pronouncing the name "Long Rifle" with a fierceness that could not be easily mistaken. Duncan pretended not to comprehend what they were talking about. After a few moments of interrogation, he looked around to find Magua who he knew could act as interpreter.

Sly Fox stood at a little distance from the prisoners. He leaned against a rock, his manner reflecting the quiet satisfaction of one who is pleased with the results of his own treachery. When the eyes of Heyward first met those of his recent guide, he turned them away in horror at the sinister though calm look on the Indian's face. Conquering his disgust, however, he was able to address his successful enemy.

"Sly Fox is too much of a warrior," said the reluctant Heyward, "to refuse telling an unarmed man what his captors say."

"They ask for the hunter who knows the paths through the woods," returned Magua, in his broken English. Then, laying his hand on the bundle of leaves that covered a wound on his shoulder, he gave a ferocious smile and continued, "Long Rifle's aim is true but it is nothing against the life of Sly Fox."

"Sly Fox is too brave to remember the hurts received in war, or the hands that gave them."

"Was it war when a tired Indian rested at the foot of a tree to eat his few pieces of corn?" asked Magua. "Was it Sly Fox who sent creeping enemies into the bushes? Whose tongue spoke words of peace while his heart was colored with blood? Not Magua!"

Duncan thought about Magua's treachery of leading them astray in the forest, but he dared not taunt his accuser with any reminder of these actions. He remained silent.

In this silence, the warriors renewed their interrogation of the prisoner.

"You hear," said Magua, with stubborn indifference, "the red Hurons call for the life of Long Rifle, or they will have the blood of the one that keeps him hidden!"

"He is gone—escaped; he is far beyond their reach."

Sly Fox smiled with cold contempt, as he answered, "When the white man dies, he thinks he is at peace; but the red men know how to torture even the ghosts of their enemies. Where is his body? Let the Hurons see his scalp."

"He is not dead, but escaped."

Magua shook his head incredulously. "Is he a bird, to spread his wings; or is he a fish, to swim without air! The white chief thinks the Hurons are fools."

"Though no fish, Long Rifle can swim. He floated down the stream when the eyes of the Hurons were not looking."

"And why did the white chief stay?" demanded the still incredulous Indian.

"The white man thinks none but cowards desert their women," Heyward replied.

Magua muttered a few words to himself before he continued, aloud, "Can the Mohicans swim, too, as well as crawl under the bushes? Where is Great Snake?"

Duncan answered reluctantly, "He also went down with the water."

"And Bounding Elk—the one you call Uncas—has he gone, too?"

"He, too, went down with the water," Duncan replied.

The Hurons had crowded around in silence

during this exchange. When Heyward ceased to speak, they turned their eyes on Magua, silently demanding an explanation of what the white chief had said. Gesturing and uttering a few words, the Fox communicated what the major had told him. At this disappointment the Hurons raised a frightful yell. They glared at the captives who still remained in their power. A few made menacing gestures.

Duncan saw a dark hand take hold of the rich tresses that flowed from Alice's head down over her shoulders. The Huron then passed a knife around her head in a mock scalping, as if suggesting what was to come. The major attempted to step to her side to defend her. But his hands were bound and at his first move the chief of the Hurons took hold of him with a vice-like grip. Duncan tried to console the sisters with a few reassuring words.

But the young major fully understood the magnitude of their danger. At any moment, any one of their captors might choose to carry out some act of violence against any one of them. While, therefore, he sustained an outward appearance of calmness and strength, his heart leaped into his throat every time one of the Hurons moved toward Alice and Cora.

His dread was, however, greatly relieved when he saw that the leader had summoned his warriors to himself in counsel. Their discussion was short and, judging by the silence of the warriors, the decision unanimous. The gestures that the group made in the direction of Fort Edward suggested that they were worried about the approach of danger from that direction.

Once the decision was made, the Hurons moved quickly to carry out their plans. The canoe they had used to gain access to the upper end of the island was carried to the foot of the falls and placed in the water near the mouth of the outer cave. The leader then made signs for the prisoners to descend the rocks and board the canoe.

As resistance was impossible, Heyward set the example by leading the way into the canoe, where he was soon seated with the sisters and the still bewildered David. One Huron sat in the stern to guide the canoe through the channels among the eddies and rapids of the river. The remaining members of the attack force plunged into the water and, clinging to the sides of the vessel, glided down the current.

In a few moments the captives found themselves on the south bank of the river, almost opposite the point where they had started their voyage upstream the evening before. The horses of the travelers had been found in their hiding place by the Hurons, and they were now led out of the woods. The attacking band now divided. The chief, mounted on Heyward's cavalry horse, led most of the Hurons across the river and disappeared into the woods, heading north. They took Gamut's horse with them. The captives were left in the charge of six fierce warriors under the command of Sly Fox.

Duncan felt renewed uneasiness as he saw what was happening. He realized that the four of them were to be kept as hopeless captives by their savage conquerors. He felt the emergency was so great that he was willing to risk a desperate trick. He decided he would attempt to bribe and flatter Magua into helping them.

Speaking to his former guide, Duncan said, in tones as friendly and confiding as he could make them, "I would speak to you, Magua, what is fit only for so great a chief as you to hear."

The Indian turned his eyes on the young soldier scornfully, as he answered, "Speak. Trees have no ears."

"But the Hurons are not deaf," said Duncan.

Magua told the Hurons to continue preparing the horses for the sisters. He then motioned for Duncan to step away from the group with him. "Now, speak," he said, "if the words are such that Magua should hear them."

"Sly Fox has proved himself worthy of the honorable name given him by his Canada fathers," said Duncan. "I can see his wisdom in all he has done for us and in the way he has deceived his enemies. I will remember these things when it is time for Magua to be properly rewarded."

"What has Sly Fox done?" demanded the Indian coldly.

"Did he not realize that the woods were filled with enemies? Did he not intentionally lose the path to blind the eyes of the Hurons? And did he not pretend to go back to the Hurons so that he could then get control over the daughters of the rich Colonel Munro in order to deliver those daughters safely to him? Yes, Magua, I see it all, and I have already been thinking how so much wisdom and honesty should be repaid. Colonel Munro will honor Magua for his great and wise service. Dollars will be as plentiful in his pouch as pebbles on the shore of Lake Horican. As for myself, I know not how to exceed the gratitude of Colonel Munro, but I—yes, I will—"

"What will the young white chief give?" demanded Magua when Heyward hesitated.

"I will make the firewater from the islands flow before the wigwam of Magua, until his heart shall be lighter than the feathers of the hummingbird."

Magua listened to Heyward gravely. After thinking for a moment, he laid his hand on the bandages of his wounded shoulder. "Do friends make such marks?" he asked, with some energy.

"Would Long Rifle make such a slight wound on an enemy?"

"Does the white chief shoot his pistol at a friend?"

"Would I miss my aim at such close range if I seriously intended to kill?" returned Duncan, smiling with well-acted sincerity.

After a long pause Magua made an expressive gesture and said, "Enough! Sly Fox is a wise chief, and what he does will be seen. Go, and be silent. When Magua speaks, it will be the time to answer."

Magua approached the horses to see if all was ready for their departure. He then signaled to Heyward to assist the sisters into the saddles.

The young major, no longer able to find any excuse for delay, complied. As he helped Cora and Alice, Duncan whispered a few encouraging words to each.

The effects of David's wound were gradually lessening and he was beginning to come to a full understanding of the difficult situation they were in.

The small party headed south with Magua in the lead. He was followed by the singing master. The sisters, on horseback, were behind David, with Heyward walking beside them. The six Hurons were on either side of them and behind them. It was clear to Duncan that there was no hope of escaping while they were on the move. At least, being on foot, he might be able to slow the progress of the group a little. He gave a final longing look in the direction of Fort Edward, in hopes that there might be some sign of approaching help.

They headed to the south, directly away from Fort William Henry. In spite of this, Duncan could not believe that his tempting offer to Magua had been that easily forgotten. As they kept on in the same direction throughout the day, however, Heyward felt less and less hopeful that Sly Fox would rise to the bait he had offered.

Only Cora remembered the scout's instructions to mark their trail so that they could be followed more easily. This, however, was difficult to accomplish because she was being closely watched by their captors. Only once was she completely successful when she broke the bough of a large sumac and, at the same time, dropped her glove. She was detected, however, and one of the Hurons returned the glove to her with a warning look so fierce that she dared not attempt it again. He then broke more of the branches so that it would appear to have been caused by some struggling animal.

Magua led the group forward at a steady pace throughout the day. He remained silent and gave no signs of considering the offer

Heyward had made. Finally, late in the day, he led the party up a steep hill. The ascent was so difficult that the women had to dismount and walk. When they reached the top, they found themselves on a level spot with a few trees. In this easily defended spot Magua was willing to let the group get some much-needed rest.

CHAPTER 11

The steepness of the hill and the fact that one side of it was too rugged to be scaled made defense of the spot easy and surprise by an attacker nearly impossible. Because they had traveled such a distance, Heyward had given up hope of rescue. He put his energy into comforting and consoling Alice and Cora.

One of the Indians had shot a faun along the trail. He and his companions gorged themselves with the uncooked flesh. Magua did not partake of this revolting meal. He sat apart, apparently buried in the deepest thought.

Heyward observed Magua's pensive mood. He believed that Sly Fox might be trying to figure out how to get the captives away from the six Hurons so that he could take them to Munro and receive the rewards. The major decided to offer assistance and to further tempt the Indian.

Walking casually to the spot where Sly Fox was seated, he said, "Has not Magua traveled south long enough to escape all danger from the Canadians? And will not the chief of Fort William Henry be better pleased to see his daughters before another night has passed? Might not too much time harden his heart to their loss and make him less liberal in his reward?"

"Do the pale faces love their children less in the morning than at night?" asked the Indian, coldly.

"By no means," returned Heyward. "The white man often forgets the burial place of his fathers, but the affection of a parent for his child is never permitted to die."

"And is the heart of the white-headed chief so soft? He is hard on his warriors and his eyes are made of stone!" Anger began to creep into Magua's voice.

Heyward tried to reassure the Indian. "He is severe to the idle and wicked, but to the sober and deserving he is a leader, both just and humane. You have seen Colonel Munro in front of his warriors, Magua; but I have seen his eyes swimming in water, when he spoke of those children who are now in your power."

Heyward tried to read the remarkable expression that gleamed across Sly Fox's face. At first it seemed as if he might be thinking about the rewards he could receive; but then the expression became so fiercely malignant that it seemed prompted by some passion more sinister than greed.

Almost instantly the Indian suppressed the expression with a face of death-like calm. He said, "Go to the dark-haired daughter and tell her that Magua waits to speak to her. The father will remember what the child promises."

Duncan assumed that Magua meant that he wanted further assurance that he would receive the promised gifts if he delivered Munro's daughters. Therefore, he returned to where Alice and Cora sat and told them what the Indian had said. He concluded by saying, "Remember, Cora, that your life, as well as that of Alice, may in some measure depend on your presence of mind and ingenuity as you speak with him."

While Heyward remained by Alice's side to comfort her, Cora walked to where Magua was sitting. "What would Sly Fox say to the daughter of Munro?" she asked with dignity.

"Listen," said the Indian, laying his hand firmly upon her arm. Cora quietly removed her arm from his grasp. He continued, "Magua was born a chief and a warrior among the red Hurons of Canada; he was twenty before he saw a pale face. And he was happy! Then his Canada fathers came into the woods, and taught him to drink the firewater, and he became a rascal. The Hurons drove him from the graves of his

fathers, as they would chase the hunted buffalo. He ran down the shores of the lakes. There he hunted and fished among the white Canadians, till the people chased him again through the woods into the arms of his enemies. The chief, who was born a Huron, became a warrior among the Mohawks."

Magua paused to suppress the anger that began to burn with too bright a flame, as he recalled of his treatment at the hands of others.

"I have heard something like this before," Cora said.

"Was it the fault of Sly Fox that his head was not made of rock? Who gave him the firewater? Who made him a villain? It was the pale faces, the people of your own color," he said, glaring at her.

"Must I be held responsible because thoughtless and unprincipled men exist and because their skin color resembles mine?" Cora calmly demanded.

"No; Magua is a man, and not a fool."

"What, then, have I to do with your misfortunes and your errors?" Cora continued.

"Listen," said the Indian, resuming his earnest attitude. "When his English and French fathers declared war, Sly Fox joined the war-post of the Mohawks and fought against his own nation. The pale faces have driven the red skins from their hunting grounds, and now when they fight, a white man leads the way. Your father, the old chief at Fort William Henry, was the great captain of our war party. The Mohawks did what he told them to. He made a law, that if an Indian swallowed the firewater and came into the shelters of his warriors, it should not be forgotten. Magua foolishly opened his mouth, and the hot liquor led him into the cabin of Munro. What did the grayhead? Let his daughter say."

"He did not forget his words, and he did justice by punishing the offender," said the undaunted Cora.

"Justice!" repeated the Indian, casting a ferocious expression at her unyielding face. "Is it justice to make evil and then punish for it? Magua was not himself; it was the firewater that spoke and acted for him! But Munro had the Huron chief tied up before all the pale-faced warriors, and whipped like a dog."

Cora remained silent. She did not know how to make amends for this imprudent severity on the part of her father.

"See!" continued Magua, tearing aside the slight shirt that very imperfectly concealed his painted breast. "Here are scars given by knives and bullets—of these a warrior may boast before his nation. But the gray-head has left marks on the back of the Huron chief that he must hide like a squaw. A Huron's spirit does not feel the blows his body suffers in battle. But when Magua felt the blows of Munro, his spirit lay under the birch. The spirit remembers forever!"

"But your spirit may be soothed. If my father has done you this injustice, show him how an Indian can forgive an injury, and take his daughters back to him. You have heard from Major Heyward—"

Magua shook his head, forbidding her to repeat offers he so much despised.

"What would you have?" continued Cora, realizing that Duncan's offer of rewards had meant nothing to the Indian.

"Magua holds the spirit of the gray-head in his hand," the Indian said quietly.

"Name your intention, Magua," said Cora, struggling with herself to speak with steady calmness. "Is there no reward, no means of easing the injury and of softening your heart? At least, release my gentle sister, and pour out all your malice on me. Gain a reward by her safety and satisfy your revenge with a single victim."

"Listen," the Indian said. "The fair-haired sister can go back to the fort of her father if the dark-haired woman will swear by the Great Spirit to do as I say."

"What must I promise?" demanded Cora, still maintaining a dignity in her presence.

"When Magua left his people his wife was given to another chief. Magua has now made friends with the Hurons, and will go back to the graves of his tribe, on the shores of the great lake. Let the daughter of the English chief go with him, and live in his wigwam forever."

Cora found the proposal unthinkable. Nevertheless, she maintained sufficient self-command to reply, "And what pleasure would Magua find in sharing his cabin with a wife he did not love, a wife who is of a different nation and a different color than his own? It would be better to take the gold of Munro, and buy the heart of some Huron maid with his gifts."

The Indian made no reply for nearly a minute, but glared so fiercely at Cora that she averted her eyes. At last Magua answered in tones of deep malignancy, "When the blows scorched the back of Magua, he knew he would find his revenge. The daughter of Munro would draw his water, hoe his corn, and cook his venison. The body of Munro would live in his fort, but his heart would lie within reach of the knife of Sly Fox."

"Monster! You live up to your treacherous name," cried Cora, unable to stop herself. "None but a fiend could dream up such a vengeance. But you overestimate your power! The heart of Munro will defy your evil!"

Magua answered this bold defiance with a ghastly smile and he motioned her away, as if to end the discussion forever. He then turned and went to join the others who were feasting on the venison.

Cora returned to Heyward and Alice. Duncan, who had been anxiously watching the conversation from a short distance, asked her what had been said. Cora, not wanting to alarm her younger sister, evaded direct reply.

When Alice asked what was going to happen to them, she pointed toward the Hurons and simply said, "There; read our fortunes in their faces. We shall see! We shall see!" The three white captives looked toward the six Indians, who were listening intensely to Magua as he spoke to them in the Huron language.

He was speaking to them with the dignity of

an Indian chief. At first, the language, as well as the action of Magua, appeared calm and thoughtful. He spoke of the long and painful route by which they had left those happy villages to the north in order to come and battle against the enemies of their Canadian fathers. He named many of the warriors who had made this journey. He praised those who had so recently fought valiantly on the island. Pointing toward Heyward, he recalled the exceptional bravery of the warrior who had struggled with the major on the rocks before falling to his death. When he mentioned the hated name Long Rifle, a loud and long yell arose from the group and echoed into the distance. He recalled the image of their fearless companion who, hanging between heaven and earth, had presented such a spectacle of horror to the whole band. He recounted how each of their friends had fallen, never failing to praise their courage.

After reciting these events, Magua demanded, "Are the Hurons dogs to bear this? There is a dark spot on the names of the Hurons, and it must be hid in blood!" His voice was no longer audible in the burst of rage that now broke into the air. Seeing that revenge was at hand, the six Hurons sprang to their feet and, with the most frantic cries, they rushed upon their prisoners in a body with drawn knives and uplifted tomahawks.

Heyward threw himself between the sisters and the first of the advancing warriors. He struggled to stop the violent advance. In that instant, Magua spoke again and proposed that, rather than killing their captives instantly, they prolong misery of their victims. His six companions quickly agreed.

The Indians then threw themselves on the four. The four struggled but each was subdued and tied to a tree. Duncan, Cora, and David then watched the warriors make their preparations. Alice sagged against the bindings that held her to the tree. Her hands were clasped in prayer while her eyes gazed at Duncan's face with infantile dependency.

The vengeance of the Hurons had now taken a new direction, and they prepared to execute it with barbarous ingenuity. Some built up the blazing fire; one was cutting splinters of pine, in order to pierce the flesh of their captives with the burning fragments; and others bent the tops of two saplings to the earth, in order to suspend Heyward by the arms between the recoiling branches.

But the vengeance of Magua sought a deeper and more malignant enjoyment. He approached Cora, and pointed out, with a malicious expression on his face, the speedy fate that awaited her. Then he added, "So, what says the daughter of Munro? Her head is too good to find a pillow in the wigwam of Sly Fox. Will she like it better when it rolls about this hill, a plaything for the wolves?"

"What does the monster mean!" demanded the astonished Heyward.

"Nothing!" Cora replied firmly. "He is a savage, a barbarous and ignorant savage, and knows not what he does. Let us find time, with our dying breath, to ask for him penitence and pardon."

Magua continued, "You can save them. Decide: will you follow Magua to the great lakes, to carry his water and feed him with corn?"

"Leave me," Cora said. "You mingle bitterness in my prayers; you stand between me and my God!"

Magua pointed toward Alice with taunting irony and continued, "Look! the child weeps! She is too young to die! Send her to Munro, to comb his gray hairs, and keep life in the heart of the old man."

"What says he, dearest Cora?" asked the trembling voice of Alice. "Did he speak of sending me to our father?"

For many moments the elder sister looked upon the younger, with a face that wavered with powerful and contending emotions. At length she spoke with a tone of tenderness that seemed maternal. "Alice, the Huron offers all of us life, if—if I will bow down this rebellious, stubborn pride of mine, and consent—" Her voice became choked. After a moment she continued, "He would have me follow him to the wilderness; go to the habitations of the Hurons; to remain there; in short, to become his wife!"

A brief silence followed. Then Cora said, "Speak, then, Alice! And you, too, Major Heyward, aid my weak reason with your counsel. Is life to be purchased by such a sacrifice? What should I do?"

Duncan immediately replied, "Cora! You jest with our misery! I could not live with myself knowing the price you paid so that I might live."

"I knew you would answer so, Duncan!" exclaimed Cora. "What says my dear Alice? If she wishes it, I will do this to save her life."

Heyward and Cora listened with painful suspense, but no sounds were heard in reply. It appeared as if the delicate and sensitive form of Alice would shrink into itself, as she listened to this proposal. In a few moments, however, she slowly raised her head. "No; better that we die as we have lived, together!" she said at last.

"Then die!" shouted Magua, unable to contain his rage now that the weakest of the captives had thwarted his plan with her sudden exhibition of firmness. At the same instant he spoke, he violently hurled his tomahawk at her.

The axe cleaved the air in front of Heyward, and cutting some of the flowing ringlets of Alice's hair, quivered in the tree above her head.

The sight maddened Duncan to desperation. Collecting all his energies in one effort he snapped the twigs which bound him and rushed upon another savage, who was preparing, with a more deliberate aim, to repeat the blow. They grappled and fell to the earth together. Heyward was unable to get a firm hold on the naked body of his adversary. The Huron glided from his grasp and rose with one knee on his chest, pressing him down with the weight of a giant. Duncan saw the knife gleaming in the warrior's hand above him, when a whistling sound swept past him. It was accompanied by the sharp crack of a rifle. He felt the pressure of the Huron's knee leave his chest. He saw the savage expression of his adversary's face change to a look of vacant wildness as the Indian fell dead on the faded leaves by his side.

CHAPTER 12

The Hurons stood aghast at the sudden death on one of their band. Before they had time to recover, there was a loud shout from a little thicket, where the warriors had piled their rifles. The next moment, Hawkeye, not taking time to reload his precious rifle that he had picked from the pile, was advancing on them, swinging Killdeer like a club with wide and powerful sweeps. Bounding past him, Uncas leaped into the middle of the group of Hurons. He placed himself directly in front of Cora and stood there whirling a tomahawk and flourishing a glittering knife. At almost the same moment, Chingachgook appeared, looking equally menacing, and placed himself by his son's side.

The Hurons recoiled before these warlike intruders. Surprised exclamations of the dreaded names fell from their lips: "Long Rifle! Bounding Elk! Great Snake!"

But Magua was not so easily confused. At a

glance he realized the intruders did not have firearms at the ready. He unsheathed his long and dangerous knife and rushed with a loud whoop at Chingachgook.

Uncas answered the whoop, and leaping on an enemy, with a single, well-directed blow of his tomahawk, opened the enemy's skull to the brain. Hawkeye brought the butt of his trusty Killdeer down on the head of another of the enemy, crushing him to the earth with the sweeping blow.

Heyward tore Magua's tomahawk from the sapling and rushed eagerly toward the fray. He hurled the weapon at an adversary, unwilling to wait until he was closer to his enemy. The weapon struck the Indian a glancing blow on the forehead. It stunned the warrior for a moment and stopped his rush toward the soldier. Seizing this delay, the impetuous young major sprang upon his enemy to fight him with his bare hands. A single instant was enough to assure him of the rashness of his action. He immediately found himself warding off the desperate thrusts made with the knife of the partially stunned Huron. Heyward threw his arms about him and succeeded in pinning the limbs of the other to his side with an iron grasp, but one that was far too exhausting to himself to continue for long.

At the next moment, the breech of Hawkeye's rifle fell on the naked head of his adversary, whose muscles appeared to wither under the shock, as he sank from the arms of Duncan, flexible and motionless.

After Uncas had brained his first antagonist, he turned, like a hungry lion, to seek another. When the battle had first started, one Huron had seized the opportunity to attempt to complete the work of revenge on the white sisters. With a shout of triumph he sprang toward the defenseless Cora, hurling his keen axe at her as he advanced. The tomahawk grazed her shoulder and cut the twigs that bound her to the tree. She eluded the grasp of the Huron, and reckless of her own safety, threw herself on Alice, striving with convulsed fingers to tear asunder the twigs which confined her sister. Seizing Cora by the rich tresses that fell about her head, he tore her from her frantic hold and bowed her down with brutal violence to her knees. The Indian drew the flowing curls through his hand, and raising them on high with an outstretched arm, he passed the knife around the head of his victim, with a taunting laugh. But this moment of fierce gratification cost him his opportunity to complete his intended actions.

It was just then the sight caught the eye of Uncas. With a leap, the young Mohawk landed on the chest of his enemy, sending him sprawling. A second later the two were in fierce combat. But the conflict was soon decided; the tomahawk of

Heyward and the rifle of Hawkeye descended on the skull of the Huron, at the same moment that the knife of Uncas reached his heart.

The only struggle still continuing was that of Sly Fox and Great Snake. The two whirled in the dust, each aiming deadly blows toward the other and each evading the deadly blows aimed by the other. Suddenly darting on each other, they closed, and came to the earth, twisted together like twining serpents. Chingachgook's companions, no longer engaged in their own battles, ran to lend aid. They were unable, however, to be of assistance. The swift circlings of the combatants seemed to incorporate their bodies into one. Any intrusion by the spectators could have easily injured the wrong party.

The whirling struggle carried Chingachgook and Magua to the edge of the little plain on top of the hill. The Mohican now found an opportunity to make a powerful thrust with his knife; Magua suddenly relinquished his grasp, and fell backward without motion, and seemingly without life. Chingachgook leaped to his feet with a cry of triumph.

"Well done! Victory to the Mohicans!" cried Hawkeye, once more raising the butt of the long and fatal rifle. "A finishing blow for Sly Fox from Long Rifle!"

But at the very moment when the dangerous weapon was descending toward Magua's head, the subtle Huron rolled swiftly from beneath the danger and over the edge of the precipice. Landing on his feet, he was seen leaping with a single bound into the center of a thicket of low bushes, which clung along the sides of the cliff.

The Mohicans, who had thought Sly Fox was dead, gave a shout of surprised dismay at the sight of their enemy's escape from this close call.

"That's just like him," cried the scout, "the lying and deceitful creature that he is. Let him go—let him go. He's but one man, without rifle or bow and many a long mile from his French comrades. Like a rattler that lost his fangs, he can do no further mischief at this point. But we had better make sure that the rest of these thieving Hurons are really dead."

Saying this, the honest scout calmly walked from one to another of the warriors who lay dead on the hilltop. At each body, he stooped and thrust his long knife into lifeless corps, as though they had been so many brute carcasses. Chingachgook, however, had already collected the scalp from each of the bodies.

Meanwhile, Heyward went to assist Alice and Cora. Uncas, in contradiction to his habits and even, almost, his very nature, joined Heyward. They released Alice, who sank into Cora's arms.

"We are saved!" she murmured. "We are

saved, to return to the arms of our dear father. And Duncan, our own brave and noble Duncan has escaped without a scratch."

Heyward, with tears in his eyes, watched over this joyful scene. Uncas, bloodstained from the combat, stood calmly watching. Although he did not shed any tears, his eyes lost the fierceness of battle and beamed with sympathy as he observed the sisters.

Meanwhile, Hawkeye, having satisfied himself that the six Hurons were in fact dead, untied the patient singing master. "There," the scout said as he released David, "you are once more master of your own limbs. And if you won't take offence, I'll give you some advice. I suggest that you trade in that musical device that you carry for some sort of weapon. A gun is far preferable to a pitch pipe in the untamed forest."

"Arms are needed for the battle, but the song of thanksgiving is needed in the victory!" answered the liberated David. "Friend," he added, thrusting his delicate hand toward Hawkeye, "I thank thee that the hairs of my head still grow where they were first rooted; I have always found my locks well suited to the brain they shelter. I would have been happy to join in the battle had I not been tied to that tree."

"You'll see plenty of other chances to join a fight if you stay here in the forest with us for any length of time," Hawkeye replied. "I have got back my old companion, Killdeer," he added, striking his hand on the breech of his rifle; "and that in itself is a victory. These Hurons outwitted themselves when they placed their firearms out of reach. I am only sorry that knave Magua escaped."

"Even so," said David, "a song of thanksgiving is needed." The singing master took out his hymnal and selected a song appropriate to the recent victory. "I invite you, friends, to join in praise for this deliverance from the hands of barbarians and infidels," he said. He named a hymn and its page number and then produced a note on his pitch pipe. He began singing and keeping time with his right hand. The sisters were too busy comforting each other to join in.

Hawkeye listened, unmoved, while he coolly adjusted his flint and reloaded his rifle. The scout shook his head, and muttering some unintelligible words, he walked away, to collect and to examine the state of the captured rifles of the Hurons. He was pleased to note that there were enough weapons and ammunition for each of the men—including David Gamut—to be armed.

When the singing master's song was finished, the scout announced that it was time for them to move. The party carefully descended the steep hill to the place where the two horses had been left. Hawkeye led the group through a thicket and across a babbling brook to a small wooded valley. Here they stopped in the shade of some elms.

Hawkeye and the Mohicans were obviously familiar with the quiet spot. Leaning their rifles against the trees, they began throwing aside the dried leaves and opening the blue clay. In a few minutes a clear and sparkling spring of bright, glancing water quickly bubbled out of the ground.

After refreshing themselves with the cool water, the Mohicans set about building a small fire so that they could cook the venison they gathered from the wallet of one of the Hurons. While the meal was being prepared, Heyward took the opportunity to ask how they had come to be rescued.

"How is it that we see you so soon, my generous friend," he asked, "and without aid from the soldiers at Fort Edward?"

"Had we gone to the fort, we would have arrived in time to rake the leaves over your bodies, but too late to have saved your scalps," coolly answered the scout. "No, instead we hid close by, under the bank of the Hudson, waiting to watch the movements of the Hurons."

"You saw our capture?" Heyward asked.

"We heard it," Hawkeye replied. "An Indian yell is plain language to men who have passed their days in the woods. But when the Hurons brought you from the island to the riverbank, we were driven to crawl like serpents, beneath the leaves; and then we lost sight of you entirely, until we placed eyes on you again tied to the trees and headed for an Indian massacre."

"Our rescue was the deed of Providence. It was nearly a miracle that you did not mistake the path, for the Hurons divided, and each band had its horses."

"Ay! There we were thrown off the scent, and might, indeed, have lost the trail, had it not been for Uncas. We took the path, however, that led into the wilderness, for we guessed, and guessed rightly, that the Hurons would take their prisoners that way. But when we had followed it for many miles, without finding a single twig broken, I began to doubt our decision, especially as all the footsteps had the prints of moccasins."

"The Hurons took the precaution making us wear moccasins," said Duncan, raising a foot and exhibiting the buckskin he wore.

"Just what you'd expect from the cunning thieves. But we weren't thrown off by so common a trick. But in truth, you owe your safety to the judgment of the young Mohican. Uncas was bold enough to say that the beasts ridden by the young ladies," continued Hawkeye, glancing toward the two horses of the ladies, "planted the legs of one side on the ground at the same time, which is different from how most horses walk."

"That type of horse is known for that unusual walk," Heyward said. "They come from the shores of Narragansett Bay and are celebrated for their strength and for the ease of this peculiar movement."

"It may be," said Hawkeye. "But I should have seen it myself. But my judgment in deer and beaver and the other creatures of the forest is greater than my knowledge in beasts of burden."

He paused for a moment, as if considering this subject. Then he continued, "I dare to say there are even stranger sights to be seen in the settlements! Nature is sadly abused by man, when he interferes with it."

After another short pause, he returned to his explanation of how they found the captives. "But it was Uncas who had noticed how the horses moved, and their trail led us to a broken bush. The outer branch, near the prints of one of the horses, was bent upward, as a lady breaks a flower from its stem, but all the rest were ragged and broken down, as if the strong hand of a man had been tearing them. So I concluded that the cunning varmints had seen the twig bent and had torn the rest, to make us believe an animal had done it. So we stayed with the trail until we found you on the top of that hill.

But I see that Uncas has built his fire, and it is time we think of eating, for the journey before us is long."

When they had eaten, Hawkeye announced his determination to proceed. The sisters resumed their saddles. Duncan and David grasped their rifles, and followed on foot. The scout led the advance, and the Mohicans brought up the rear. The whole party moved swiftly through the narrow path, toward the north, leaving behind them the soothing waters of the spring—and the unburied bodies of the dead to fester on the hilltop.

CHAPTER 13

Hawkeye led them back across the same wooded hills and valleys that Magua had brought them over that morning. As the sun dipped lower in the sky, the oppressive heat of the day faded and they were able to make good time. Long before twilight they had covered many miles on their journey north, in the direction of Fort William Henry.

The scout did not hesitate, seeming to read the signs of the route by instinct. Gradually the light among the trees began to fade as the mass of clouds to the west turned a warm golden color tinged with ruby streaks.

Hawkeye turned suddenly and, pointing upward toward the gorgeous heavens, spoke, "Yonder is the signal that man to seek his food and natural rest. Our night, however, will soon be over, for when the moon rises, we must be up and moving again. Chingachgook and I fought the Maquas not far from here, the first time I ever drew blood. It was years ago, but I remember the spot well. We put up a small blockhouse to fight from. If I am not mistaken, the place should lie not more than a hundred yards to our left."

With that the sturdy hunter moved boldly into a dense thicket of young chestnuts, shoving aside the branches as he went. In a few moments, the group emerged into an open space that surrounded a low, green hillock. On top of the small mound was the decayed blockhouse Hawkeye had spoken of. In the years that had passed since the scout fought here, the building had quietly crumbled, neglected and nearly forgotten. The roof of bark had long since fallen, and mingled with the soil, but most of the huge logs of pine, which had been hastily thrown together, still stood in their original positions.

Heyward, the sisters, and David were reluctant to approach a building so decayed. Hawkeye and the Indians, however, entered within the low walls with obvious interest. While the scout surveyed the ruins, Chingachgook related to his son the brief history of the skirmish that had been fought, in his youth, in that secluded spot. As he talked, his voice was filled with pride.

After the scout had completed his study, the vigilant Duncan approached him and asked,

"Wouldn't we be safer in a resting place less known and less visited than this?"

"Few live who know the blockhouse was ever built," Hawkeye replied slowly. "Not much is written about scrimmages like the one that took place here. It was fought between the Lenape and the Mohawks, in a war they waged against each other. I was a youngster. I fought on the side of the Mohicans because I knew they were a wronged race. Forty days and forty nights the Mohawks craved our blood around this pile of logs, which I designed and helped the Lenape build. We were outnumbered but we fought bravely and eventually defeated the hounds. Not a man of them ever got back to tell the fate of his party. But I was young then, and new to the sight of blood. I didn't like the thought that creatures who had spirits like myself should lay on the bare ground, to be torn apart by beasts, so I buried the dead with my own hands. I buried them under that very little mound you and the women are sitting on."

Instantly, Heyward and the sisters arose from the grassy grave with alarmed looks on their faces.

"They are gone, and they are harmless," continued Hawkeye, waving his hand. "They'll never shout the war-whoop or strike a blow with the tomahawk again! And of all those who fought side by side with us, Chingachgook and

I are the only ones still living! The brothers and family of the Mohican formed our war party; and you see in Chingachgook and Uncas all that are now left of his race."

Heyward, Alice, and Cora involuntarily turned their eyes to the dark forms of the two Mohicans who sat within the shadows of the blockhouse. The son was listening intently to his father's story of honorable warriors who fought there years before.

"You see before you a chief of the great Mohican Sagamores!" Hawkeye said. "Once his family could chase their deer over tracts of country so wide that they could run for days without crossing brook or hill that was not their own; but what is left to their descendants? He may find his six feet of earth when he dies. And he can keep that in peace, if he has a friend who will take the trouble to bury him deep enough that the plowshares cannot reach him."

"Enough!" said Heyward, worried that further discussion of the subject might unnecessarily upset Alice and Cora. "We have journeyed far, and some of us are in need of rest."

"It is quite reasonable to suppose that the gentle ones are ready to rest, after all they have seen and done this day," Hawkeye said. He then turned to the Mohicans who had just emerged from the ruins. "Uncas, clear out the spring that we may have water to refresh ourselves.

Meanwhile, your father and I will make a roof of these chestnut shoots and a bed of grass and leaves for the gentle sisters."

Shortly, Alice and Cora were drifting to sleep on a fragrant bed of sweet shrubs and dried leaves. Duncan had prepared himself to spend the night standing guard near them, but the scout pointed toward Chingachgook and said, "The eyes of a white man are too heavy and too blind for such a watch as this! The Mohican will be our sentinel, therefore let us sleep."

In spite of Hawkeye's words, the young major had resolved not to close his eyes until he had delivered Munro's daughters into the arms of their father at Fort William Henry. For many minutes after all the others except Chingachgook had gone to sleep, Duncan succeeded in keeping his senses on the alert to every moaning sound that arose from the forest. Before long, however, the young man sank into a deep sleep and was dreaming that he was a knight in armor hoping to win the favor of a princess through his devoted protection of her.

How long the tired Duncan slumbered, he never knew himself, but he was awakened by a light tap on the shoulder. He sprang upon his feet in confusion. "Who comes?" he demanded. Habit made him reach for his sword which he forgot lay broken on the island in the waterfalls. "Speak! friend or enemy?"

"Friend," replied the low voice of Chingachgook. "Moon comes and white man's fort is far off; time to move, when sleep shuts the eyes of the Frenchman."

"You are right!" Duncan said, looking up at the bright moon. "Call up your friends, and bridle the horses while I wake my own companions for the march."

"We are awake, Duncan," said the soft, silvery tones of Alice within the building, "and ready to travel very fast after so refreshing a sleep. But you have stood watch over us all night and must be exhausted."

An exclamation from Chingachgook saved Duncan from having to respond to Alice.

"The Mohicans hear an enemy!" whispered Hawkeye, who by now was awake and stirring. "They scent danger in the wind!"

"God forbid!" exclaimed Heyward. "Surely we have had enough of bloodshed!"

While he spoke, however, the young soldier seized his rifle and advanced, prepared to make up for his shortcomings as a sentinel. As he heard the sounds which had aroused the Mohicans he whispered, "It is some creature of the forest prowling around us in quest of food."

"Shhh!" returned the attentive scout. "It is man; even I can now tell his tread, poor as my senses are when compared to an Indian's! That scampering Sly Fox has joined one of General

Montcalm's outlying parties of Hurons, and they have found our trail. Lead the horses into the blockhouse, Uncas; and the rest of you take cover there too. Poor and old as it is, it still offers protection."

Within moments the whole party, including the horses, was silently gathered within the shelter of the ruined building. The sound of approaching footsteps was now distinctly audible to everyone in the group. The advance of the group came to a halt when they reached the place where the scout had led his party off the trail and into the thicket that surrounded the blockhouse. The voices of about twenty men could be heard in noisy discussion.

Hawkeye, in a whisper, affirmed to Heyward that it was the language of the Hurons. The young major only grasped his rifle more firmly and fastened his eyes upon the narrow opening through which he gazed upon the moonlight view with increasing anxiety.

A moment later, the rustling of leaves and crackling of dried twigs made it apparent that the Hurons were separating in pursuit of the lost trail. Fortunately for the pursued, the light of the moon was not strong enough to penetrate the deep shadows of the thicket and allow the searchers to see the footprints they looked for.

It was not long, however, before the restless Hurons were heard beating the brush, and gradually approaching the inner edge of that dense border of young chestnuts that encircled the little area.

"They are coming," muttered Heyward, attempting to thrust his rifle through the chink in the logs. "We must fire on their approach."

"Stay in the shadows," returned the scout. "A single shot would bring the hungry varlets on us in a body."

Curbing his impatience, the young major again looked out on the area and awaited the result in silence. At that instant the thicket opened, and a tall and armed Huron advanced a few paces into the open space. As he gazed upon the silent blockhouse, the moon fell upon his swarthy face, and revealed his surprise and curiosity. In a low voice, he called a companion to his side.

The two Hurons stood together for several moments pointing at the crumbling edifice and conversing in low tones. They then approached, though with slow and cautious steps, pausing every instant to look at the building, like startled deer struggling between curiosity and apprehension.

At this moment, Heyward observed that the scout loosened his knife in its sheath and lowered the muzzle of his rifle. Imitating these movements, the young man prepared himself for the struggle that now seemed inevitable.

The two were so near that the least motion in one of the horses, or even a breath louder than common, would have betrayed the fugitives. But, noticing the mound where Hawkeye had buried his Mohawk enemies years earlier, the Hurons examined it. They spoke together, and the sounds of their voices were low and solemn, as if influenced by a reverence that was deeply blended with awe. Then they drew warily back, keeping their eyes riveted on the ruin, as if they expected to see the ghosts of the dead issue from its silent walls. Reaching the boundary of the area, they moved slowly into the thicket and disappeared.

Hawkeye dropped the breech of his rifle to the earth, and drawing a long breath, exclaimed in an audible whisper, "Ay! They respect the dead, and it has this time saved their own lives and maybe ours as well."

Heyward did not reply but kept his attention on the spot where the two Hurons had disappeared into the brush. A moment later he heard them leave the bushes as they emerged back on the trail. It was soon plain that all the pursuers were gathered about them, in deep attention to their report. After a few minutes of earnest and solemn dialogue, the sounds grew fainter and more distant, and finally were lost in the depths of the forest.

Hawkeye waited until a signal from the

listening Chingachgook assured him that every sound from the retiring party was completely swallowed by the distance. Then he motioned to Heyward to lead forth the horses, and to assist the sisters into their saddles. The instant this was done they left the blockhouse through the broken gateway. They stole out of the open area in the direction opposite to that by which they had entered. The sisters cast furtive glances at the silent and crumbling ruin, as they left the soft light of the moon, to bury themselves in the gloom of the woods.

CHAPTER 14

Hawkeye led the party in silence until they were buried deep in the woods, far from the blockhouse. From time to time they would stop briefly while the scout consulted the Mohicans about their route. During these pauses Heyward and the sisters strained to detect any sounds that might indicate that enemies were close by.

After a time they came to a little stream. Here Hawkeye led the group into the water. They traveled for nearly an hour in the bed of the shallow stream in order to hide their trail. By the time they left the stream to continue their journey on dry land, the moon was sinking behind an immense pile of black clouds that hung above the western horizon.

The path soon became more uneven, and the travelers could see that the mountains were closing in on either side of the trail. They were approaching a gorge between two mountains when Hawkeye stopped. In the quiet and darkness of the place, the scout spoke in low and cautious tones.

"It is yet a long path to Fort William Henry," he told the group, "but we must think carefully about how we approach the fort. The wilderness all about has many outposts of our French enemies. But look there," he continued, pointing to a spot through the trees where the stars were reflecting from the calm surface of a small body of water. That is the so-called 'bloody pond.' I have not only traveled this area many times but also, a few years ago, fought the enemy here."

Heyward said, "I have heard of the pond but have never been here before. So that sheet of dreary water is the grave of the brave men who died in the battle."

"We fought three battles against the French soldiers that day," Hawkeye said. "In the first, they surprised us and scattered us like deer. Next, we took a stand and fought them from behind the trees. Hundreds of Frenchmen saw the sun that day for the last time. We stopped them, but we, too, lost many friends in the fight."

"It was a noble fight," Heyward said. "I have heard of it many times."

"But that wasn't the end of it," the scout continued. "The Major sent me to slip past the remaining French and take news of the battle to Fort Edward on the Hudson River. On the way I met a troop of British soldiers coming to aid us. I led them to where the French soldiers were resting and taking their meal. They did not dream that the bloody work of the day was not yet finished. When it was over, the dead, and some say the dying, were cast into that little pond. Its waters became the color of blood. Some say you can still see blood in the water."

"I trust it will prove a peaceful grave for the soldiers," the young major said.

"Not everyone thinks so. Some believe that a man who is buried while there is still breath in his body cannot rest at peace. It is certain that, in the hurry of that evening, the doctors had little time to say for sure who was living and who was dead." Then, grasping Heyward's shoulder with superstitious terror, the scout said, "Shhh! Do you see something walking on the shore of the pond?"

"It isn't likely that there would be anyone besides ourselves walking in this dreary forest tonight," Heyward answered.

"By heaven, there is a human form, and it approaches! Have your weapons ready, my friends, for we know not whom we encounter."

"*Qui vive?*" demanded a stern, quick voice.

"France!" cried Heyward, advancing from the shadow of the trees to the shore of the pond, within a few yards of the sentinel.

"Where are you coming from and where are you going at this early hour?" the sentinel asked in French.

"I've been scouting and am going to rest," Heyward responded in the same language.

"Are you an officer of the French king?"

"Certainly, friend. I am a cavalry captain," Heyward continued in French, "and I have captured the daughters of the commander at Fort William Henry. I am taking the prisoners to General Montcalm."

"Well, ladies," the sentinel said to Alice and Cora, still in French, "I am sorry for you. But those are the fortunes of war! However, you will find General Montcalm a very courteous man."

Cora replied, in French, "That is a characteristic of a good soldier. Good-bye, my friend. I wish you a more agreeable duty to perform."

The soldier bowed and thanked Cora.

Heyward said, "Good night, my friend," in French. He then led the group deliberately forward, leaving the unsuspecting sentinel pacing on the banks of the silent pond.

Before they had gone more than a few yards into the trees, a long and heavy groan arose from the bank of the pond. Glancing around, Hawkeye noticed that Chingachgook was missing. Another groan, more faint than the first, was succeeded by a heavy and sullen plunge into the water. Then all was still again. A moment later, the form of the Indian was seen gliding out of the thicket. As the chief rejoined them, with one hand he attached the scalp of the unfortunate young Frenchman to his belt, and with the other he replaced his knife.

Heyward felt a moment of sadness for the young sentinel, in spite of the fact that he had been one of the enemy. Then, turning to Hawkeye, he said, "It is obvious that the French have taken up positions within the wilderness surrounding Fort William Henry and that we will only run into more of them if we proceed. What do you suggest we do?"

"You are right," Hawkeye answered. "We must, then, retrace our steps and get outside the line of their lookouts. Once we are beyond danger from them, we will go west and enter the mountains. I can hide you safely there."

Following the scout, the little band returned along the trail that had brought them into this dangerous situation. They moved silently, constantly on the lookout for enemy patrols and sentinels.

Hawkeye soon deviated from the line of their retreat, and led his followers toward the mountains at the western boundary of the narrow plain. With swift steps they quickly moved deep within the shadows that were cast from high and broken summits ahead of them. The route was difficult, lying over ground that was ragged with rocks and intersected with ravines. Their progress was slow. Soon they were ascending steeply, winding their way between boulders.

After a time they came out of the stunted woods that clung to the barren sides of the mountain and onto a flat and mossy rock that formed the summit. The morning sun came blushing above the green pines of a hill that lay on the far side of Lake Horican.

The scout now told the sisters to dismount. Taking the bridle saddles off the weary horses, he turned them loose.

"Go," he said, "and seek your food where you can find it; and beware that you not become food to ravenous wolves yourselves."

"Don't we need them any longer?" asked Heyward.

"Judge with your own eyes," the scout said, leading the group toward the eastern edge of the mountaintop.

When the travelers reached the edge they saw, at a glance, why the scout had climbed to this commanding view. The mountaintop on which they stood was elevated perhaps a thousand feet above the wooded plain that bordered Lake Horican. Mist was rising from the lake as well as from the ponds that dotted the area.

Directly on the shore of the lake, at its southeastern edge, lay the extensive earthen ramparts and low buildings of Fort William Henry. The trees had been cleared for a considerable distance on the land around the fort. In its front were scattered sentinels, who held a weary watch

against their numerous enemy. Within the walls themselves, the travelers looked down upon men still drowsy from a night of watchful guarding. Extending to the southeast from the fort, Hawkeye pointed out the encampment of the auxiliary regiments that had left Fort Edward the same morning Heyward, Alice, Cora, and David had begun their journey. The scout then directed Heyward's attention to the narrow plumes of dark smoke that showed large numbers of enemy forces lay in that direction.

But the spectacle that most concerned the young soldier was on the western bank of the lake, near its southern end. On a strip of land, which extended many hundreds of yards from the shores of Lake Horican to the base of the mountain, were the white tents and military engines of an encampment of ten thousand French soldiers.

As the spectators looked down on this scene, the roar of artillery rose from the valley and passed off in thundering echoes along the eastern hills.

"Morning is just touching them below," said the scout, "and the sentinels are waking up the sleepers by the sound of cannon. We are a few hours too late! General Montcalm has already filled the woods with his accursed Huron confederates."

"The whole area around the fort is indeed occupied," returned Duncan. "But is there no way we can reach the fort? Being captured there by the French would be far preferable to falling again into the hands of roving Hurons."

"Look!" exclaimed the scout, unconsciously directing the attention of Cora to the quarters of her own father. "That shot made the stones fly from the side of the commandant's house! Ay! These French will pull the fort to pieces faster than it was put together, solid and thick though it is."

"Heyward, I am sickened at the sight of danger that I cannot share," said the undaunted Cora. "Let us go to General Montcalm, and ask to be allowed to enter the fort. He cannot deny the request of a daughter to be with her father in his desperate situation."

"You will lose your scalp long before you find the tent of the French general," said the blunt scout. "But luck may be with us! Do you see that fog coming down the lake? If you are up to it, follow me. I am as anxious to get to that fort to help fight the varmints as you are to get there to join your father. Are you with me?"

"We are equal to the task," said Cora, firmly. "On such an errand we will follow through any danger."

"I wish I had a thousand strong men that feared death as little as you do!" the scout said with an approving smile. "I'd send those French rascals back to Canada before the week was out. But we must hurry. The fog is rolling in with such speed that will just have time to get down to the plain before it settles. Then we can use it as a cover."

He waved his hand for them to follow, and threw himself down the steep path with quick but careful footsteps. The trail they descended brought the travelers to the plain about half a mile from the main gate of the fort. They arrived at the edge of the plain before the fog had settled in. Here they paused to wait hidden among the trees for the mist that would hide their progress to the fort. Hawkeye and the two Mohicans took advantage of this pause to steal out of the woods and size up the situation.

When they returned a few moments later, the scout had a disappointed look on his face. "The confounded French have posted a detachment of soldiers and Indians directly in our path," he said. "We are as likely to fall into their midst as to pass them in the fog!"

"Can't we circle around them to avoid the danger," asked Heyward, "and come back to the path when we are past them?"

Hawkeye shook his head. "Once you bend from the line of march in a fog such as that of Lake Horican, you may never find it again."

He was yet speaking, when a crashing sound was heard, and a cannonball entered the thicket, striking the body of a sapling, and rebounding to the earth. After studying the situation for a moment, Uncas spoke earnestly with his father and Hawkeye.

"It may be so, lad," muttered the scout, when he had finished. "Come, then, the fog is shutting in. Let's get going."

"Stop! cried Heyward, "First explain your plan."

"It is risky," Hawkeye replied, "but it is better than nothing. This cannonball has plowed a line in the dirt in its path from the fort. If all other means fail, we will hunt for the furrow it has made and follow that. But enough talk. We must go while we still have the advantage of the fog."

Heyward took Alice and Cora by the arm and followed the dim figure of the scout into the mist. Before they had proceeded twenty yards, the fog had become so thick that it was difficult for the travelers to see one another.

They circled to the left of where they had seen the French detachment and were beginning to curve back to the right when they heard a fierce voice not twenty feet from them: "*Qui va là?*"

"Push on!" whispered the scout, once more bending to the left.

The question was repeated by a dozen menacing voices.

"It is me," Duncan answered, in French, as he dragged the sisters quickly forward.

A voice from the mist said in French, "Brute! Who are you?"

"A friend of France," Duncan answered.

"You seem more like an enemy of France," the voice said. "Halt! Damn you, or I'll make you a friend of the devil. You won't halt? I warned you—Fire, men, fire!"

The order was instantly obeyed, and the fog was stirred by the explosion of fifty muskets. Fortunately, the bullets missed their mark. But they were close enough that, to the unpracticed ears of David Gamut and the sisters, it sounded as if they came within inches of the fugitives. The order was given to fire again and to pursue the fugitives.

Heyward translated the order for Hawkeye who immediately responded, "We will return fire. They will believe it to be an attack by the besieged soldiers in the fort and will pull back to wait for reinforcements."

The plan did not succeed for, as soon as they fired back, the plain came alive with French muskets firing in their direction.

"If we aren't careful, we'll bring the whole French army down on ourselves," Duncan said. "Lead on, or we'll all be killed for sure."

Hawkeye attempted to do as the major had said, but in the confusion of the shooting, had lost the direction. At this moment, Uncas came upon three gouges in the ground made by the skipping cannonball. From these, the scout was able to regain his bearings. The seven raced forward through the fog.

Suddenly a strong glare of light flashed across the scene, the fog rolled upward in thick wreaths, and the roar of several cannons belched across the plain. "It's the fort!" Hawkeye cried. "This way quickly!"

In order to better aid Alice in their flight, Duncan willingly relinquished the support of Cora to the arm of Uncas. Cora readily accepted the welcome assistance. French soldiers, hot and angry in pursuit, were close at their heels, and each instant threatened their capture, if not their death.

Suddenly, an English voice above them exclaimed, "Stand firm, and be ready, my gallant

Sixtieths! Wait to see the enemy, then fire low and sweep the slope with your bullets!"

"Father! Father!" exclaimed a piercing cry from out the mist. "It is Alice! Your own Alice! Don't fire! Save your daughters!"

"Hold your fire!" shouted the voice from above them. It continued in the awful tones of parental agony "It is she! God has restored me to my children! Throw open the gate! To the field, Sixtieths, to the field; do not shoot, lest you kill my lambs! Drive off these dogs of France with your swords."

Duncan heard the grating of the rusty hinges, and darting to the spot, he met a long line of warriors dressed in red, passing swiftly toward the slope in front of the fort. He knew they were his own battalion of the Royal Americans. Racing to the head of the line, he soon swept every trace of his pursuers from before the fort.

For an instant, Cora and Alice stood trembling and bewildered by this unexpected disappearance of Heyward. But immediately an officer of gigantic build and white hair rushed out of the mist, and folded them in his arms, while large scalding tears rolled down his pale and wrinkled cheeks. He exclaimed, in a Scottish accent:

"For this I thank thee, Lord! Let danger come as it will, thy servant is now prepared!"

CHAPTER 15

Fort William Henry had already been under siege for a day when the fugitives arrived at its gates. General Montcalm and his French soldiers continued to pound at the fort for four more days. The British troops, under the valiant command of Colonel Munro, continued to bravely battle back. In spite of the fact that they were vastly outnumbered, the British had been successful so far in keeping the enemy from taking the fort. It appeared as if General Webb, with his army, which lay slumbering on the banks of the Hudson River, had utterly forgotten the trouble that Munro's troops were in.

On the fifth day of the siege a truce was declared. Both sides took advantage of the temporary break in the fighting to rest. Late in the afternoon Heyward took the opportunity to look out across the peaceful Lake Horican from one of the bastions on that side of the fort. The sun poured down its parting glory on the scene, the heat of the day gone. The mountains looked green, and fresh, and lovely as thin vapors floated between them and the sun. The numerous islands that dotted Lake Horican appeared to hover above the water in little hillocks of green velvet.

Some of the young French soldiers could be seen relaxing on the pebbly beach of the lake. Others rowed about the lake in skiffs or fished its calm waters. Still others took walks into the surrounding hills. In short, everything wore the appearance of a day of pleasure, rather than of an hour stolen from the dangers of a bloody and vindictive warfare.

Duncan stood watching this peaceful scene for a few moments when his attention was drawn to the main gate by the sound of approaching footsteps. Coming up the slope to the fort he saw Hawkeye, tired and dejected. He was in the custody of French soldiers. His arms were tied behind his back and his beloved Killdeer was not to be seen. Duncan knew that the scout had been sent to carry a message to General Webb two days earlier. Surprised to see the scout was a captive, he turned to descend to the main gate to find out what had happened.

As he turned, however, the sounds of voices caught his attention and for a moment caused him to forget his purpose. This was the first time he had seen Alice and Cora since he had deserted them in front of the fort in order to help repulse the attacking French soldiers.

"So there you are," Alice said in a teasing voice. "I can't blame you for hiding from us after the way you deserted us in front of the gate. You should know better than to run away from two women in distress that way!"

"You know that Alice means to give you our thanks and our blessings," added the more serious Cora. "In truth, we have wondered what had become of you. We have wanted to convey our gratitude to you."

"Your father himself could tell you that, though absent from your presence, I have been fighting for your safety from the French," replied the young man. "I felt that was my duty. But, in doing it, I am ashamed to say, I have neglected to show you the proper respect of my attention."

"Oh, Duncan!" Alice exclaimed, a tear forming in the corner of her eye. "If I had thought my teasing would hurt your feelings, I would remain silent forever. Cora can tell you how deep our gratitude is for your steadfast attention to your duty."

Duncan turned his eyes to Cora. As she returned the look, he saw that her face was filled with an expression of anguish. "You are not well, dearest Miss Munro!" he exclaimed. "We have been joking while you are in suffering!"

"It is nothing," she answered. "I cannot see

the sunny side of life the way my enthusiastic sister can. But that is the penalty of experience, and perhaps, the misfortune of my nature. Look around you, Major Heyward," she continued, nodding at the French encampment, "and tell me what hope there is for the daughter of a soldier whose greatest happiness is his honor and his military fame."

"Neither will be tarnished by circumstances over which he has had no control," Duncan replied. "But your words recall me to my own duty. I am on my way now to your gallant father, to see if he has received any news that would influence his plan for our defense."

Saying good-bye to the sisters, he quickly descended and went to Colonel Munro's headquarters. The Colonel was pacing the narrow room with gigantic strides as Duncan entered. He seemed disturbed.

"You have anticipated my wishes, Major Heyward," he said. "I was about to send for you."

"I am sorry to see, sir, that the messenger I so strongly recommended has returned in custody of the French! I hope there is no reason to distrust his faithfulness."

"The fidelity of Long Rifle is well-known to me," returned Munro, "and is above suspicion; but his usual good fortune seems, at last, to have failed. Montcalm captured him. And with the accursed politeness of the French, he has sent him back saying that he knows how much I value the fellow and he therefore could not think of keeping him. It is a sly way for the French General to let me know what an impossible position he has me in."

"But what about aid being sent by General Webb?" asked Duncan.

"Oh, yes!" said Munro with a bitter laugh. "Didn't you notice all those thousands of British soldiers coming to help us as you entered my quarters? Hoot! You're an impatient young soldier. Don't you know that they need to travel at a leisurely pace?"

"They are coming, then? Is that the message from General Webb?"

"The dunce has neglected to tell me when they are coming and what route they are taking. But he did give Long Rifle a letter to bring to me—a letter that General Montcalm has intercepted and chosen not to pass along."

"But what does the scout say?" asked Heyward. "He has eyes and ears, and a tongue. What verbal report does he make?"

"All he can report is that he saw no signs at Fort Edward of any intention of sending soldiers to relieve us." Then, changing his bitter manner, he continued more thoughtfully, "And yet there must be something in that letter that we should know! Otherwise, Montcalm would not have kept it from us."

"Our decision should be speedy," said Duncan. "You are well aware, sir, that our soldiers camped next to the fort will not be able to hold their position much longer. And, I am sorry to add, things do not look much better for the fort itself. Half of the guns have burst. The walls are crumbling about our ears, and we are running short of provisions. Even the men show signs of discontent and alarm."

"Major Heyward," said Munro, turning to him with dignity, "I have served his majesty for half a century and have earned these gray hairs. I am well aware of all you say and of the pressing nature of our situation. But everything possible must be done to defend the honor of the king and of ourselves. While there is hope of aid, I will defend this fortress, even if I must do it with pebbles gathered on the lake shore. It is important that we learn what was in that letter so that we can know what General Webb's intentions are."

"Can I be of service in the matter?" Heyward asked.

"Sir, you can. General Montcalm has invited me to a personal interview. He says that he wishes to pass on some additional information. Now, I think it is not wise to show any undue eagerness to meet him, and so I will send you, an officer of rank, as my substitute."

Duncan cheerfully agreed to meet with General Montcalm as Colonel Munro's representative. Within ten minutes the young major was making his way through the main gate of Fort William Henry. He was received by a French officer who led him to the distant tent of the leader of the army of France.

General Montcalm welcomed the youthful messenger graciously. As Heyward entered Montcalm's quarters, he saw that the general was surrounded by his principal officers. In addition, there was a group of the native chiefs who had brought their warriors to the battlefield in support of the French army. Heyward stopped short when, in glancing rapidly at the Indians, he saw the malignant face of Magua. The Indian returned his look with a calm but sullen expression. Although Heyward was surprised, he hid every appearance of emotion. He turned to the hostile general, who had already stepped forward to greet him.

Speaking in French, Montcalm said, "Sir, it is my great pleasure to—bah! Where is that interpreter?"

"I believe, sir, that an interpreter won't be necessary," Heyward said in French. "I speak the language a little."

"That is a relief," Montcalm said. "I hate those rascals. One is never sure where one stands with them." Then he continued, still speaking French, "Very well, sir. Although I would have been proud to receive the commandant of the fort, I am very happy that he sent an officer as distinguished and as pleasant as you."

Duncan bowed low, pleased with the compliment.

Montcalm paused, as if to collect his thoughts, and then continued, "Your commandant is a brave man, and well qualified to repel my assault. But, sir, isn't it time to begin to pay more attention in humanity and less in courage?"

"We consider the qualities as inseparable," replied Duncan, smiling. "But while we find in the vigor of your excellency's troops a strong motive to stimulate our courage, we can, as yet, see no particular call to turn from courage to humanity."

Montcalm, in his turn, slightly bowed to acknowledge the compliment. Then, after musing a moment, he added: "It is possible my eyes have deceived me, and that your fort resists our cannon better than I had supposed." Then, with a sly smile, he continued, "Although you think it is too soon to listen to the call of humanity, I trust you have not forgotten how to be gallant. The daughters of the commandant, I understand, have entered the fort since the siege began."

"It is true, sir; but, instead of weakening our

efforts, they set us an example of courage in their own bravery," Duncan responded.

"We have a wise rule in our military laws that says that the army of the king of France must never draw its courage from a woman," Montcalm remarked dryly. Then, changing back to his frank and casual tone, he said, "I trust, sir, you come authorized to discuss the surrender of the fort?"

"Has your excellency found our defense so feeble as to believe that we are ready to surrender?" Duncan asked.

Ignoring the question and glancing toward the group of chiefs, Montcalm said, "I would be sorry to have the siege drawn out so long as to irritate my Indian friends, there. I find it difficult, even now, to keep them under control."

Heyward was silent as he recalled his recent troubles with the Hurons and remembered the images of the defenseless sisters who had been at their mercy.

"It is unnecessary to tell you how difficult it is to restrain them when they are angry," Montcalm continued, pressing his advantage. "Well then, sir! Shall we speak of the terms of surrender?"

"I am afraid that your excellency has been deceived as to the strength of William Henry, and the resources of its garrison," Heyward countered, recovering himself.

"I know that it is but an earthen work fort and that it is defended by twenty-three hundred gallant men," said Montcalm bluntly.

"The fort is only an earthen work structure, certainly, but it has seen the defeat of others in the past. And there is also a powerful force at Fort Edward, which is but a few hours' march from here."

"There are a mere five or six thousand men there," Montcalm remarked, with apparent indifference. "And General Webb wisely feels it safer to keep those men there than risk them in the field against us."

Both men thought in silence for a short while. Then they renewed the conversation. Montcalm attempted to convince Heyward of the wisdom of surrendering. Heyward, meanwhile, attempted to deceive the general into revealing the contents of the captured letter. Neither man succeeded.

As Heyward left the tent, General Montcalm once again extended an invitation to Colonel Munro to come in person and meet with him. They parted and Duncan was escorted back to the fort, where he went immediately to the headquarters of his own commander.

CHAPTER 16

Major Heyward, in his eagerness to report on his conversation with General Montcalm, entered Colonel Munro's quarters unannounced. He came upon a scene of family tenderness. Alice was playfully running her fingers through her father's white hair. When he would pretend to be angered, she would kiss the frowning forehead. Cora was sitting close by, watching her younger sister with maternal fondness. The troubles and dangers of their situation were momentarily forgotten in their joy at being together.

On Heyward's entrance, all three looked at him.

"You're back already, Major! You're young and quick," Munro chuckled. Then, turning to his daughters, he said lovingly, "Away with you, my dears! There are troubles enough for a soldier, without having his camp filled with such impudent and bewitching creatures as you two!"

Alice laughingly followed her sister, who instantly led the way from the room. Munro, instead of demanding the result of the young man's mission, paced the room for a few moments, with his hands behind his back, and his head inclined toward the floor, like a man lost in thought. At length he raised his eyes, glistening with a father's fondness, and exclaimed, "They are two excellent girls, Heyward, and such as any one may boast of."

"I have not come to discuss my opinion of your daughters," Duncan replied.

"True, lad, true," interrupted the impatient old man. "All the same, I recall that you were about ready to discuss that matter the day you arrived here. But I did not think it becoming in an old soldier to be talking of nuptial blessings and wedding jokes when the enemies of his king were beating down the doors of the fort. But I was wrong, Duncan, boy, I was wrong there; and I am now ready to hear what you have to say."

"Your invitation gives me pleasure, sir, but just now I have a message from Montcalm—"

"Let the Frenchman and all his troops go to the devil, sir!" exclaimed the hasty veteran. "He is not yet master of Fort William Henry, nor shall he ever be, if General Webb proves himself the man he should. No, sir, thank heaven we are not yet in such a difficult situation that I am too busy to pay attention to the care of my own family. Duncan, your mother was the only child of my best friend. I will hear what you wish to say about my daughters even if every last Frenchman is storming the main gate!"

Heyward realized that the colonel took malicious pleasure in showing such contempt for the message from the French general. And he was happy to discuss his feelings about Alice with her father. He said, as indifferently as he could, "My request, as you know, sir, went so far as to wish the honor of being your son-in-law."

"Ay, boy, you found words to make yourself very easily understood. But, let me ask you, sir, have you been as open to the girl?"

"On my honor, no," exclaimed Duncan, warmly. "That would have been an abuse of trust, if I had taken advantage of my situation for such a purpose."

"You are a true gentleman, Major Heyward. But Cora Munro is a maiden too sensible to need the protection of a father."

"Cora!"

"Ay — Cora! We are talking of your wish to marry Miss Munro, are we not, sir?"

"I—I—I was not conscious of having mentioned her name," said Duncan, stammering.

"And are you planning to marry? Do you wish my consent, Major Heyward?" demanded the old soldier, speaking with the dignity of offended feeling.

"You have another child who is just as lovely."

"Alice!" exclaimed the father with astonishment.

"That is the direction of my wishes, sir."

The young man waited in silence while the full impact of his unexpected wishes settled in to Munro's mind. For several minutes Munro paced the room with long and rapid strides, his rigid features working convulsively. At length, he paused directly in front of Heyward. Riveting his eyes on the young major, he said, with a lip that quivered violently:

"Duncan Heyward, I have loved you for the sake of my dear friend, your grandfather; I have loved you for your own good qualities; and I have loved you, because I thought you would contribute to the happiness of my child. But all this love would turn to hatred, if your reasons for your choice are what I fear they may be."

"God forbid that any act or thought of mine should cause such a change!" exclaimed the young man, whose eye never quailed under the penetrating look of the colonel.

Munro recognized the impossibility of Heyward's understanding those feelings that were hidden in his own heart. However, he was encouraged by the steadfast look on the young man's face and so, with a softened voice, he continued:

"You wish to be my son, Duncan, but you're

ignorant of the history of the man you wish to call your father. Sit you down, young man, and I will open to you the wounds of a seared heart."

The message from Montcalm all but forgotten by both men at this point, the two drew up chairs. After a silence, the old man spoke.

"You already know, Major Heyward, that my family is both ancient and honorable," the Scotsman began. "But my family was not wealthy. I was about your age when I pledged my love to a woman named Alice Graham. She was the only child of a rich man who lived nearby. Her father was opposed to our marrying for several reasons, including my poverty. Honoring her father's wishes, I broke off my engagement and left the country with the military. Eventually my service to the king took me to the West Indies. There I married a woman who became the mother of Cora. This woman, the daughter of a wealthy gentleman in the West Indies, was remotely descended from a slave. But if I ever find a man who dares to look down on my Cora because of her ancestors, he will feel the weight of a father's anger! Major Heyward, you are yourself born in the south, where these unfortunate beings are considered of a race inferior to your own."

"It is unfortunately true, sir," said Duncan, unable to prevent his eyes from sinking to the floor in embarrassment.

"And you cast it on my Cora as a reproach! You scorn to mingle the blood of the Heywards with one so degraded—no matter how lovely and virtuous she is?" fiercely demanded the jealous parent.

"Heaven forbid that I should feel a prejudice so unworthy of my reason!" returned Duncan. "The sweetness, the beauty, the witchery of your younger daughter, Colonel Munro, might explain my motives without unjustly accusing me of such a feeling."

"You are right, sir," replied the old man, again changing to a gentler tone. "The girl is the image of what her mother was at her age. When Cora's mother died, I returned to Scotland, enriched by the marriage. And, would you think it, Duncan! That angel Alice Graham had remained unmarried all those twenty long years, and that for the sake of a man who could forget her! What's more, her father now long dead, she took me for her husband."

"And what happened to her?" asked Duncan.

"She died giving birth to my beloved Alice. I had her but a single year. It was a short term of happiness for one who had seen her youth fade in hopeless pining."

There was something so commanding in the distress of the old man that Heyward did not dare to speak a syllable of consolation. Munro sat utterly unconscious of the other's presence, while heavy tears fell from his eyes and rolled unheeded from his cheeks. At length he moved, and seemed suddenly recalled to his duties. He arose and, approaching his companion with an air of military grandeur, demanded:

"I believe you have, Major Heyward, some communication that I should hear from General Montcalm?"

Duncan immediately recounted his unsuccessful meeting with the French general. He concluded by saying that Montcalm had refused to reveal the contents of the confiscated letter and that he would divulge that information only to Munro in person. He wished to meet with him on the ground between the fort and his own lines of troops.

"So, he wishes to confer with Munro in person!" the veteran said with some anger. "I am inclined to indulge the man, if only to let him see our firmness in spite of his numbers and his summons. There might be not bad policy in such a move, young man."

Duncan believed that it was of great importance for them to learn the contents of the letter. He therefore encouraged Munro to meet with the French general. He said, "I believe it would be a good show of firmness on our part to talk with him. What do you wish to do, sir?"

"I will meet the Frenchman, and without

delay," the colonel said decisively. "Go, Major Heyward, and send word to Montcalm that I am coming. You will come with me. And we will take a small guard with us. It may be prudent to have some help close at hand just in case the French rascals plan some treachery in all this."

The day was fast coming to a close by the time Duncan had made the necessary arrangements. He met Colonel Munro at the gate of the fort and they proceeded, with a small escort, from the fort and down the slope in front of it. Munro carried himself with great dignity. They had walked only a hundred yards from the fort when the French general appeared with his own small escort.

As the two leaders approached each other, Munro spoke to Duncan in an undertone: "Tell the men to be on the lookout and to keep their guns at the ready."

The wary Scotsman halted with his guard close at his back. Montcalm moved toward them with a quick but graceful step, removed his hat with its white plume, and bowed deeply in courtesy. Neither leader spoke for a few moments, each regarding the other with curious and interested eyes. Then Montcalm broke the silence. After uttering the usual words of greeting, he turned to Duncan, and continued, with a smile of recognition, speaking always in French:

"I am pleased, monsieur, that you have given us the pleasure of your company on this occasion. There will be no necessity to employ an ordinary interpreter; for, in your hands, I feel the same security as if I spoke your language myself."

Montcalm then ordered his escort to drop back. Before Major Heyward would imitate this proof of confidence, he glanced around the plain. He noticed with uneasiness the numerous groups of Hurons who looked out from the margin of the surrounding woods, curious spectators of the interview.

"Sir, you can plainly see the difference in our situation," he said, pointing at the same time toward those dangerous foes who were to be seen in almost every direction. "If we dismiss our guard, we will stand here at the mercy of our enemies."

"Sir, you have the promise of a gentleman of France for your safety," returned Montcalm, laying his hand impressively on his heart. "It should be enough."

"It is," Duncan said. Then he turned to the officer who led the escort and said, "Fall back, sir, and wait for orders."

Munro was uneasy at seeing his escort pull back and demanded an explanation from Heyward. The major told him, "Montcalm pledges his word for our safety, and I have ordered the men to withdraw in order to prove how much we depend on his assurance."

Munro replied in a quiet voice, "It may be all right, sir, but I have no great trust of these French noblemen. I am not certain that they have true honor."

"Yes, but we have his word as a distinguished officer. From a soldier of his reputation we have nothing to fear," Heyward said reassuringly.

The old man made a gesture of resignation, though his rigid features still showed a distrust of and contempt for his enemy. Once the short discussion was finished, Montcalm stepped forward to open the subject of their meeting.

"I have requested this interview with your superior, sir," he said, "because I believe he will allow himself to be persuaded that he has already done everything he can for the honor of his king. I hope that he will now listen to the cautions of humanity. I will always report that his resistance has been gallant and was continued as long as there was hope."

When this opening was translated to Munro, he answered with dignity, "However I may prize such testimony from General Montcalm, it will be more valuable when it is better merited."

The French general smiled, as Duncan translated this reply, and observed, "Does the colonel wish to see my camp, and witness for himself our numbers, and the impossibility of his resisting them with success?"

"I know that the king of France has many soldiers," returned the unmoved Scotsman, as soon as Duncan ended his translation; "but my own king has as many and as faithful troops."

"But they are not close by, fortunately for us," said Montcalm, without waiting for the interpreter. "A brave man knows how to accept destiny in war with the same courage he shows when he faces his foe."

"Had I been conscious that General Montcalm was master of the English, I would have spared myself the trouble of so awkward a translation," Duncan said, with some annoyance. He was remembering with embarrassment his recent side conversation with Munro.

"Your pardon, sir," replied the Frenchman. "There is a vast difference between understanding and speaking a foreign tongue; you will, therefore, please to assist me still." Then, after a short pause, he added, "These hills give us every opportunity of reconnoitering your fort, gentlemen, and I may be as well acquainted with their weak condition as you yourselves are."

"Ask the French general if his lookouts can see Fort Edward," Munro said proudly, "and if he knows when and where to expect General Webb's army."

"Let General Webb be his own interpreter," returned the politic Montcalm, suddenly extending an open letter toward Munro. "You will learn there, sir, that his movements are not likely to prove a problem to my army."

Munro eagerly seized the paper from Montcalm's hand. As his eye passed hastily over the words, his face changed from its look of military pride to one of deep disappointment; his lip began to quiver; and allowing the paper to fall from his hand, his head dropped upon his chest, like that of a man whose hopes were dashed. Duncan picked up the letter from the ground and read its cruel words. General Webb, rather than encouraging them to resist, advised a speedy surrender, offering, as a reason, the utter impossibility of his sending a single man to their rescue.

"The man has betrayed me!" Munro bitterly exclaimed. "He has brought dishonor to the door of one who never knew disgrace before, and he has heaped shame heavily on my gray hairs. We will go back to the fort and fight to the finish!"

"Sirs," said Montcalm, advancing toward them a step, "you do not know me well if you believe me capable of profiting by this letter to humble brave men, or to build up a dishonest reputation for myself. Listen to my terms before you leave me."

"What does the Frenchman say?" demanded the veteran, sternly. "Does he praise himself for having captured a scout, with a note from headquarters?"

Duncan explained the other's meaning.

"General Montcalm, we will hear you," the veteran said, more calmly, as Duncan ended.

"To retain the fort is now impossible," said Montcalm. "It is necessary to the interests of my king that it be destroyed; but as for yourselves and your brave comrades, you will all be given every privilege a soldier could want."

"Our flag?" demanded Heyward.

"Carry it to England, and show it to your king."

"Our arms weapons?"

"Keep them; none can use them better than you."

"Our march; the surrender of the place?"

"It shall all be done in a way most honorable to yourselves."

Duncan now turned to explain these proposals to his commander, who heard him with amazement; he was deeply touched by so unusual and unexpected generosity.

"Go, Duncan," he said; "go with the honorable general, for he is indeed a man of honor; go to his tent and arrange it all. I have lived to see two things in my old age that never did I expect to behold: an Englishman afraid to support a friend and a Frenchman too honest to profit by his advantage."

So saying, the veteran again dropped his head to his chest, and returned slowly toward the fort.

The proud feelings of Munro never recovered from the shock of this unexpected blow. From that moment there was a change in his determined character, which accompanied him to a speedy grave.

Duncan remained to settle the terms of the surrender. He returned to the fort during the first watches of the night, and immediately after a private conference with the commandant, he left again. It was then openly announced that hostilities must cease—Munro having signed a treaty by which the place was to be yielded to the enemy in the morning. The garrison was to retain their arms, the colors, and their baggage, and, consequently, according to military opinion, their honor.

CHAPTER 17

The hostile armies, which lay in the wilds by Lake Horican, passed the night of the ninth of August, 1757, as they would have on any other battlefield. While the conquered were still, sullen, and dejected, the victors celebrated their triumph. Eventually, all settled into such stillness that a listener would not know that those armed powers rested there.

In the deep silence of the hour before daybreak, General Montcalm emerged from his tent. He was wrapped in a cloak that protected him from the damp air of the woods and that concealed his identity. He was challenged by the sentries as he made his way through the French camp in the direction of Fort William Henry. Each time, he gave the password and was permitted to proceed without further question.

Passing the French sentinel at the outpost closest to the enemy fort, Montcalm continued until he reached a spot on the edge of Lake

Horican near the western bastion of the fort. Stopping in the shadow of a tree trunk he stood for a few minutes gazing at the outlines of the English fort.

As he was about to turn and go, he saw a figure approach the edge of the rampart. He recognized the outline of his English counterpart. As Montcalm watched from the shadow of the tree on the lake shore, it appeared that Colonel Munro was studying the tents of the French encampment. Montcalm, feeling it improper to secretly intrude on Munro's melancholy contemplation, turned to slip silently back toward the French camp.

As he turned, an almost inaudible grating sound of the pebbles of the beach caught his ear. In a moment he saw a dark form rise, as it were, out of the lake, and steal without further noise to the land, within a few feet of the place where he himself stood. The figure then silently raised a rifle and aimed it in the direction of the rampart where the English commander stood. Before the treacherous shot could be fired, Montcalm put his hand on the rifle.

Sly Fox gave a quiet exclamation of surprise when his shot was so unexpectedly interrupted.

Without saying anything, the French officer laid his hand on the shoulder of the Indian, and led him in silence to a spot where they could speak quietly without being heard by the watcher on the rampart.

Opening his cloak so that Sly Fox could see who he was, Montcalm sternly demanded: "What is the meaning of this? Does Sly Fox not know that the hatchet is buried between the English and the French?"

"What can the Hurons do?" returned the savage, speaking imperfectly in French. "Not a single warrior has claimed the prize of a scalp, and yet the pale faces make friends!"

"I think, Sly Fox, that you are too anxious for the blood of our former enemy who is now our friend," Montcalm said. "You have much power over your people."

"Magua is a great chief," the sullen Indian replied.

"Then prove it, by teaching your nation how to conduct themselves toward our new friends. I was ordered to drive the English squatters off this piece of land. They have consented to go and now they are no longer enemies. You have pledged not to hurt the friends of France. The enemies of France are enemies of the Hurons; the friends of France are friends of the Hurons."

"Friends!" repeated the Indian in scorn. "Does the French chief know what this is?" he demanded, pointing to the deep scar on his chest.

"What warrior does not? It is the mark left by a bullet wound," Montcalm answered.

"And what about this?" Magua asked, turning his naked back toward the general.

"This!—Sly Fox has been sadly injured here; who has done this to you?" Montcalm said, looking at the scars on Magua's back.

"Magua slept hard in the English wigwams, and the sticks have left their mark," returned the Indian, with a hollow laugh. His fierce temper was nearly choking him. Then, with sudden dignity, he added: "Go. Teach your young men of this peace. Sly Fox knows how to speak to the Huron warriors."

Without waiting for any answer, the Indian cast his rifle into the hollow of his arm, and moved silently through the encampment toward the woods where his own tribe rested.

Montcalm lingered on the shore where he had been left by his companion. He brooded deeply on the temper that his ungovernable ally had just revealed. He became keenly aware of the deep responsibility one assumes when he disregards the means to attain the end; and he thought about the danger of setting in motion a force which that is too great for human power to control. He then turned away from Lake Horican and returned to the center of the French camp.

On arriving at his tent, he gave the order for the troops to be assembled. The rays of a brilliant sun were reaching the camp as the soldiers triumphantly prepared for the formal surrender.

A very different scene presented itself within the lines of the British-American army. Here there were all the signs of a hurried and forced departure. The sullen soldiers shouldered their empty rifles and fell into their places. The wish for revenge and the wounded pride were hidden beneath the military decorum.

Women and children ran from place to place in the fort. Some carried the scanty remnants of their baggage, and others searched in the ranks for the faces of their loved ones.

Munro appeared among his silent troops firm but dejected. It was evident that the unexpected blow had struck deep into his heart, though he struggled to maintain a show of dignity.

Duncan was touched at the quiet and impressive exhibition of his grief. He approached the old man to ask how he might be of service.

"My daughters," was the brief reply.

"Have no arrangements been made for them yet?" asked Duncan with some alarm.

"Today I am only a soldier, Major Heyward," said the veteran. "Everyone here is my child today."

Duncan had heard enough. He flew toward the quarters of Munro to find the sisters. They were on the threshold of the low building, already prepared to depart. They were surrounded by a clamorous and weeping group of women who had gathered there to seek strength at this most difficult time. Cora looked pale and anxious, but she had lost none of her firmness. Alice's eyes were inflamed, betraying how long and bitterly she had wept.

"The fort is lost," she said, with a melancholy smile; "though, I trust, the good name of Colonel Munro still remains untarnished."

"It is brighter than ever. But it is time to think less of others, and to make some provision for yourself. Your father and I must lead the troops. We need to find someone to be with you as we leave the fort. Although I cannot be by your side, I cannot let you endure this alone."

At this moment, the three of them heard the voice of the singing master coming from the next building. As Duncan entered, David Gamut was pouring out his pious feelings in the low and serious sounds of the sacred music. As David finished the song, Duncan touched him on the shoulder to get his attention. In a few words he explained his request.

"It will be your duty to see that no one bothers the colonel's daughters or taunts them about the misfortune of their brave father."

"Even so," replied Gamut.

"We understand each other," Duncan said. "It is time for us to assume our respective duties."

Gamut cheerfully agreed, and together they went to the sisters who thanked Duncan for his kind attention. The young major told them he would rejoin them as soon as he had led the advance a few miles toward the Hudson. Then he took his leave.

By this time the signal for departure had been given, and the head of the English column was in motion. French soldiers had already taken possession of the main gate of the fort. The French flag waved near the entrance.

"Let us go," said Cora. "This is no longer a fit place for the children of an English officer."

Alice clung to the arm of her sister, and together they left the parade ground, accompanied by the moving throng that surrounded them.

Every vehicle and each beast of burden was occupied by the sick and wounded. Cora and Alice, along with everyone else who was able, traveled on foot. Even many of the maimed and wounded soldiers were compelled to drag themselves at the rear of the columns, for there was no room in the wagons. The whole body of nearly three thousand people was in motion; the weak and wounded, groaning and in suffering; their comrades silent and sullen; and the women and children in terror, of they knew not what.

The living masses of the English left the confines of the fort and were moving slowly across the plain, heading for the point where the Hudson River cut a wide gap in the tall trees of the forest. The French army stood at a little distance to the right, waiting to occupy Fort William Henry. Along the sweeping borders of the woods hung a dark cloud of natives, eyeing the passage of their enemies, and hovering at a distance, like vultures who were only kept from swooping on their prey by the presence of a superior army. A few of the Indians had straggled among the conquered columns, where they stalked in sullen discontent as passive observers of the vanquished.

The forward line of troops, with Heyward at its head, was already slowly disappearing into the woods. Cora's attention was drawn to a collection of stragglers by the sounds of an argument. One of the soldiers who had fallen behind the rear of the line, was struggling with an Indian for possession of some item of his baggage. Voices grew loud and angry, and a hundred savages appeared, as it were, by magic, where only a dozen had been seen a minute before. It was then that Cora saw Magua gliding among his countrymen, and speaking with his artful eloquence. The mass of women and children stopped and hovered together like alarmed and fluttering birds. The argument was resolved when the soldier gave up his possession to the Indian. The straggling soldiers moved slowly onward.

The Indians now fell back and seemed content to let their enemies advance without further molestation. But, as the crowd of women and children approached them, the gaudy colors of a shawl attracted the eyes of one Huron. He advanced to seize it. In terror, the woman wrapped her child in the shawl and held it close to her. The Huron let go of the shawl and tore the screaming infant from her arms. Abandoning the shawl to the hands of other Indians, the mother darted to reclaim her child. The Indian smiled grimly, and extended one hand, in sign of a willingness to exchange his prize, while, with the other, he dangled the baby over his head.

"Here—here—take anything," exclaimed the breathless woman, tearing pieces of clothing from herself with trembling fingers. "Take anything, but give me my baby!"

He rejected the worthless rags the woman offered. Then, seeing that the shawl had fallen into the hands of another Indian, his sullen smile changed to a gleam of ferocity. He dashed the head of the infant against a rock and cast its quivering remains to her feet. For an instant the mother stood, like a statue of despair, looking wildly down at the object that had been her child. Then she raised her face toward the sky, as if to call a curse from the heavens down on the murderer. Maddened by his disappointment and excited at the sight of blood, the Huron drove his tomahawk into her brain. The mother sank under the blow and fell, grasping for her child with the same engrossing love that had caused her to cherish it when living.

At that dangerous moment, Magua placed his hands to his mouth and raised the fatal and appalling whoop. The scattered Indians echoed the well-known cry, until the plain and the surrounding woods overflowed with the noise.

More than two thousand raging Indians broke from the forest at the signal, and raced across the fatal plain. A scene of unimaginable horror followed. Death was everywhere. Resistance only served to inflame the murderers, who inflicted their furious blows long after their victims no longer could feel them. The flow of blood was like the outbreaking of a torrent.

The soldiers ran back to the mass of screaming women and children and attempted to fight off the attackers. But too often their empty rifles were ripped from their hands and used to bludgeon them to the ground with savage fury.

For minutes that seemed like hours the sisters stood riveted to one spot, horror-stricken and nearly helpless. The other women and children had crowed in around them when the first blow was struck. Now that most of their screaming companions had fallen under the blows of the Hurons, it still was not possible to fly because the murderers were all around them.

On every side arose shrieks, groans, exhortations, and curses. At this moment, Alice caught a glimpse of the vast form of her father, moving rapidly across the plain, in the direction of the French army. He had bargained for an escort in the terms of surrender but it had not yet been provided. He was trying to reach Montcalm to demand the condition be met. He moved forward, fearless of every danger. The Hurons, even in their fury, respected his rank and his calmness; although they threatened his progress, they permitted the white-haired veteran to brush their weapons aside and pass unharmed.

"Father—father—we are here!" shrieked Alice, as he passed at no great distance. "Come to us, father, or we die!"

The cry was repeated, but it was unanswered. Once, the old man appeared to catch the sound, for he paused and listened; but Alice had dropped senseless on the earth, and Cora had sunk at her side, hovering in tenderness over her lifeless form. Munro shook his head in disappointment, and proceeded, determined to carry out his duty as an officer.

"Lady," said Gamut, who, helpless and useless as he was, had not yet dreamed of deserting his trust, "this is the jubilee of the devils and not a good place for Christians to remain. Let us fly from this spot."

"Go," said Cora, gazing at her unconscious sister; "save yourself. You can not be of further help to me."

David understood the unyielding character of her resolution. He gazed for a moment at the dusky forms that were acting their hellish rites on every side of him. Then his tall person grew more erect while his chest heaved, and his whole body became a picture of dignity.

"In the Bible, David was able to tame the spirit of Saul by the sound of his harp and the words of sacred song," he said. "It may not be amiss to try the potency of music here."

Then raising his voice to its highest tone, he poured out a strain so powerful as to be heard even amid the din of that bloody field. More than one Huron rushed toward them, thinking to bear away the scalps of the sisters; but when they found this strange and unmoved figure riveted to his post, they paused to listen. Astonishment soon changed to admiration at the firmness with which the white warrior sang his death song; they went on to other and less courageous victims, leaving David singing, and the sisters unharmed.

David, assuming his song was exerting a holy influence over the murderous attackers, continued to sing. The music soon attracted the attention of Magua, who uttered a yell of pleasure when he realized his former prisoners were again at his mercy.

"Come," he said, laying his bloody hands on Cora's dress. "The wigwam of the Huron is still open. Is it not better than this place?"

"Monster!" cried Cora. "There is blood, oceans of blood, on your soul. Your spirit has caused this scene."

"Magua is a great chief!" returned the exulting Huron. "Will the dark-hair go to his tribe?"

"Never! Kill me if you will, and complete your revenge," she answered.

He hesitated a moment, and then taking the unconscious form of Alice in his arms, the subtle Indian moved swiftly across the plain toward the woods.

"Stop!" shrieked Cora, following wildly on his footsteps. "Release the child! What are you doing?"

But Magua ignored her voice. He knew his power and was determined to maintain it.

"Stay—stay, dear lady," called Gamut to the unhearing Cora. "The holy charm is beginning to take effect. Soon you will see this horrid tumult stilled."

Realizing that she was not heeding him, the faithful David followed the distracted sister. As he ran he raised his voice again in sacred song, sweeping the air in time with his long arm. In this manner they crossed the plain, through the wounded and the dead. Cora would have fallen more than once under the blows of her enemies, but for the figure of the singing David following her. To the astonished Indians she appeared to be under the protection of a spirit of madness.

Magua, with Alice over his shoulder, entered the woods through a low ravine. Here another Huron waited with the two horses that the travelers had abandoned before crossing the plain in the fog five days earlier. He placed the still unconscious Alice across the saddle of one of the horses. He then signaled to Cora, who had been just a few steps behind him, to mount the other horse.

Not wanting to be separated from her sister, she obeyed. She then held forth her arms for her sister, with an air of entreaty and love that even the Huron could not deny. Placing Alice, then, on the same animal with Cora, he seized the bridle and led the horse deeper into the forest.

David, who had stopped singing as they entered the woods, realized that he was left alone. He had been ignored as a subject too worthless to kill. Seeing the sisters he had promised to protect disappearing into the woods, he threw his long limb across the saddle of the horse they had deserted and followed them as best he could along the difficult path.

They soon began to ascend. Alice revived a bit and Cora divided her attention between comforting her sister and listening to the still audible cries from the plain behind them.

In a little while they reached the flattened surface of the mountaintop. Cora recognized it as the place the scout had led them to before they approached the fort. Magua signaled them to dismount and then directed their attention to the sickening sight on the plain below them.

The cruel work was still going on. On every side the captured were flying before their relentless persecutors, while the armed columns of the French army stood watching in an apathy which has never been explained. Nor was the sword of death stayed until greed overcame the desire for revenge. Then, as the Hurons increasingly turned their attention to taking trinkets from the bodies, the shrieks of the wounded, and the yells of their murderers grew less frequent. Finally, the cries of horror were lost to their ear or were drowned in the long and piercing whoops of the triumphant attackers.

CHAPTER 18

Toward the end of the third day after the surrender of the fort and the massacre of the conquered, there was nothing but stillness and death in the area. The bloodstained conquerors had departed; and their camp, which had so lately rung with the merry rejoicings of a victorious army, lay a silent and deserted city of huts. The fortress was a smoldering ruin; charred rafters, fragments of exploded artillery, and smashed mason-work covered its earthen mounds in confused disorder.

A frightful change had also occurred in the season. The August sun had been hidden by a damp mist that was driven by a cold north wind. Hundreds of human forms, which had blackened beneath the fierce heats of August, were stiffening in their deformity before the blasts of a premature November. The sparkling mirror of Lake Horican was gone; in its place, the green and angry waters lashed the shores, as if indignantly casting back its impurities to the polluted pebbled beach.

The wind blew unequally; sometimes it swept heavily along the ground, seeming to whisper its moanings in the cold ears of the dead; sometimes it rose in a shrill and mournful whistling and entered the forest with a rush that filled the air with the leaves and branches it scattered in its path. A few hungry ravens struggled against the wind and then dropped down onto the plain to partake of the hideous banquet offered there.

About an hour before sunset on the third day, five men could be seen coming from the place where the path to the Hudson River entered the forest. These were the first living human beings to approach the place since the departure of the conquerors. The progress of the five was slow and guarded, as though they entered with reluctance amid the horrors of the place. They moved in the direction of the ruined fort. They watched carefully, alert for the smallest sign of danger from the plain or from the surrounding forest.

Uncas, who led the group, threw serious but furtive glances at the mangled victims, as he stepped lightly across the plain; he was too inexperienced to quell entirely powerful influence of the grotesque sights. Chingachgook was more practiced and so was able to maintain a steadiness of purpose and a calm eye as he passed the groups of the dead. Munro, although a man long experienced in scenes of war, was not ashamed to groan aloud whenever a spectacle of more than usual horror came under his view. Heyward, walking beside the colonel, shuddered, but seemed to suppress his feelings of horror under acts of tenderness toward his companion. Hawkeye, who followed last, appeared alone to betray his real thoughts, without fear of observation or dread of consequences. He gazed at the most appalling sight with eyes that did not waver, but with muttered oaths so bitter and deep as to denote how much he denounced the crime of his enemies.

When Uncas had reached the center of the plain, he raised a cry that drew his companions in a body to the spot. The young warrior had halted over a group of women who lay in a cluster, a confused mass of death. In spite of the revolting horror of the scene, Munro and Heyward flew toward the festering heap, attempting, with a love that could not be extinguished, to discover whether any vestiges of those they looked for lay among the tattered and many-colored garments. The father and the lover found instant relief in the discovery that the sisters were not part of this heap.

They were standing, silent and thoughtful, around the melancholy pile, when the scout approached. Eyeing the sad spectacle with an angry look, the sturdy woodsman, for the first time since his entering the plain, spoke aloud: "Never have I found the hand of the devil so plain as it is here to be seen! Should any of those Frenchmen ever come within range of my Killdeer, they will pay for this horror they permitted. But look, Chingachgook, there lies a dead and scalped Indian. He may be one of your missing people; and if so, he should have the burial of a brave warrior."

Chingachgook approached the mutilated form. Turning it over, he found the distinguishing marks of one of those six allied tribes who, although they fought on the British side, had long been enemies of his own people. Scornfully rejecting the loathsome object with his foot, he turned from it with the same indifference he would have left an animal carcass.

An exclamation from Uncas drew their attention.

"What is it, lad?" whispered the scout, crouching, like a panther about to leap. "I hope it's a sneaking Frencher, looking for plunder. Killdeer is itching for a shot at him."

Uncas, without replying, bounded away from the spot. In the next instant he was racing from a bush and waving in triumph a fragment of the green riding-veil of Cora. The movement and the cry that burst from the lips of the young

Mohican, instantly drew the whole party about him.

"My child!" said Munro, speaking quickly and wildly; "give me my child!"

"Uncas will try," was the Mohican's short and touching answer.

"There are no dead in this vicinity," Heyward said, with hope in his voice. "The violence seems not to have passed this way."

"It's clear," returned the undisturbed scout, "that either she, or they that have robbed her, have passed this bush. Uncas, you are right; the dark-hair has been here, and she has fled to the woods like a frightened fawn. We must search for the marks she left."

The young Mohican darted away at the suggestion. A moment later they heard him raise a cry of success from the edge of the forest. On reaching the spot, the anxious party discovered another portion of the veil fluttering on the lower branch of a beech tree.

"Gently, gently," said the scout, extending his long rifle in front of the eager Heyward. "We must not disturb the trail if we are to hope to be able to follow it. A step too soon may give us hours of trouble. We have them, though; that much is beyond denial."

"Bless you, bless you, worthy man," exclaimed Munro. "Where, then, have they fled? Where are my daughters?"

"If they are alone, they are as likely to travel in a circle as in a straight line and may be within a dozen miles of us," Hawkeye responded; "but if the Hurons have taken them, they are probably near the border of Canada by now. But don't worry. Here are the Mohicans and I on one end of the trail and we will find the other end no matter how far it is!"

Chingachgook gave an exclamation. He had been examining the ground near the underbrush and now he stood pointing downward with the air of a man who was looking at a disgusting serpent.

"Here is the impression of the footstep of a man," cried Heyward, bending over the spot Chingachgook pointed to. "The mark cannot be mistaken. They are captives."

Uncas examined the track closely. At length he arose from his knees, satisfied with the result of the examination.

"Well, lad," demanded the attentive scout, "what does it say? Can you make anything of it?"

"Sly Fox!"

"Ha! That rampaging devil again! There will never be an end of his loping till Killdeer has said a friendly word to him," Hawkeye declared. "But let me have a look at it."

After examining the track, the scout said, "You are right, Uncas; here is the print we saw so often in the chase from Glenn's Falls. It's definite, then. Cora and Magua have passed this way."

"And not Alice?" demanded Heyward.

"Of her we have not yet seen the signs," returned the scout, looking closely around at the trees, the bushes, and the ground. "What have we there? Uncas, bring me the thing you see dangling from that thornbush."

The young Mohican brought the object to Hawkeye. The scout held it up and laughed. "Why it's the tooting weapon of the singer. He has left his pitch pipe behind."

"At least he has been faithful to his trust," said Heyward. "And Cora and Alice are not without a friend. As we now possess these infallible signs, let us follow the trail immediately."

"It is not the swiftest leaping deer that gives the longest chase," returned Hawkeye. "We know that the rampaging Huron has been here, and the dark-haired sister, and the singer. But where is the sister of the yellow locks and blue eyes? There is no sign that she has come this way. We must push deeper on the trail. If nothing turns up, we must go back to the plain and try again. Move on, friends; the sun is getting behind the hills."

"Is there nothing that I can do?" demanded the anxious Heyward.

"You?" said the scout. "Yes, you can keep in our rear and be careful not to trample on clues."

Before they had proceeded a hundred yards,

the Mohicans stopped and gazed at some signs on the earth with more than their usual keenness.

"What have we here?" asked the scout, joining his two Indian companions. "Why, these are the prints of those one-sided Narragansett horses again. They were tied to this sapling, waiting. Yes, and here they were mounted. And there runs the broad path away to the north, heading for Canada."

"But still there are no signs of Alice," said Duncan.

"Unless the shining bauble Uncas has just lifted from the ground should prove one. Pass it here, lad, that we may look at it."

Heyward instantly knew it for a trinket that Alice was fond of wearing. The young major seized the prized jewel and, as he proclaimed the fact, he pressed it warmly against his heart. After a moment he said, "We must not delay our march. Let us go immediately."

"Patience, my boy," Hawkeye declared. "We are not going on a squirrel hunt or to catch a deer. We will be in the wilderness for days and nights, most likely. It is land where men seldom go. An Indian never starts on such an expedition without considering it over his council-fire; although I am not an Indian, I honor that custom in this circumstance. We will, therefore, go back, and light our fire tonight in the ruins of the old fort, and in the morning we shall be fresh, and ready to undertake our work like men, and not like eager boys."

Heyward saw that argument would be useless. And he noticed that Munro had again sunk into that apathy which had frequently overcome him in the past three days. The young man took the veteran by the arm and followed in the footsteps of the Indians and the scout, who had already begun to retrace the path that led them to the plain.

CHAPTER 19

The shades of evening had increased the dreariness of the ruins of Fort William Henry by the time the five men entered the place. The scout and his companions immediately made their preparations to spend the night there. They went about their work with a seriousness that reflected how much the unusual horrors they had just witnessed played on their feelings.

Uncas leaned a few fragments of rafters against a blackened wall and covered them with brush. This served as a shelter for the grieving Munro.

While Hawkeye and the Mohicans built a fire and prepared a frugal meal of dried bear's meat, Heyward walked on a rampart of the dilapidated fort and looked out across Lake Horican. The wind had died down. The clouds had drawn back into black masses along the horizon while light mists hung above the water's surface and clung to the mountaintops.

Here and there, a red and fiery star struggled through the drifting vapor, giving a lurid gleam of brightness to the dull aspect of the heavens. Within the encircling hills, an impenetrable darkness had settled, and the plain lay like a vast and deserted house of the dead, without omen or whisper to disturb the slumbers of its numerous and luckless tenants.

Duncan stood on the mound for many minutes, peering into the gloom and remembering the horrid pictures he had seen so recently. He soon imagined that inexplicable sounds arose from the place, but sounds that were so faint and indistinct that he could not be certain of their existence. Feeling foolish for being so apprehensive, he tried to turn his mind to other matters. A moment later, an audible and swift trampling seemed to rush across the darkness. Unable to quiet his uneasiness any longer, Duncan spoke in a low voice to the scout, asking him to come up to the place where he stood.

Hawkeye threw his rifle across his arm and left the fireside to join Heyward. He appeared to be unmoved and calm, as if he were sure that they were safe in their position.

"Listen!" said Duncan, when the scout stood beside him on the rampart. "There are suppressed noises on the plain. It may be that a Huron has remained behind seeking plunder among the dead—Listen! You hear the noise I mean?"

"An Indian rarely lurks about the graves of his victims. After the spirit has left the body, he forgets his enmity and is willing to let the dead find their natural rest."

"No doubt—no doubt. I thought I heard it again! Do you hear it?"

"Ay, ay; when food is scarce, and when food is plentiful, a wolf grows bold," said the unmoved scout.

Duncan, understanding the cause of the noises he heard, became less vigilant.

Hawkeye continued casually, "Yes, the wolves would pick among the skins of the devils if they had the chance—what goes there?"

"Isn't it the rushing of the wolves you have mentioned?"

Hawkeye slowly shook his head and beckoned for Duncan to follow him to a spot further from the glare of the fire. The scout placed himself in an attitude of intense attention and listened long and keenly for a repetition of the low sound that had so unexpectedly startled him.

His efforts, though, were in vain. After a pause he whispered to Duncan, "We must call Uncas. The lad may hear what is hid from us."

Hawkeye gave a cry like the sound of a moaning owl. Uncas, who was talking quietly with his father by the fire, sprang to his feet. A moment later he silently appeared next to Duncan and Hawkeye on the rampart.

Hawkeye explained his wishes in a few words. Immediately, Uncas threw himself flat on the ground. To the eyes of Duncan, the Mohican appeared to lie there quiet and motionless. But, on moving to the spot where he thought the Indian lay, he discovered that Uncas had vanished into the darkness.

"What has become of the Mohican?" he asked, stepping back in amazement.

"Shhh! speak lower. We know not what ears are open, and the Mingoes are a quick-witted breed. Uncas is out on the plain, and the Maquas, if there are any, will find their equal in him."

"You think the Hurons are still out there?" asked Heyward. "We must warn Colonel Munro and Chingachgook to be ready for a fight."

"Not a word to either man, if you value your life. Look at the Sagamore. He sits by the fire like a grand Indian chief. If there are any skulking Mingoes out in the darkness, they will never discover, by his appearance, that we suspect danger at hand."

"But he can be plainly seen by the light of the fire. If they see him it will mean his death," Heyward said impatiently.

"What you say is undeniable," returned the scout, showing more anxiety than usual. "Yet what can be done? A single suspicious look might bring on an attack before we are ready. Chingachgook knows, by the call I gave to

Uncas, that we suspect something; I will tell him that we are on the trail of Mingoes; his nature will teach him how to act."

The scout put his fingers to his mouth and raised a low hissing sound. Duncan jumped aside, believing that he heard a snake. Chingachgook, who had been sitting with his head on his hand, reacted to the warning by sitting up straight. His dark eyes moved to either side. Otherwise, he showed no signs of surprise or alarm. His rifle lay untouched within reach of his hand. He appeared to be at rest. The chief awaited the result with calmness and strength.

A moment later the silence was interrupted by the flash and report of a rifle. The air was filled with sparks of fire. When Heyward looked again, Chingachgook had disappeared in the confusion. The scout threw his rifle forward, ready for action. But with the solitary and unsuccessful attempt on the life of Chingachgook, the attack appeared to have terminated. Once or twice the listeners thought they could distinguish the distant rustling of bushes, as bodies of some unknown description rushed through them. After an impatient and breathless pause, a plunge was heard in the water, and it was immediately followed by the report of another rifle.

"There goes Uncas!" said the scout. "I know the sound of that rifle, for I carried the gun myself until I got Killdeer."

"What can this mean?" demanded Duncan.

"Certainly, no good was intended," Hawkeye replied.

After a moment Duncan saw Chingachgook reappear within the circle of light around the fire. The Indian quietly resumed his seat. As they joined the Mohican chief by the fire, Hawkeye asked, "How goes it, Sagamore? Are the Mingoes on us in earnest or is it only one of those reptiles hanging around looking for missed scalps?"

Chingachgook did not make any reply until after he had examined the burning piece of wood that had been struck by the bullet intended for him. Then he said, "One."

"I thought as much," returned Hawkeye. "And as he had got the cover of the lake before Uncas got a shot at him, I suspect he got away."

Chingachgook turned a calm and incurious eye toward the place where the bullet had struck, and then resumed his former composed attitude, undisturbed by so trifling an incident. Just then Uncas glided into the circle and seated himself at the fire with the same appearance of indifference as his father showed.

They sat in silence for several moments. Finally, Duncan could no longer contain himself. "What has become of our enemy, Uncas?" he demanded. "We heard your rifle and hoped your shot found its target."

The young chief removed a fold of his hunting skirt and quietly exposed the fatal tuft of hair, the symbol of victory. Chingachgook laid his hand on the scalp and considered it for a moment with deep attention. Then dropping it, with disgust depicted in his strong features, he said: "Oneida!"

"Oneida!" repeated the scout. "By the Lord, if the Oneidas are outlying on the trail, we will be flanked by devils on every side of us!"

"The poor fellow must have mistaken us for French," said Heyward. "He would not have attempted to take the life of a friend."

"He mistake a Mohican in his war paint for a Huron! That isn't possible," returned the scout. "No, no, the serpent knew his errand. There is but little love between a Mohican and a Mingo, no matter which white man's flag they may fight under. Even though the Oneidas serve the same king as we do, I would have let Killdeer kill that rascal if I'd had the chance."

"You can't mean that," said Heyward. "That would have been against our treaties."

"White cunning has managed to throw the tribes into great confusion, as respects friends and enemies," Hawkeye said. "As a result, the Hurons and the Oneidas, who speak the same tongue, take each other's scalps, and the Lenape are divided among themselves. The white man's quarrels have armed friend against friend, and brought natural enemies to find themselves fighting side by each side. Everything is thrown into disorder, destroying all the harmony of warfare. Allegiances among the Indians are not likely to alter with every shift in the white man's policies. The love between a Mohican and an Oneida is much like the regard between a white man and a snake."

"I'm sorry to hear that," the young major said. "I had thought that all the tribes that live within our boundaries had identified themselves completely with our quarrels."

"An Indian is no different from a white man in respect to quarrels," the scout replied. "It is only natural to give preference to one's own quarrels over the quarrels of strangers."

And so, putting the matter to rest, the woodsman fell into silence as he turned to help the Mohicans replenish the fire. Heyward went back to the rampart. He was too uneasy and too little accustomed to the warfare of the woods to remain at ease under the possibility of such insidious attacks. He felt safer under the cover of darkness.

Not so, however, with the scout and the Mohicans. Their acute senses, after having detected the danger, had enabled them also to recognize when it had passed. Not one of the three appeared in the least to doubt their perfect security. They were preparing to sit in council to decide how to best proceed with the pursuit of the sisters.

Duncan positioned himself where he could watch the ritual from a short distance.

After a short and impressive pause, Chingachgook lighted a pipe whose stone bowl was curiously carved. The pipe was passed from man to man three times. Finally, Chingachgook broke the silence and, in a few calm and dignified words, proposed the subject for deliberation. The quiet discussion then took place. It was clear to Duncan that Chingachgook and Hawkeye had different views. In spite of this, the entire council was conducted with the utmost courtesy and respect. There were long pauses during which the words of the other were considered.

Although Heyward could not understand the language, he was able to follow the general thread of the argument. By the frequency with which the Indians gestured toward the forest, it was evident they urged a pursuit by land; the repeated sweep of Hawkeye's arm toward Lake Horican indicated that he was in favor of traveling across its waters.

In support of his argument, the scout noted the difficulties of the overland route, particularly for Munro, who seemed to be weakening by the day. He also indicated dangers they would face on land from other Oneida warriors. Finally, his points convinced the Mohicans that they would do better to travel on Lake Horican.

The instant the matter in discussion was decided, the debate and everything connected with it, except the result, appeared to be forgotten. Hawkeye gave no appearance of feeling he had triumphed. He merely stretched out on the ground before the dying embers and went to sleep.

Chingachgook and Uncas the Mohicans seized the moment to devote some attention to one another. Chingachgook began speaking to his son in the soft and playful tones of affection. Uncas gladly met the familiar air of his father. The eyes of the father followed the flowing and musical voice of the son, and he never failed to smile in reply to the other's contagious but low laughter.

After an hour had passed in this comfortable manner, Chingachgook abruptly announced his desire to sleep, by wrapping his head in his blanket and stretching his form on the naked earth. The merriment of Uncas instantly ceased; and carefully raking the coals in such a manner that they should give their warmth to his father's feet, the youth also stretched out on the ground and went to sleep.

Finding renewed confidence from the security of these experienced foresters, Heyward, too, prepared to sleep. For long hours the five seemed to slumber as heavily as the unconscious multitude whose bones were already beginning to bleach on the surrounding plain.

CHAPTER 20

The heavens were still studded with stars when Hawkeye came to arouse the two sleepers in the temporary shelter that Uncas had built the previous afternoon. Casting aside their cloaks Munro and Heyward were on their feet instantly. As they came out of the rough shelter, the only greeting the scout gave them was a significant gesture for silence.

"Speak not a syllable; it is rare for a white voice to pitch itself properly in the woods," he warned them. "Follow me. And walk only on the stones and the fragments of wood as you go."

Although the two soldiers did not know the reason for such extreme caution, they followed the scout over the stones and pieces of wood of the ruined fort. Soon all three were standing on the shore of Lake Horican.

"That's a trail that nothing but a nose can follow," said the satisfied scout, looking back along their difficult way. "Wood and stone take no footprint from a moccasin." Then turning toward the water, he said, "Shove in the canoe closer to the land, Uncas, but softly, lad, softly; it must not touch the beach, or the rascals will know by what road we have left the place."

Uncas brought the canoe close to shore. The scout laid a board between the edge of the ruins and the waiting vessel. He then signaled them to get into the canoe. After making sure that no trace of their exit from the fort remained, Hawkeye entered the canoe. The two Mohicans cautiously maneuvered across the glassy waters and into the broad and dark shadows that fell from the mountains to the east.

Once they were at some distance from the fort, Heyward asked, "Why must we make such a secret and hurried departure?"

"Have you forgotten the skulking reptile that Uncas killed last night?" returned the scout.

"No. But you said he was alone. Is there any reason to fear a dead man?"

"Ay, he was alone in his deviltry! But his tribe has many warriors. It is not likely they would leave his death unavenged for long," Hawkeye replied. Then, looking back at the dim shore of Fort William Henry, which was now fast receding, he continued, "No. I have put a trail of water between us; and unless the imps can learn from the fishes who has paddled across their pond this fine morning, we will put the length of Lake Horican behind us before they have made up their minds which path to take."

"With enemies in front of us and enemies behind us, we are likely to have a dangerous journey," Heyward noted.

"Dangerous!" repeated Hawkeye, calmly; "no, not dangerous. We can manage to keep a few hours ahead of the rascal. No, not dangerous. But it is probable that we shall have what you might call a brisk push of it; and it may happen that we will have a brush or a scrimmage, or some such diversion. But nothing dangerous!"

Heyward, unable to take such a relaxed attitude toward their journey, did not reply. Instead, he sat in silence while the canoe glided over several miles of water.

Just as the day dawned, they entered the narrows of the lake and stole swiftly and cautiously among numberless little islands. They knew that General Montcalm had come by this route as he returned north from Fort William Henry. It was possible that he had left some of the Hurons to protect the rear of his forces and ambush anyone who might try to follow him. Therefore, they approached the passage in their customary silent and guarded manner.

Chingachgook laid aside his paddle while Uncas and the scout urged the light vessel through crooked and intricate channels. Every foot that they advanced exposed them to the danger of some sudden confrontation. The eyes of the Sagamore moved warily from islet to islet, and thicket to thicket, as the canoe proceeded.

Heyward was just beginning to think that maybe he was overly concerned about the dangers of their trip when the paddles ceased moving in response to a signal from Chingachgook. The Indian gravely raised his arm and pointed in the direction in which his own steady look was riveted. A hundred yards in front of them lay another of the wooded islets, but it appeared as calm and peaceful as if its solitude had never been disturbed by the foot of man.

"I see only mist above the island," Duncan said, as he looked where Chingachgook pointed.

"But what is the edging of blacker smoke that hangs along its lower side, and which you may trace down into the thicket of hazel trees? It is from a fire; but one that has been allowed to burn low," Hawkeye replied. "We must make a push, and if the Indians or Frenchers are in the narrows, run the gauntlet between them. Does that make sense to you, Chingachgook?"

The Indian made no other answer than to drop his paddle into the water and urge the canoe forward. All three paddled vigorously and in a very few moments could see the entire north shore of the island.

"There they are," whispered the scout, "two canoes and a fire. The knaves haven't yet got their eyes out of the mist, or we should hear the accursed whoop. Together, friends! We are leaving them."

They heard the crack of a rifle and a bullet came skipping across the placid surface of the water. A shrill yell from the island announced that they had been spotted. In another instant several Hurons were seen rushing into canoes, which were soon dancing over the water in pursuit.

"Hold them there, Chingachgook," said Hawkeye, looking coolly backward over his left shoulder, while he still plied his paddle. "Keep them just at that distance. The Hurons have never a rifle in their nation that will shoot this far. But Killdeer has a barrel that can do the job."

While the two Mohicans paddled, Hawkeye raised his rifle to take aim. He then lowered it again without firing and asked his companions to let the Hurons gain on them a little. He was raising his rifle again when an exclamation from Uncas made him stop.

"What now, lad?" demanded Hawkeye. "You save a Huron from death by that word. What do you see?"

Uncas pointed toward a rocky shore a little in front of them. From the spot, another war canoe was darting directly across their course.

The scout laid aside his rifle, and resumed

paddling. Chingachgook steered the bow of the canoe a little toward the western shore, in order to increase the distance between them and this new enemy. In the meantime they were reminded of the presence of those behind them by wild and exulting shouts. The stirring scene awakened even Munro from his apathy.

"Steer her more along the land, Chingachgook; we are surpassing the vermin," Hawkeye said.

When the Hurons found their course was likely to throw them behind prey, they gradually adjusted their bearing until the two canoes were gliding on parallel lines within two hundred yards of each other. It now became entirely a trial of speed. But the pursuers had the advantage of numbers. It was clear that the fugitives could not keep up such severe exertion for any great length of time.

Duncan noticed with uneasiness that the scout began to look anxiously about him, as if searching for some further means of saving themselves.

"Edge her a little more from the sun, Chingachgook," said the stubborn woodsman. "I see one of the rascals has put down his paddle for a rifle. A single broken bone might lose us our scalps. Edge more from the sun and we will put that island between us and them."

A long, low island lay at a little distance

before them. As they closed with it, the chasing canoe was forced to take the side opposite to that on which the scout and his companions passed. As soon as they were hidden by the island, Hawkeye and the Mohicans now redoubled their efforts at the paddles. When the two canoes came within sight of each other again at the far end of the island, the fugitives had taken the lead. However, the pursuers were now almost in a direct line behind them.

"They are preparing to shoot," said Heyward; "and as we are in a line with them, they can scarcely miss."

"Get into the bottom of the canoe," returned the scout; "you and the colonel; it will make the target that much smaller."

Heyward smiled, as he answered, "It would be a poor example for the highest in rank to duck, while the warriors were under fire."

"Lord! Now that is a white man's courage!" exclaimed the scout; "and like too many of his notions, not supported by reason. Do you think the Chingachgook, or Uncas, or I would hesitate to take cover in the scrimmage, when an open body would do no good?"

"What you say is very true, my friend," replied Heyward. "Still, our customs must prevent us from doing as you wish."

A volley from the Hurons interrupted the discussion, and as the bullets whistled about them, Uncas turned his head and looked back at Heyward and Munro. His expression showed amazement at finding men willing to encounter so useless an exposure to danger.

Another shot rang out and the bullet knocked the paddle from the hands of Chingachgook. It was driven through the air, landing far in advance of the canoe. A shout arose from the Hurons, followed by more shots. Uncas cut an arc in the water with his own paddle, and as the canoe passed swiftly on, Chingachgook recovered his paddle. Waving it in the air, he gave the war-whoop of the Mohicans, and then lent his strength and skill again to the important task.

The clamorous sounds of "Great Snake!" "Long Rifle!" "Bounding Elk!" burst from the canoes behind. The scout seized Killdeer in his left hand, and elevating it about his head, he shook it in triumph at his enemies. The Hurons answered the insult with a yell, and immediately another volley followed.

Hawkeye turned his head toward Duncan and said, "The fools love to hear the sound of their own rifles. Notice that the dumb devils have taken another man off the paddle to assist in the shooting. We are beginning to pull away from them again!"

The Hurons soon fired again, and a bullet struck the blade of Hawkeye's paddle without doing any damage.

"That will do," said the scout, examining the slight indentation. "That bullet would not have cut the skin of an infant, much less of men. Now, major, if you will try to use this piece of flattened wood, I'll let Killdeer take a part in the conversation."

Heyward seized the paddle, and applied himself to the work with an eagerness that made up for his lack of skill. Meanwhile, Hawkeye prepared his rifle. He then took a swift aim and fired.

The Huron in the bow of the leading canoe had risen to fire on them, and he now fell backward, allowing his gun to slip from his hands into the water. In an instant, his companions suspended their efforts, and the chasing canoes clustered together and became stationary.

Chingachgook and Uncas took advantage of the interval to catch their breath, but Duncan continued to paddle with vigor. A few large drops of blood were trickling down the shoulder of the chief. When he noticed that the eyes of Uncas dwelt too long on the sight, he raised some water in the hollow of his hand and washed off the stain to demonstrate the slightness of the injury.

"Softly, softly, major," said the scout, who by this time had reloaded his rifle. "We are a little too far already for even my rifle. Let them come up within striking distance."

"We forget our purpose," returned Duncan. "For God's sake let us profit by this advantage and increase our distance from the enemy."

"Give me my children," said Munro, hoarsely; "Do not prolong a father's agony. Restore to me my daughters."

Throwing a last and lingering glance at the distant canoes, Hawkeye laid aside his rifle, and, relieving the wearied Duncan, resumed the paddle. The Mohicans also took up their efforts again. Within a few moments the stretch of water between them and their enemies had become great enough that Heyward once more breathed freely.

The lake now began to expand as they left the narrows behind them. There were high and ragged mountains on either side here, but the islands were few and easily avoided. They continued along the eastern shore for several hours until they reached a bay near the northern end of the lake. Here the canoe was driven onto the beach, and the whole party landed. Hawkeye and Heyward ascended an adjacent bluff. After considering the expanse of water beneath him for some moments, the scout pointed out a small black object, hovering under a headland, at the distance of several miles.

"It is a canoe paddled by fierce and crafty Mingoes. The moment it is dark they will be on our trail, as true as hounds on the scent. We must throw them off, or they may put an end to our pursuit of Sly Fox. These lakes are useful at times but they give no cover."

Hawkeye and the major descended to the shore. There the scout explained the situation to the Mohicans. After a short consultation, the three instantly set about carrying out their plan.

They lifted the canoe from the water and carried it into the woods, leaving as broad and obvious a trail as possible. They soon reached a brook, which they crossed. They continued on until they came to a large sheet of bare rock. At this point, where their footsteps might be expected to be no longer visible, they retraced their route to the brook, walking backward, with great care. Then they walked in the bed of the little stream to the lake. There they immediately launched their canoe again.

Along the edge of the lake for some distance were dense and overhanging bushes. Under the cover of these they paddled along the water's edge until the scout determined that it was safe for them to land again.

Here they rested until evening. Then they resumed their route, and, under the cover of darkness, pushed silently and vigorously toward the western shore. After some time Chingachgook steered them into a secluded spot.

The boat was again lifted and carried into the woods where it was carefully concealed under a pile of brush. The adventurers collected their arms and packs, and the scout announced to Munro and Heyward that he and the Mohicans were at last ready to proceed.

CHAPTER 21

The party had landed in the rugged country that stretches to the northwest from Lake Horican. But because Hawkeye and the Mohicans had often traveled the mountains and valleys of this vast wilderness, they did not hesitate to plunge into its depth. They were searching for the path that lead the Hurons north to their homeland.

They traveled across this untamed terrain well into the night, using the stars as their guide. Finally, the scout called a halt. After a short consultation with the Mohicans, he announced that they would spend the remainder of the night where they were. Imitating the example of the scout and his two companions, Duncan and Munro put aside their fears and slept soundly.

The morning sun was shedding a strong and clear light in the forest by the time the travelers resumed their journey.

After proceeding a few miles, the progress of Hawkeye became more deliberate and watchful. He often stopped to examine the trees and the streams. He consulted frequently with Chingachgook. During these discussions, Uncas would stand patient and silent.

At last the scout spoke in English and explained the embarrassment of their situation: "I know that the home path of the Hurons must run north and that it would lie in the valleys of this wilderness. But here we have almost reached the waters of Schroon Lake and still found no sign of the trail. It is possible that we may not have followed the proper scent."

"How can we have made such a mistake!" Duncan exclaimed. "Should we retrace our steps, looking more carefully? Does Uncas have any ideas what is best?"

The young Mohican glanced at his father, who gestured for him to speak. The look on the son's face changed from grave composure to a gleam of joy. Bounding forward like a deer, he sprang up the side of a little slope, some yards in advance. There he stopped and stood, exultingly, over a spot of fresh earth that looked as though it had been recently upturned by the passage of some heavy animal.

"See!" said Uncas, pointing north and south, at the evident marks of the broad trail on either side of him; "the dark-hair has gone toward the forest."

"It's the trail!" exclaimed the scout, advancing to the spot. "The lad is quick of sight and keen of wit for his age." Then, springing forward on the trail, he said with a laugh, "A hound never ran on a more beautiful scent. We are favored with a clear trail to follow. Here are the prints of both your waddling horses! This Huron travels like a white general!"

The renewed spirit of the scout raised the hopes of the whole party. They advanced rapidly, with the confidence of a traveler on a wide highway. Magua had attempted to make the way confusing by frequent turns and false trails, but his pursuers were never fooled for long.

By the middle of the afternoon they had passed Schroon Lake and were following the route of the declining sun. After descending a small hill to a spot where a swift stream glided, they suddenly came to a place where the party of Sly Fox had made a halt. The remains of a fire lay near a spring and the trees showed evidence of having been browsed by the horses. But while the earth was trodden, and the footsteps of both men and beasts were so plainly visible around the place, the trail appeared to have suddenly ended.

The tracks of the horses indicated that the creatures had just wandered without guides. Uncas followed the tracks and, in a short time, returned leading the two Narragansetts. The condition of their saddles indicated that they had been permitted to run a will for several days.

"What does this suggest?" asked Duncan with deep concern.

"That our march is come to a quick end, and that we are in an enemy's country," returned the scout. "I know what you are thinking, but even a Mingo would not ill-treat a woman unless it was the only way to save his own skin. No, no. I have heard that the Hurons come to these woods to hunt. We are getting close to their camp. Magua is back in friendly territory. It is true that the horses are here, but the Hurons are gone; let us, then, hunt for the path by which they left."

Hawkeye and the Mohicans searched with renewed vigor. But their search was unsuccessful. The scout and his companions again made the circuit of the halting place, each slowly following the other, until they assembled in the center once more, no wiser than when they started.

"Such cunning is not without its deviltry," exclaimed Hawkeye, when he met the disappointed looks of his assistants. "We must search again, Chingachgook, beginning at the spring and going over the ground inch by inch."

Setting the example himself, the scout engaged in the examination with renewed zeal. Not a leaf was left unturned. Still no discovery was made.

Finally Uncas returned to the spring. There he raked the earth across the muddy little stream that ran from the spring and diverted its course into another channel. When the narrow streambed below the dam was dry, he stooped over it with keen and curious eyes. A cry of exultation immediately announced the success of the young warrior. The whole party crowded to the spot where Uncas pointed out the impression of a moccasin in the moist soil.

"This lad is an honor to his people," said Hawkeye, regarding the trail with admiration, "and a thorn in the sides of the Hurons. But that is not the footstep of an Indian! The weight is too much on the heel, and the toes are squared. It appears to be the footprint of the singer, judging by the great size of it. But he has been made to exchange his shoes for moccasins."

Chingachgook nodded in agreement with Hawkeye's conclusion.

"I can now read the whole of it, as plainly as I see the trickery of Sly Fox," the scout continued; "the singer was made to go first, and the others have trod in his steps, so hiding their own footprints. I'd be willing to bet my Killdeer that we will see the prints of the whole pack—including those of the gentle sisters—before many miles."

The whole party moved forward, following the course of the little stream. The foresters watched the ground on either side to determine where the Hurons had exited from the watery trail. After more than half a mile they came to a place where the stream rippled close to a sheet of rock.

Knowing that this was a likely spot for the Hurons to leave the stream, they paused to search for signs. The quick and active Uncas soon found the impression of a foot on a bunch of moss, where an Indian had accidentally stepped. Uncas then entered a nearby thicket. Here he found the trail, as fresh and obvious as it had been before they reached the spring. A shout brought the others to his side.

"Well done, lad," the scout said to Uncas. "Here we have three pair of moccasins, and two of little feet. It is amazing that any mortal beings can journey on limbs so small!"

"The tender limbs of my daughters are not equal to the hardships of this journey," said Munro, looking at the light footsteps of his children, with a parent's love. "I fear that we shall find their fainting forms in this wilderness."

"There is little cause to fear that," returned the scout, slowly shaking his head; "this is a firm and straight, though a light step. See, the heel has hardly touched the ground; and there the dark-hair has made a little jump, from root to root. No, no; my knowledge for it, neither of them was anywhere close to fainting. On the other hand, the singer was beginning to be foot-sore and leg-weary, as is plain by his trail. There, you see, he slipped and here he has traveled wide from the path and tottered. Ay, a man who uses his throat so much, can hardly give his legs proper training."

Cheered by these assurances, the party made a short halt to take a hurried meal. When the meal was ended, the party pushed forward with renewed energy. Except for an occasional glance at the setting sun, the scout kept his eyes on the clear trail ahead. Before an hour had elapsed, however, Hawkeye slowed his pace. His head, instead of maintaining its direct and forward look, began to turn suspiciously from side to side, as if he were conscious of approaching danger. He soon stopped again and waited for the whole party to come up.

"Over there is open sky, through the tree-tops. We are getting too close to the encampment of the Hurons," he said, pointing ahead in the quickly fading twilight. "Chingachgook, you will take the hillside, to the right; Uncas will bend along the brook to the left, while I will continue on the trail. If anything should happen, the call will be three croaks of a crow."

The Indians each left without reply, while Hawkeye cautiously proceeded with the two soldiers. Heyward, eager to catch a glimpse of the enemy, stayed close by Hawkeye's side. The scout told Duncan to move ahead to the thicket at the edge of the woods and to wait for him there. He, in the meantime would examine certain suspicious signs off the other side of the trail. Duncan obeyed and soon found himself looking out on an extraordinary sight.

In the dimness of the mild summer evening, the young major could see that the trees had been felled across many acres. A short distance from where he peered out of the thicket, the stream seemed to have expanded into a little lake. The was a waterfall at the lower end of the lake, but it was so smooth and even that it appeared to have been built by human hands. A hundred earthen dwellings stood on the edge of the lake, and even in its waters, as though the water had overflowed its usual banks. The whole village seemed surprisingly carefully constructed and well ordered.

At first, the place appeared deserted. After a few moments, thought, he believed he saw several human forms crawling about on all fours. Each was dragging some large and seemingly heavy object behind him. Alarmed at these suspicious and inexplicable movements, he was about to attempt the signal of the crows, when the rustling of leaves at hand drew his eyes in another direction.

The young man started and recoiled a few paces instinctively, when he found himself within a hundred yards of an Indian he did not recognize. Realizing that making any sound could prove fatal, he kept silent and watched the stranger.

It was clear the Indian had not seen him, for this stranger was occupied in observing the village and the stolen movements of its inhabitants. It was impossible for Duncan to discover the expression of his features because they were concealed under a grotesque mask of paint. But he did seem to be more melancholy than savage. His head was shaved, as usual, with the exception of the crown. His clothing was ragged but he was wearing a pair of good deerskin moccasins. Altogether, the individual appeared forlorn and miserable.

Duncan was still curiously observing the stranger when the scout stole silently and cautiously to his side.

"You see we have reached the hunting encampment of the Hurons," whispered the young man; "and over there is one of the savages himself."

Hawkeye studied the figure of the stranger that Heyward pointed toward. Then he said, "The imp is not a Huron, nor of any of the Canada tribes; and his clothes look to have been ripped from a white man. Did you see where he put his rifle or his bow?"

"He appears to have no arms; nor does he

seem to be viciously inclined," Duncan replied.
"Unless he gives the alarm to his fellows, who,
as you see, are dodging about the water over
there, we have little to fear from him."

The scout turned to Heyward, and stared at
him for a moment with unconcealed amazement. Then opening his mouth wide, he
indulged in unrestrained and heartfelt silent
laughter.

Repeating the words, "Fellows who are
dodging about the water!" he added, "So much
for book learning and growing up in the settlements!" Then, turning his attention back to the
stranger, he continued, "The imp has long legs,
though, and shall not be trusted. Keep your rifle
trained on him while I creep in behind, through
the bush, and take him alive. But do not fire a
shot under any circumstances unless I say so."

In the next moment he was concealed by
the leaves. Duncan waited several minutes in
feverish impatience before he caught another
glimpse of the scout. Then he reappeared,
creeping along the earth. When he was within a
few yards of the stranger, he arose to his feet,
silently and slowly. The Indian was busy studying the dark forms that were moving about near
the lake. Hawkeye raised his hand above the
head of the stranger. Then, for no apparent reason, he withdrew it again. Instead of grasping
his victim by the throat, he tapped him lightly

on the shoulder and exclaimed aloud: "How now, friend! Have you a mind to teach the beavers to sing?"

"Even so," was the ready answer. "It would seem that the Lord that gave them power to improve His gifts so well would not deny them voices to proclaim His praise."

CHAPTER 22

Heyward found himself surprised on several counts. His lurking Indians were suddenly converted into four-footed beasts, the lake into a beaver pond, and the suspected enemy into a former traveling companion, David Gamut. The discovery of the singing master gave him great hope that he could get news of Munro's daughters. He sprang from the bushes and joined the scout and the singer.

Hawkeye's merriment was unstoppable. He spun Gamut around and complimented the man on his appearance. He slapped him on the back and shook his hand with a firm grip, wishing him joy in his new manner of life.

"But now," Hawkeye said with a laugh, "tell me what you think of this fine song!" And with that he let forth with three croaks of a crow.

"See!" continued the laughing scout. He pointed toward the remainder of the party, who were already approaching an answer to the signal. "This is music which has its natural virtues; it brings two good rifles to my side. But we see that you are safe; now tell us what has become of the young women."

"They are captives to the heathen," said David. "And, though they are greatly troubled in spirit, both are safe and comfortable."

"Both!" echoed the breathless Heyward.

"Even so," David said. "Our journey has been difficult, but we have had little other cause for complaint. We were treated well, except the violence done our feelings by being led into a far land."

"Bless you for these very words!" exclaimed the trembling Munro. "My children shall be returned to me, spotless and angel-like, as they were when I lost them!"

"I do not believe that their delivery is at hand," responded David. "The leader of those savages seems possessed with an evil spirit."

"Where is the thief?" the scout interrupted bluntly.

"He hunts the moose today, with his young men; and tomorrow, I hear, they pass further into the forests and closer to the borders of Canada. The older sister has been taken to a tribe in the next valley while the younger one is being kept among the women of the Hurons, less than two miles from here."

"Alice, my gentle Alice!" murmured Heyward. "She has lost the comfort of her sister's presence."

"But why are you permitted to wander about, unwatched?" asked the scout.

"It is the power of my song," Gamut answered. "Although it was unable to stop the horror on that field of blood, it has regained its strength. My song has influenced the souls of these heathens and they permit me to come and go at will."

The scout laughed and tapped his own forehead. He then gave his explanation for David's freedom from restraint: "The Indians never harm a person they believe is not in his right mind."

"Even so," David went on, "I felt it my duty to stay with the young women and encourage them as I might with my hymns."

The scout shook his head as he handed David the pitch pipe he had found on the trail. He said, "Here, friend; I had intended to kindle a fire with this tooting-whistle of yours; but, as you value the thing, take it, and blow your best on it."

Gamut received his pitch pipe with great pleasure. He immediately tested it out and was preparing to launch into one of the songs from his little book.

Heyward, however, hastily interrupted the singing master's pious purpose by continuing questions about the captive sisters. From David's answers, they were able to piece together what had happened after the capture of the sisters.

It seems that Magua had waited on the mountain until a safe moment to begin his journey north. He had taken the route along the western side of Lake Horican. Because of the respect Indians give to a person whose intellect has been visited by the Great Spirit, David was permitted to follow along. At night the captive women were both protected from harm and guarded against escape. At the spring, Sly Fox had taken measures to prevent anyone from discovering their trail. When they had arrived at the encampment of his people, Magua had separated the prisoners, as was the policy of his people. Cora had been sent to a tribe that was temporarily occupying the next valley. David knew only that they were also allies of General Montcalm.

At this point, the scout interrupted Heyward's questioning. He wanted to know more about this tribe in the next valley. "Did you see the style of their knives?" he asked. "Were they of English or French make?"

"My thoughts were on no such matters, but rather concentrated on the consolation of the maidens," David responded.

"Did you see anything that might tell us who they are?" Hawkeye pressed.

"I have seen strange and fantastic images drawn in their paint—especially one, and that was a foul and loathsome object."

"Was it a serpent?" the scout asked quickly.

"Much the same. It was in the likeness of a creeping tortoise."

Both of the Mohicans gave an exclamation. Chingachgook then spoke a few words in the language of the Lenape. As he spoke, he pulled aside the shirt that hung across his chest. His action revealed an image of a tortoise that was beautifully, though faintly, worked in blue tint, on the swarthy breast of the chief.

"We have found that which may be good or evil to us," said Hawkeye. "Chingachgook is of the high blood of the Lenape, and is the great chief of their Tortoises! It is a very dangerous path we move in; for a friend whose face is turned from you often bears more hatred toward you than the enemy who seeks your scalp."

"Explain," said Duncan.

"It is a long and melancholy tradition. And it is one I don't like to think of because the evil has been mainly caused by the white man. But it has ended in turning the tomahawk of brother against brother, and brought the Mingo and the Lenape to travel in the same path."

The impatient Duncan now made several hasty and desperate proposals for attempting to rescue the sisters. Munro seemed to shake off his apathy, and listened to the wild schemes of the young man with serious interest. But the scout, after a little, found means to convince him of the folly of racing into action. This was a matter that would require their coolest judgment and utmost strength of mind.

"It would be best," the scout added, "to let the singer go back to the camp, as usual. He can get word to the gentle ones that we are in the area. When we are ready we will signal him to come out, to consult with us. Do you know the whistle of the whip-poor-will, friend?"

"It is a pleasing bird," returned David, "and has a soft and melancholy note, though the time is rather quick and ill-measured."

"Well, since you like his whistle, it shall be your signal." said Hawkeye. "Remember, then, when you hear the whip-poor-will's call three times repeated, you are to come into the bushes where the bird might be supposed—"

"Wait," interrupted Heyward; "I will accompany him."

"You!" exclaimed the astonished Hawkeye. "Are you tired of seeing the sun rise and set?"

"David is a living proof that the Hurons can be merciful."

"Yes, but to them he appears to be a madman."

"I too can play the madman, the fool, the hero. I'll do anything and everything to rescue the woman I love. There is no more argument. I am determined," Heyward said with finality.

Hawkeye regarded the young man a moment in speechless amazement. But Duncan now assumed a superior manner that was not easily resisted. The major waved his hand and then, in more tempered language, he continued: "You can disguise me; change me; paint me if you will; in short, alter me to anything—a fool."

"When you send your parties to war," muttered the discontented scout, "it is good judgment to at least have some plan in mind. That way, you at least know where the friendly troops are."

"Listen," interrupted Duncan, "and see if this plan satisfies you. We have learned that Alice is still held by our enemies, the Hurons, but that Cora is now held by a tribe you believe to be part of the Lenape nation. It makes sense for me, in disguise, to rescue Alice, or at least die trying. Meanwhile, you negotiate with your friends to secure Cora's release."

The awakened spirit of the young soldier gleamed in his eyes. His very physical presence became imposing under its influence.

Hawkeye, although he recognized the great danger in the major's plan, was not prepared to combat this sudden resolution in the younger man. At the same time, there was something about the boldness and daring of Heyward's idea that appealed to the scout. His opposition to the scheme gave way and he agreed to support

Duncan in his attempt.

"Come," he said, with a good-humored smile; "Chingachgook has as many different paints as the king's wife, and he knows how to use them, too. Seat yourself on the log. I guarantee that he can soon make a natural fool of you, and it will be to your liking."

Duncan sat down and Chingachgook went to work with his paints. The Mohican worked quickly and carefully. He used only designs that Indians considered signs of a friendly and joking nature and avoided any line that could be interpreted as war-like.

While Chingachgook worked, the scout reflected that it was just possible that the plan would work. With Duncan's disguise and his knowledge of French, he might pass for a juggler from the nearby French fort, Ticonderoga.

Once the disguise was complete, Hawkeye suggested where and when they should meet if they were successful. He also told Duncan that he planned to leave Munro in some safe place under the care of Chingachgook while he and Uncas went to negotiate with the Lenape.

The scout concluded their discussion with words that touched Duncan deeply: "And, now, God bless you! You have shown a spirit that I like; it is the gift of youth, especially one of a brave heart. But be constantly alert for it is not easy to outdo the cunning of a Mingo. God bless you! If the Hurons get your scalp, I promise that the Mohicans and I will make them pay for their victory."

Duncan shook Hawkeye's hand warmly. Then he motioned to David to proceed. Hawkeye gazed after the high-spirited and adventurous young man for several moments, in open admiration; then, shaking his head doubtingly, he turned, and led the rest of the party into the concealment of the forest.

The route taken by Duncan and David lay directly across the clearing of the beavers and along the edge of their pond. When the young major found himself alone with the singing master, he began to fully appreciate the difficulties of the task he had undertaken. But then the glowing image of Alice filled his mind and the thoughts of danger faded. Cheering David on, he moved forward into the darkness with the vigorous step of youth and certainty.

Within half an hour they came to the edge of another opening. A very natural sensation caused Duncan to hesitate a moment, unwilling to leave the cover of their sheltered path. It was as if he were collecting all his energies before moving forward with this hazardous experiment that he knew would require them. The halt also gave him a chance to observe the open space before them.

On the opposite side of the clearing the

brook tumbled over some rocks from a higher level. Near the waterfall were some fifty or sixty Indian lodges, constructed of logs, brush, and earth. They were arranged without any order, and seemed to be constructed with very little attention to neatness or beauty. To his surprise, he saw in the doubtful twilight twenty or thirty forms rising alternately from the cover of the tall, coarse grass, in front of the lodges, and then sinking again from the sight. The glimpses he caught of these figures made them seem more like dark phantoms than creatures of flesh and blood. A gaunt, naked form was seen, for a single instant, tossing its arms wildly in the air, then disappearing, only to be replaced by another in some other location.

David noticed what had caught Heyward's attention. He said, "For three nights I have gathered together these urchins to join me in sacred song. But all they have responded with is whoopings and howlings that have chilled my soul!"

"Who are you talking about?" Duncan asked.

"Of those children of the devil, who waste the precious moments in those idle antics you are looking at. Ah! the wholesome restraint of discipline is unknown among this self-abandoned people. Sadly, the choicest blessing the Lord has given us—the voice—is wasted in such cries as these."

As a yell from the playing children rang shrilly through the forest, David put his hands over his ears.

Duncan, laughing at himself for having let his imagination distort the scene he looked at, regained his composure. "We will proceed," he said firmly.

Without taking his hands from his ears, David led the way toward what the sing master thought of as the "tents of the vulgar heathen."

CHAPTER 23

It is unusual to find an encampment of Indians guarded by the presence of armed men. Duncan and David, therefore, were able to walk unchallenged into the midst of the playing children. But as soon as the children saw them, the young pack raised a shrill and warning whoop. Then it sank, as if by magic, from before the sight of their visitors. It seemed as if the earth had swallowed up their forms as they blended into the tall withered grass. But as Duncan glanced curiously around him, he found his look met everywhere by dark, quick eyes.

The startling moment made the young major doubt the wisdom of his plan. It was, however, too late to appear to hesitate. The cry of the children had drawn a dozen warriors to the door of the nearest lodge.

David, to some extent familiar with the encampment, led the way with steadiness into this very building. It was the main building of the village. It was in this lodge that the tribe held its councils and public meetings during their temporary stay in this wilderness.

Duncan found it difficult to maintain an appearance of calm unconcern as he brushed past the dark Hurons and followed David into the very center of the lodge. Imitating the example of Gamut, he pulled a bundle of fragrant brush from the corner and seated himself in silence.

Once the two were seated, the group of warriors fell back from the entrance. Three or four of the oldest and most distinguished among them sat down across from the white men. The other warriors stood about casually leaning against the vertical posts that supported the rough building.

A flaring torch was burning and by its light Duncan was able to make out the faces of the Hurons. But he was not able to read the reserved, unemotional expressions he saw. The silence continued. Finally, an older warrior stepped forward from a dark corner of the lodge. He spoke in the language of the Hurons. Although Heyward could not understand the words, he felt that the gestures suggested courtesy more than anger.

The major shook his head and then replied in French, "Do none of my brothers speak French or English?"

A long and grave pause followed. There was no movement of a limb or expression in a face to tell him how his words had been received. Although the lack of reaction made him uncomfortable, Duncan was glad to have the silence to arrange his thoughts.

At length the same warrior who had addressed him replied, by dryly demanding, in French: "When our Great Father speaks to his people, is it with the language of the Huron."

"General Montcalm, the one you call the Great Father knows no difference in his children, whether the color of the skin be red, or black, or white," returned Duncan, evasively; "but he is pleased with the brave Hurons."

"Will he still be pleased," demanded the wary chief, "when the runners show him the scalps which five nights ago grew on the heads of the Yankee soldiers and their women and children?"

"They were his enemies," said Duncan, shuddering involuntarily at the memory of the massacre that had taken place on the day of the surrender. "Doubtless, the great Montcalm will say, it is good; the Hurons are very gallant."

"Yet our Great Father does not offer us any reward. He has turned his back on the Hurons. What can this mean? Does he no longer respect the Hurons?" asked the chief with some displeasure.

"It cannot be. I am a man who knows the art of healing. The great Montcalm has sent me to his children, the Hurons of the great lakes, to ask if any are sick."

Another silence followed this statement by Duncan. Looking at the chief's cold solemn face, Heyward could not tell if the explanation he had just given for his presence had convinced the Huron or not.

"Do the men of Canada paint their skins?" the chief coldly asked. "We have heard them boast that their faces are white."

"When an Indian chief comes among his white fathers," returned Duncan, with great steadiness, "he lays aside his buffalo robe to wear the shirt that is offered him. My red brothers have given me paint and I wear it."

A low murmur from the Hurons in the lodge announced that the compliment to the tribe was favorably received. Duncan began to breathe more freely, believing that the pressure of his examination was past. He had come up with an explanation for being at the encampment and his hopes of ultimate success grew brighter.

After a silence of a few moments, another warrior stood up to speak. But before he could begin, a low, fearful sound arose from the forest. It was immediately overshadowed by a high, shrill yell. The yell was drawn out until it almost sounded like the sorrowful howl of the wolf. At the same moment, the warriors glided in a body from the lodge. Then the outer air was filled with loud shouts that nearly drowned those awful sounds, which were still ringing beneath the arches of the woods.

Duncan, unable to contain his curiosity, stepped from the lodge. He found himself in the midst of men, women, and children who were all exclaiming and shouting with a joy that seemed frantic.

Coming from the woods was a line of warriors. They were led by a Huron carrying a short pole from which were suspended several human scalps. The unexpected return of this successful war party was the cause of the fierce rejoicing in the camp.

Duncan felt relief that this event had turned the attention away from him for the moment. He watched with a combination of horror and fascination as the events of the return unfolded.

The cries of the warriors, intended to represent both the wailings of the dead and the triumph of the victors, continued until they reached the buildings of the encampment. One of the warriors spoke to the crowd that had come out to meet them. Following his words, the whole encampment, in a moment, became a scene of violent commotion. The warriors in the camp drew their knives, and flourishing them, arranged themselves in two lines, forming a lane that extended from the war party to the lodges. The women seized clubs, axes, or whatever weapon they could find and rushed eagerly to act their part in the cruel game that was about to begin. Even the children grabbed weapons and raced to join in.

Large piles of brush lay scattered about the clearing, and an aged squaw set fire to these to illuminate the coming exhibition. As the flame rose, it made the whole scene more distinct and more hideous.

The war party then fell back to reveal a prisoner standing straight and firm, bravely prepared to meet his fate. From where Duncan stood he could not see the man's face clearly in the light, but he admired the dignity and nobility with which the man faced the deadly race he was about to run.

Just then the signal yell was given, and the momentary quiet which had preceded it was broken by a burst of cries. The tall prisoner bounded from his place at the cry, with the swiftness of a deer. He started down the lane of poised knives and tomahawks. But before a single blow landed, he turned short and leaped over the heads of some children. This surprise move threw the Hurons into wild confusion as they broke from their lines to chase him.

The blazing piles now shed their lurid

brightness on the place, which resembled some supernatural arena in which malicious demons had assembled to act their bloody and lawless rites.

The fugitive continued to elude the weapons of his pursuers. For a moment, it seemed as if he might get to the edge of the forest and freedom, but a half-dozen fiends outflanked him, closing that path and driving him back into the center of the relentless mass. With the swiftness of an arrow, he leaped through a pillar of flame and evaded the mob of brutes, only to be cut off again. He wheeled and ran into the midst of the throng, as if to seek safety in the chaos.

Nothing could be distinguished but a dark mass of human forms tossing in inexplicable confusion. Arms, gleaming knives, and formidable clubs, appeared above them, but the blows were evidently given at random. The awful effect was heightened by the piercing shrieks of the women and the fierce yells of the warriors.

A moment later the stranger emerged from the swirling mass, running toward the spot where Duncan stood. The captive seemed conscious that human power could not much longer endure so severe a trial. He appeared to be racing to reach the painted pole near the principal lodge. Reaching it would not win him his freedom, but at least it would end the frantic chase. He had managed to get clear of the mob but was closely followed by a tall and powerful Huron who was gaining on him. As the fugitive brushed past Heyward, the pursuer came within striking distance. He raised his arm to give the fatal blow.

At that moment Duncan thrust out his foot and sent the eager savage sprawling headlong, many feet in advance of his intended victim. Taking advantage of this momentary reprieve, the fugitive turned sharply and raced to the painted post and safety from the mob.

Disappointed at their failure to execute this enemy, the crowd fell into gloomy and sullen mutterings as they dispersed among the dwellings. Duncan, relieved that his part in helping the captive had not been detected, returned toward the main lodge.

A crowd of women stood near their escaped prey, taunting him with insults. He stood with one hand holding the protecting post, breathing hard from the chase. He ignored the insults, standing with quiet dignity. His face was turned to the darkness, but his indifference to the insults was clear from the way he held himself.

Duncan could not help but admire the calm and quiet manner. As he passed close to the post, he looked a composed figure. For an instant, the captive turned his head and Heyward found himself looking into the firm and piercing eyes of Uncas.

Duncan feared that, in his surprise, some exclamation might have escaped from his lips. But if it did, it went unnoticed, for at that moment a Huron warrior motioned the women aside and approached the prisoner. Taking Uncas by the arm the Huron led him toward the council lodge. As the chiefs and the distinguished warriors crowded into the lodge, Duncan managed to enter without attracting any dangerous attention to himself.

Uncas stood calmly at the center of the lodge in the light of the glaring torch. His captors had arranged themselves around him according to their rank. When each individual had taken his proper place, the gray-haired chief who had interviewed Duncan earlier spoke from the silence.

"Lenape," he said, "though you are one of a nation of women, you have proved yourself a man. If you are so skillful, why are you now our prisoner?"

"I followed in the steps of a flying Huron coward and fell into a trap," Uncas responded defiantly.

A short and sullen pause succeeded this bold statement. Then the chief replied, "Two of my young men are in pursuit of your companion. When they get back, then will our wise man say if you live or die."

"Has a Huron no ears?" scornfully

exclaimed Uncas. "Twice, since I became your prisoner, have I heard a gun that I know. Your young men will never come back! Tomorrow the crows will feast on them!"

After another brief pause the chief said coldly, "Rest in peace till the morning sun, when our last words shall be spoken."

The chief then dashed the torch to the earth, casting the lodge into gloom. He and the other Huron warriors glided from the lodge like troubled spirits, leaving Duncan and Uncas in the darkness.

CHAPTER 24

Duncan stood in silence in the dark for a moment. Then a hand powerfully grasped his arm and the low voice of Uncas muttered in his ear: "The Hurons are dogs. Chingachgook and the gray hair are safe. The rifle of Hawkeye is not asleep. Go. You and I are now strangers. It is enough."

Heyward would gladly have heard more, but a gentle push from his friend urged him toward the door and reminded him of the danger of any Huron seeing them talking to one another. Slowly and reluctantly he left the council lodge.

Duncan wandered among the lodges, unquestioned and unnoticed, attempting to find some trace of Alice. He continued to stray from hut to hut without success until he had made the entire circuit of the village. He retraced his steps to the council lodge. Since he could find no signs of Alice, he decided to seek the help of David Gamut.

On reaching the council lodge the young major found that the warriors had reassembled there. They were now calmly smoking, while they conversed gravely on the events of their recent expedition to Fort William Henry at the other end of Lake Horican.

He was not anxious to risk further questioning about his reasons for being there, but the need to talk with David strengthened his resolve. Without seeming to hesitate, he walked into the lodge and took his seat with a seriousness that matched that of his hosts. A hasty but searching glance told him that, though Uncas still remained where he had been, David had not reappeared.

Heyward sat in the silence of the group, considering what he should do next. Before he came up with a plan, he was addressed by one of the elder warriors:

"My Canada father Montcalm does not forget his children," said the chief. "I thank him. An evil spirit lives in my daughter. Can the clever stranger frighten him away?"

Heyward recognized that he might be able to use this situation to his advantage. He answered, with an air of mystery, "Spirits differ; some yield to the power of wisdom, while others are too strong."

"You, my brother, are powerful in the art of healing," replied the chief. "You must try."

Heyward nodded in assent. The chief then settled into silence again, awaiting the proper moment to move. To Duncan, who was impatient to get on with his search, the minutes passed slowly. Finally, the Huron began to stir. But before he had a chance to rise, a warrior of powerful frame entered and stalked silently among the attentive group. He seated himself near Duncan.

The young major cast an impatient look at his new neighbor and felt his flesh creep with uncontrollable horror when he found himself gazing at Magua.

Several minutes passed while the Indians smoked their pipes in silence.

At length, one warrior uttered, "Welcome! Has my friend found the moose he sought?"

"My two days of journeying have been successful. The young men stagger under their burdens," returned Magua.

"That is good," replied the elder Huron. "The Lenape have been like bears after the honey pots, prowling around my village. But who has ever found a Huron asleep?"

A dark cloud passed over Magua's features as he exclaimed, "The Lenape from the Lakes?"

"Not so," replied the chief. "The Lenape from the river beyond Lake Horican. One of them has run the gauntlet this very night."

"Did my young men take his scalp?" Magua asked.

"His legs were good and he reached the post. He stands there," the chief said, pointing to the unmoving form of Uncas.

Magua did not look at Uncas but continued to smoke his pipe meditatively for a quiet interval. When he had finished his pipe, he shook out the ashes. Then, standing up, he turned to look at the prisoner, who stood a little behind him. Sensing the movement, Uncas turned suddenly to the light. Their looks met. For nearly a minute these two bold and untamed spirits stood regarding one another steadily in the eye, neither quailing in the least before the fierce gaze he encountered.

Gradually, a look of ferocious joy spread over the face of Magua, and heaving a breath from the very bottom of his chest, he pronounced aloud the formidable name of: "Bounding Elk!"

The warriors in the lodge sprang to their feet in surprise and repeated the well-known name as if with one voice. The women and children, who lingered around the entrance, took up the words in an echo. Then quiet again prevailed as the warriors sat down again to regard this enemy who had so often proved himself against the proudest of the Hurons.

Magua raised his arm and shook it at the captive while in a voice filled with vengeance he exclaimed, "Mohican, you die!"

"The healing waters will never bring the dead Hurons to life," returned Uncas. "The tumbling river washes their bones. Their men are squaws; their women owls. Go! Call together the Huron dogs, that they may look upon a warrior."

The insults rankled. Magua saw his opportunity. He was a powerful speaker and he rarely spoke without making converts to his opinions. On this occasion, his natural powers were stimulated by the thirst of revenge.

He again recounted the events of the attack on the island at Glenn's Falls, the death of his associates and the escape of their most formidable enemies. Then he described the surprise attack by Long Rifle and the two Mohicans on the flat hilltop in which the three had killed the six Hurons who had been guarding the four white prisoners. Then, dropping his voice, he described the qualities of each of the Huron warriors who had been killed in those two confrontations. His words vibrated in the hearts of the Hurons gathered in the council lodge.

"Are the bones of my young men," he concluded, "in the burial-place of the Hurons? You know they are not. Their spirits are gone toward the setting sun. But they departed without food, without guns or knives, without moccasins, naked and poor as they were born. Shall this be? Brothers, we must not forget the dead. We will load the back of this Mohican until he staggers under our bounty and dispatch him after my young men. It is true that many white men have paid for the death of my brave men. But the earth is still pale. A stain on the name of Huron can only be hidden by blood that comes from the veins of an Indian. Let this Lenape die."

The effect of Magua's powerful speech could scarcely be mistaken. His listeners lost every trace of humanity in a wish for revenge. One warrior in particular, a man of wild and ferocious appearance, had settled into a look of deadly malice as the speech progressed. As Magua finished, this man rose, uttering a yell like a demon. He whirled his tomahawk about his head and sent it toward the hated enemy. But at the moment of release, Magua had darted forward and struck the arm of the Huron. His blow had diverted the aim so that the sharp weapon cut the war plume from the hair of Uncas and then passed through the frail wall of the lodge.

"No!" said Magua, after satisfying himself of the safety of the captive. "The sun must shine on his shame; the squaws must see his flesh tremble, or our revenge will be like the play of boys. Go! Take him where there is silence; let us see if a Lenape can sleep at night, and in the morning die."

With that, three young warriors bound Uncas' arms and led him away.

Magua, content with the success of his speech and the promise of revenge, turned and left the lodge. He had so concentrated his efforts on the hated Mohican that he had failed to notice Duncan in his disguise. Heyward felt relief sweep over him as the dangerous and subtle foe left.

The excitement produced by the speech gradually subsided. The warriors resumed their seats and clouds of smoke once more filled the lodge. For near half an hour, not a syllable was uttered.

When the chief who had asked the aid of Duncan finished his pipe, he made move to depart. He motioned for the supposed physician to follow. Passing through the clouds of smoke, Duncan was relieved to be able at last to breathe the pure air of a cool and refreshing summer evening.

Instead of going among the lodges, the chief led Heyward toward the base of a mountain that overhung the temporary village. A crooked path took them through a thicket of brush. The path then opened onto a grassy space. In the gloom, a dark and mysterious-looking being rose in front them. The Indian paused, as if doubtful whether to proceed, and studied the large black ball that moved in front of them. Then Duncan realized that the creature was a bear. Though it growled loudly and fiercely, it gave no other indications of hostility.

The Huron, at least, seemed assured that the intentions of this unusual intruder were peaceable. After giving it an attentive examination, the chief quietly pursued his course. Duncan, who knew that bears were often domesticated among the Indians, followed the example of his companion, assuming that this was some favorite of the tribe.

They passed it unmolested. Heyward's uneasiness, however, was not diminished when he realized that the beast was following them. He would have spoken, but the Indian at that moment shoved aside a door of bark, and entered a cavern in the side of the mountain.

Relieved to have so easy a way to escape the bear, Duncan stepped after him. He was gladly closing the slight cover to the opening, when he felt it drawn from his hand by the beast, whose shaggy form immediately darkened the passage.

They were in a straight, long chasm in the rock. The bear made retreat impossible. Making the best of the circumstances, Heyward pressed forward, keeping as close as possible to the Huron. The bear growled frequently at his heels and once or twice placed its enormous paws on him, as if trying to stop him.

There was a glimmer of light in front of them and they soon arrived at its source. They were in a large cavity in the rock. The space was open to the sky and was illuminated by fires and torches. It was divided into several rooms by walls of rock and wood that the Hurons had built. Here was the place where the Hurons stored their valuables. They had brought the ill woman to the place in hopes that the surrounding rocks might better protect her from the supernatural power that they believed to be tormenting her.

Duncan was led into the room where the sick woman lay. She was surrounded by several young women. Heyward was surprised to see that his missing friend David was there too. A single look at the woman told the pretend doctor that she was far beyond his powers of healing. She lay in a sort of paralysis, indifferent to the objects which crowded before her sight, and happily unconscious of suffering.

Heyward was relieved that the woman was too far gone to be aware of the medical deception he was about to invent. He collected his thoughts so that he could play his part appropriately and not arouse suspicion.

Before he had a chance to take any action, David Gamut indicated that he was about to try to use the power of music to heal the woman. He sounded a note on his pitch pipe and then launched into his hymn. As he sang, he was startled to hear the strains of the song repeated in a half human, half ghostly voice coming from behind him. Looking around, he beheld the shaggy monster seated in a shadow of the cavern, where it repeated, in a sort of low growl, sounds, if not words, which bore some slight resemblance to the melody of the singer.

The effect of so strange an echo overwhelmed David. His eyes opened wide; his voice became instantly mute. The singer had planned to use the song to communicate some important information to Heyward. But his shock was so great that the plan was driven from his mind. All he could do was to exclaim aloud, "She expects you, and is at hand." Then he left the cavern.

CHAPTER 25

Heyward was too preoccupied to notice the strange blend of the ridiculous and the solemn in the whole situation. He felt that the words David Gamut had hurriedly spoken just before he left the cavern must have some secret meaning. But before he had time to think much about the message, the Huron chief stepped to the bedside of his deathly ill daughter. After sending the young women from the cavern, he turned to Heyward and said, "Now let my brother show his power."

Knowing that he now had to live up to the role he had invented for himself, he prepared to begin a chant that he hoped would convince the Huron that he really was a healer. Just as he began he was interrupted by a fierce growl from the bear who still sat in the shadows. Again Duncan tried to begin, but again a fierce growl stopped him.

The third time this happened the Huron said,

"The cunning ones are jealous. My daughter is the wife of one of our bravest young men. Deal justly by her, my brother." Then, beckoning to the discontented bear, he added, "Peace! I go."

A moment later the echo of the distant closing door was heard. Duncan found himself alone in that desolate abode with the helpless invalid and the dangerous beast. The bear began to approach him. Expecting to be attacked, the young major looked anxiously about him for some weapon to defend himself with.

It seemed, however, as if the humor of the animal had suddenly changed. Instead of continuing its discontented growls, its shaggy body shook violently. The huge and unwieldy talons pawed stupidly about the grinning muzzle. Then, while Heyward kept his eyes riveted on its movements, the grim head fell on one side. In its place appeared the honest face of Hawkeye. His whole body was shaking with silent laughter.

"Shhh!" said the scout, interrupting Heyward's exclamation of surprise. "The varlets are close by. Any sounds that are not natural to your healing witchcraft would bring them down on us like a pack of demons."

"What are you doing here? What caused you to try such a desperate disguise? What has become of Colonel Munro?" asked Duncan.

"The best plans often fall prey to accident," Hawkeye replied. "Just be patient, my friend, and I'll explain it all. After we parted, I placed the Colonel and Chingachgook in an old beaver lodge. They will be safe from the Hurons there. Then Uncas and I started for the Lenape encampment as planned. Have you seen the lad?"

"Unfortunately, yes," Duncan answered. "He is captive and condemned to die at sunrise."

"I suspected that would be his fate," the scout said, with a touch of anxiety in his voice. "His bad fortune is the true reason of my being here. Wouldn't those imps love it if they could tie Bounding Elk and Long Rifle to the same stake!"

"Finish your story," said the impatient

Heyward. "The Hurons may return at any moment."

"Don't worry about that. They'll give you plenty of time to work your magic," Hawkeye replied. Then he continued, "Well, Uncas and I ran into a party of the varlets returning to the camp. Uncas was well ahead of me and one of the Huron dogs led him into an ambush. Once they had Uncas, I stayed in the area to see what I could do to help. I ran into two straggling warriors, but Killdeer took care of them. Then, as luck would have it, I came across one of their famous medicine men—or shaman, as they call him—preparing to do his work. I hit him on the head, tied him between two saplings, and dressed myself in his costume that you see here. I figured that might be a way to sneak into the camp unnoticed. Then I ran into you and that chief, so I followed you here."

"You certainly fooled the chief," said Duncan, feeling a little foolish for having thought it was a real bear that followed them into the cavern.

"That is true," Hawkeye agreed. "But we have work to do. Where are they keeping Alice?"

"Heaven knows. I have examined every lodge in the village and can't find the slightest trace of her."

"You heard what the singer said, as he left us: 'She is at hand, and expects you'? I expect that he meant that she is in one of the other chambers close by. I'll find out." And saying that, the scout climbed up the wall of the compartment they were in.

A moment later he dropped back to the ground and whispered to the anxiously waiting Heyward, "She is here and you will find her right through that door."

. Hawkeye had intended to warn Duncan that his painted appearance might frighten the young woman. But before he could say as much, the young major had already sprung through the door.

Alice, who was asleep, was awakened from a nightmare by the sound of someone entering the chamber. In the flickering light of the small fire she saw a wildly painted stranger rushing toward her. She gasped with horror and drew back.

"Alice!" cried Duncan, moving into the light of the fire.

Recognizing the voice, she looked closely and realized who the intruder was. "Duncan!" she exclaimed, rushing to him. "I knew that you would not desert me." In the confusion of the moment she looked anxious and terrified, but lovely.

Her relief at seeing him faded as she said, "But you are alone! I am grateful you are here, but I wish you were not alone."

Duncan observed that she trembled so

much that she could barely stand. He gently eased her into a seat on one of the boxes scattered about the room. He then briefly filled her in on the current situation. Alice listened with breathless interest. When he mentioned the sorrow her father was in, unstoppable tears ran down her cheeks.

With soothing tenderness, Duncan quieted this burst of emotion and she listened with undivided attention while he finished explaining what was going on. He concluded by saying, "And now, Alice, you see that much is expected of you. With the assistance of the scout, we may find our way from this savage people. You must be strong. Remember that you fly to the arms of your worthy father. His happiness, as well as your own, depends on your courage in what lies ahead."

As he finished, he gently pressed her hands between his. Then he added, "And my happiness, too, depends on our success. I have the permission of your father to hope for a nearer and dearer bond between us."

Alice trembled violently. Then looking him full in the face with a touching expression of innocence and dependency, she said, "Give me, Duncan, the sacred presence and the holy sanction of my father before you urge me further."

The young major was about to answer when he was interrupted by a light tap on his shoulder. Jumping to his feet, he turned, and his look fell on the dark form and malignant face of Magua. The deep guttural laugh of the savage sounded to Duncan like the hellish taunt of a demon. In spite of the paint, Magua recognized his enemy in the light of the fire.

The Indian drew warily back before the menacing stare of the young major's fiery eye. He regarded both his captives for a moment with a steady look. Then he stepped to a second entrance to the room—the one he had used—and dropped a log of wood across it. Realizing they were trapped, Heyward drew Alice to himself, prepared to meet whatever fate brought next.

But Magua intended no immediate violence. After studying the two motionless figures he said, "The pale faces trap the cunning beavers; but Sly Fox knows how to take the Yankees."

"Huron, do your worst!" exclaimed Heyward. "You and your vengeance are alike despised."

"Sly Fox is a great chief!" the Indian said. "I will bring my young men, to see how bravely a pale face can laugh at tortures."

He turned and was about to leave by the door through which Duncan had entered when a growl caught his ear. He hesitated. The figure of the bear appeared at the door. In the dim light Magua eyed it for a moment. Then, recognizing the costume of the well-known shaman, he prepared to pass the creature in cool contempt. He was not one to believe in the superstitions of his tribe.

Magua moved toward the door. This brought another growl. "Fool!" exclaimed the chief, in Huron. "Go play with the children and squaws; leave men to their wisdom."

As Magua attempted to push past the creature, it raised its arms and grasped him firmly. Immediately, Heyward grabbed a strip of buckskin from the debris on the floor. While Hawkeye held the surprised Huron's arms firmly to his sides, Duncan secured them. Once Magua's arms, legs, and feet were completely bound, Hawkeye released his hold, and Duncan laid the enemy on his back, utterly helpless.

The scout then removed the head of his costume and looked into Sly Fox's face. The Huron gave an exclamation of disgust.

"Ay, you've found your tongue," Hawkeye said. "Now, in order that you shall not use it to our ruin, I must stop your mouth." And so saying, he gagged the Huron.

"Now," the scout said, "we must get out of here and to the woods."

"It's impossible!" Duncan said. "Alice is overcome with fear and has fainted. Besides, we'd never get past the Hurons waiting at the entrance for me to cure the dying woman."

"We'll manage," replied Hawkeye. "There, wrap her in those blankets. Conceal her completely."

When Duncan had wrapped Alice in the blankets, the scout said, "Now take her in your arms, and follow. Leave the rest to me."

They passed swiftly through the natural gallery, to the entrance. As they approached the little door of bark, a murmur of voices outside announced that the friends and relatives of the invalid were gathered, patiently waiting to re-enter.

"My English will tell the varlets that the enemy is among them," Hawkeye said. "You must talk to them in that French talk of yours, major. Say that we have shut the evil spirit in the cave and are taking the woman to the woods in order to find strengthening herbs. Keep your wits about you, for our lives depend on it."

The scout boldly threw open the door and left the place, enacting the character of a bear as he went. Duncan kept close at his heels, and soon found himself in the center of a cluster of twenty anxious relatives and friends.

The crowd fell back a little and permitted the father to approach.

"Has my brother driven away the evil spirit?" demanded the chief. "What are you carrying?"

"Your child," returned Duncan, gravely. "The disease has gone out of her; it is shut up in the rocks. I take the woman to the woods where I will strengthen her against any further attacks. She will be in the lodge of her husband when the sun comes again."

When the father had translated the meaning of Heyward's words into the Huron language, a murmur of satisfaction ran through the crowd. The chief himself waved his hand for Duncan to proceed, saying, in a firm voice, "Go; I am a man, and I will enter the rock and fight the wicked one."

Heyward had already moved past the group when these startling words made him stop. "Is my brother mad?" he exclaimed. "Is he cruel? You will drive out the disease, and it will chase your daughter into the woods. No; it is best to wait outside the entrance. If the spirit appears, beat him down with clubs. When he sees how many are ready to fight him, he will bury himself in the mountain."

The warning accomplished its purpose. The chief and the others drew their tomahawks and posted themselves outside the entrance to the cavern, prepared to attack the spirit if it should try to come out.

The two counterfeit healers continued quickly along the path with their supposedly ailing burden. They skirted the village so they would not be observed. By the time they had entered the forest, the night air had revived Alice.

"Now let me make an effort to walk," she said, embarrassed that she had been a burden to Duncan. "I have revived."

"No, Alice, you are still too weak."

But the young woman insisted so Heyward reluctantly released his precious bundle.

When they had traveled some distance into the woods, Hawkeye stopped. Turning to Alice and Duncan, he said, "This path will lead you to the brook. Follow its northern bank until you come to a waterfall; climb the hill on your right, and you will see the fires of the Lenape encampment. Go there and ask for protection; if they are true Lenape, you will be safe. The young woman does not have the strength for a long flight through the wilderness at this point. The Hurons would follow our trail and easily overtake us. Go, and Providence be with you."

"And you?" Heyward said with surprise. "Are we to part company here?"

"The Hurons still hold Uncas. He is the last of the high blood of the Mohicans," Hawkeye replied. "I must try to help him."

Duncan and Alice tried to convince the scout that the danger was far too great when there was so little chance of success. But Hawkeye remained unmoved.

"I taught the lad how to use a rifle," the scout said. "We have fought side-by-side in many a bloody battle; with him on one side of me and his father on the other, I knew that there was no enemy at my back. Winter and summer, night and day, we have roamed the wilderness together, eating the same food, one sleeping while the other watched. There is but a single Ruler of us all, whatever may be the color of the skin; and Him I call as my witness, that before the Mohican lad shall perish for the want of a friend, Killdeer shall become as harmless as the tooting weapon of the singing master."

Duncan released his hold on the arm of the scout, who turned and steadily retraced his steps toward the Huron lodges. After pausing a moment to gaze the woodsman disappearing into the darkness, Heyward and Alice sadly continued on their way together toward the distant village of the Lenape.

CHAPTER 26

Hawkeye was fully aware of the danger that lay ahead of him as he made his way toward the Huron encampment. But he hoped that his masquerade in the bear costume of the shaman might give him some degree of safety. As he approached the buildings, his steps became more deliberate and nothing escaped his watchful eye.

A neglected hut was at the edge of the village. But the light of a low fire inside told the scout that it was occupied. He cautiously peered in through a crack and saw the inhabitant was David Gamut.

The singing master was lost in thought. He was thinking about the apparently miraculous incident of the bear that had tried to join with his singing of a hymn at the bedside of the dying young woman in the cavern. He was not a superstitious man and he could not understand how such a thing had been possible.

Hawkeye was relieved to see that the singing master was alone. He got down on all fours, crawled through the low entrance of the hut, and sat down in front of the fire, facing Gamut. Nearly a minute elapsed, during which the two sat regarding each other without speaking. The suddenness of the surprise reappearance of the bear almost proved too much for David. He fumbled for his pitch pipe and arose with a confused intention of attempting a musical exorcism.

"Dark and mysterious monster!" he exclaimed, while with trembling hands fumbled for his trusted book of psalms. "I know not your nature nor intention; but if you mean to harm this humble servant of the Lord, listen to the inspired words of my hymn and repent."

The bear shook his shaggy sides in silent laughter, and then a well-known voice replied: "Put up the tooting weapon and teach your throat modesty. A half dozen words of plain English will be worth more than an hour of squalling right now."

"Can these things be?" David asked, as the truth began to dawn on him. "I have found many marvels during my travels among the heathen, but surely nothing to excel this."

"Come, come," returned Hawkeye, removing the bear head. "You see an honest face before you, and one that you know well. Now, let's get down to business."

"First tell me of the maiden and of the young soldier who so bravely sought her," interrupted David.

"They are happily freed and on their way toward safety. But can you tell me where Uncas is?"

"The young warrior is bound and, I greatly fear, condemned to death. I mourn that such a fine human should die and I hope that a hymn might help his—"

"Can you lead me to him?" the scout said impatiently.

"The task will not be difficult," replied David, hesitating. "Though I greatly fear your presence would make his unhappy fortune worse rather than better."

"No more words, but lead on," returned Hawkeye, concealing his face under the bear head again.

The encampment was mostly asleep by this time. As they made their way, the scout learned that Gamut had been allowed access to the prisoner because of his privileged status as a man whose mind was believed to have been visited by the Great Spirit. He also learned that one of the warriors guarding Uncas spoke a little English.

The lodge in which Uncas was confined was in the very center of the village. Its location made it impossible to approach or leave without being seen. But, counting on his disguise, he had Gamut lead him by the most direct route.

At the entrance to the lodge were half a dozen warriors. As they saw the possessed singer approaching, accompanied by one in the well-known masquerade of their most distinguished shaman, they made way for them both. But they remained clustered near the entrance out of interest in seeing what these two magicians might do.

Following instructions that Hawkeye had given him, David spoke to the warrior who understood some English. "The Lenape are women!" he exclaimed, playing his part well. "Does my brother wish to hear Bounding Elk ask for his petticoats and to see him weep before the Hurons, at the stake?"

The warrior nodded his head. The thought of such a display of weakness in his enemy gave him pleasure.

"Then let the shaman breath upon the dog. But beware. You must stand further off. If the breath of the shaman blows upon you, it will take away your courage, too."

The Huron explained the meaning of David's words to his companions. They immediately withdrew to a point that was out of earshot but where they could still watch the entrance to the lodge.

As if satisfied of the safety of the warriors, the pretend shaman slowly entered the place. It was silent and gloomy and dimly lighted by the dying embers of a fire. Uncas lay in a distant corner, his hands and feet tightly bound. As the frightful beast entered, the young Mohican looked scornfully at it.

While David made certain they could not be observed by the warriors outside, the scout signaled Uncas by giving a low hissing sound.

"Hawkeye!" he whispered.

"Cut his bindings," Hawkeye said to David.

While David did as ordered, Hawkeye removed his disguise. The scout then handed Uncas a long, glittering knife. Then placing his hand significantly on a similar weapon tucked into his belt, he said, "The Hurons are outside. We must be ready."

"We will go," said Uncas.

"Not so fast," replied Hawkeye. "There are six of them and this singer is as good as nothing. But in war, what can't be done by force must be done by trickery. Put on the bear skin; I suspect you can play the animal nearly as well as I do."

Uncas did as the scout directed.

"And you, friend," Hawkeye said to David, "an exchange of garments will be an improvement over your current covering. Here, take my hunting shirt and cap, and give me your blanket and hat. You must trust me with your book and spectacles, as well as the tooter, too. If we ever meet again, in better times, you shall have all back again, with many thanks into the bargain."

As soon as the singer and the woodsman had exchanged garments, the scout turned to David to explain the plan.

"Are you much given to cowardice?" he bluntly asked.

"I am a man of peace and a believer in mercy and love," David said, "and I have never forgotten my faith in the Lord, even under the most trying circumstances."

"You must decide if want to make a run for it or stay here. If you stay here, you must sit down in the shadow and pretend to be Uncas until the Hurons find out otherwise. Your greatest danger will be at the moment when the savages find out that they have been deceived. If you survive that, you can expect to die an old man in your bed, for you will be protected by the fact that the Hurons think you are a madman. So choose for yourself—to make a rush or remain here."

"Even so," said David, firmly; "I will wait here in the place of the Mohican. Bravely and generously has he battled in my behalf. This, and more, will I dare do for him."

"You have spoken as a man and a true friend," Hawkeye said. "Once we have gone, keep silent as long as may be; and it would be wise, when you do speak, to break out suddenly in one of your shoutings. That will remind the

Hurons that you are not in your right mind and, therefore, not altogether as responsible as men should be. If however, they take your scalp, you can depend on it that Uncas and I will not forget the deed. We will avenge your death as becomes true warriors and trusty friends."

"Hold!" said David, seeing that they were about to leave him. "Should I die, do not make victims of those who destroyed me, but rather forgive them. If you remember them at all, let it be in prayers for the enlightening of their minds and for their eternal welfare."

Hawkeye gave a sigh and then said, "It is what I would wish to practice myself, though it is not always easy to do. God bless you, friend; I do not believe your way of life is wrong, when all is considered. Much depends on the natural gifts of a man. Each must take the path that life leads him down."

So saying, the scout returned and shook David cordially by the hand. After this act of friendship, he immediately left the lodge, accompanied by the new representative of the beast.

As soon as Hawkeye found himself being watched by the Hurons, he launched into his imitation of a hymn while he waved his hand vigorously as if conducting the music. Fortunately, the Hurons were not familiar enough with this sort of music to be able to tell that he was not the singing master. The warriors showed him the respect they always give to someone they believe to be the subject of mental illness. They let the two pass unchallenged.

The Mohican and the woodsman continued through the encampment at a deliberate pace. They did not wish to betray themselves by appearing to hurry. Hawkeye's attempt at singing brought some of the Hurons to the doors of their huts. But none attempted to stop them. The darkness of the night and the boldness of their attempt greatly aided in their success.

The adventurers got clear of the village and were swiftly approaching the shelter of the woods when a loud and long cry arose from the lodge where Uncas had been confined. The Mohican turned and threw off the bear skin, as though he was about to make some desperate effort to help the one who had taken his place.

"Hold!" said the scout, grasping his friend by the shoulder. "Let them yell again! That was just a shout of surprise."

At the next instant a burst of cries filled the air and ran along the whole extent of the village. Hawkeye tapped Uncas lightly on the shoulder and glided ahead. He then knelt and produced two rifles from a hiding place beneath the bushes. Handing one to Uncas, the scout waved Killdeer in the air and said, "Now let the devils find our trail! At least two, and maybe more, will find it leads only to their deaths."

Then the two dashed forward on the path and were soon buried in the somber darkness of the forest.

CHAPTER 27

The Hurons who guarded the lodge where Uncas was imprisoned heeded the warning to keep their distance. They feared the possibility of the conjurer's breath taking their courage, just as it would from Uncas. But then they saw the shaman and the madman leave the lodge. Or, at least, they saw two people who they thought were the shaman and the madman leave. And after a time, their curiosity overcame their fear. They crept close to the building and peered in through the cracks. In the dim light they mistook David for the prisoner. But after several minutes, David, not realizing he was being watched, turned his neck to stretch it. In doing so, the light of the dying embers of the fire illuminated his face.

Seeing that the figure was not the Mohican, the warriors rushed into the lodge and grabbed the imposter. As they did so, they gave the first cry that was heard by the fugitives in the edge of the forest. David, certain that he was about to be killed, began singing the opening verse of a funeral anthem. This reminded the warriors of the man's supposed mental infirmity; they immediately let go of him and rushed out to alert the village that the Mohican was gone. This had been the second cry heard by the two in the forest.

Almost instantly two hundred warriors were on their feet and ready for action. News of the escape was soon known by all and within minutes all of the warriors were crowded into the council lodge awaiting instructions from their chiefs. Magua's absence at this time of crisis was quickly noticed. Messengers were sent to his lodge to bring him.

In the meantime, a number of the young men were sent to make a circuit of the edge of the woods to make certain that the Lenape from the next valley were not up to some mischief. Women and children ran everywhere. The whole camp was in a state of wild confusion. But in the council lodge, the oldest chiefs were assembled in grave consultation.

A clamor of voices outside the lodge announced that someone was being brought who might be able to help explain the mysterious escape. It was the shaman who had been tied up by the scout and had had his bear costume stolen. After he explained to the chiefs what had happened to him, the father of the sick woman told what he knew. On the basis of these pieces of information, ten chiefs were selected to go to the cavern to investigate.

These men entered the cavern and made their way to the room that had been occupied by the ill woman. In the silent gloom, she could be seen lying on the bed. Her father could not understand how this was possible. He had seen her carried from the cavern with his own eyes. He stepped to the side of the bed, as if distrusting his eyes. His daughter was dead.

The chief stared at the young woman in silence. Then he turned to the others and said, "My daughter has left us! The Great Spirit is angry with his children."

After a short pause, one of the elder Indians was about to speak when a dark-looking object came rolling out of an adjoining compartment and into the very center of the room where they stood. The whole party drew back a little in surprise. Then the face came into the dim light enough to reveal the fierce and sullen features of Magua. The discovery was followed by a general exclamation of amazement.

Magua was quickly cut from him bonds and the gag removed. Once freed, he leaped to his feet. He cast his eyes across the assembled party, grating his teeth together like iron rasps. His anger and frustration brought him close to being a madman. Several minutes passed before a word was uttered.

"Let the Mohican die!" exclaimed Magua, in a voice of thunder.

Another longer and expressive silence was followed. At last it was broken by the oldest of the assembled party. "The Mohican is swift of foot, and leaps far," he said; "but my young men are on his trail."

"Is he gone?" demanded Magua, in tones so deep and guttural that they seemed to proceed from his inmost chest.

"An evil spirit has been among us, and the Mohican has blinded our eyes."

"An evil spirit!" Magua repeated, mockingly. "It is the spirit that has taken the lives of so many Hurons; it is the spirit that slew my young men at the waterfall; that took their scalps at the healing spring; and who has, now, bound the arms of Sly Fox. It is the dog called Long Rifle."

Hearing the familiar name and being reminded of all he had done against the Hurons enraged the chiefs. They gnashed their teeth and burst out with angry yells. Magua stood silently during this demonstration of frustration and anger. Once it had run its course, he spoke quietly and with a thoughtful dignity.

"Let us go to my people," he said. "They wait for us."

His companions consented in silence, and

the whole of the party left the cavern and returned to the council lodge. When they were seated, all eyes turned on Magua.

He described in detail the whole deception created by Duncan and Hawkeye. In doing so, he emphasized how insultingly and shamefully and disgracefully they all had been tricked. When he finished, he resumed his seat. It was now time for them to consider the best way to exact revenge for the shameful deeds.

Magua listened in respectful silence as several different plans were proposed by various elder warriors. During this time, some of the runners who had been sent out to search the nearby woods returned. They reported that the enemies had been traced far enough to make it clear that they were headed for the neighboring camp of the Lenape.

Magua remained silent until all of the others had spoken. Then, with his usual cautious and convincing manner of speaking, he offered his own opinions. He had been working hard to erase all questions about his authority that might have been raised by the foolishness and disloyalty he had shown in his youth. And he had made good progress in regaining the respect and confidence of the Hurons. He used this occasion to put the final touches on his reestablishment of himself as leader.

In the course of his presentation he reminded

the others how much he had done to cultivate a good relationship with their powerful and dangerous neighbors, the Lenape. And he knew well how to flatter each of the elders and warriors gathered in the council lodge by praising their courage and wisdom. He referred to many different occasions when the Hurons had shown their power and pride through the punishment of those who had insulted them.

He then went on to show the risks and pitfalls of the plans for revenge that the others had proposed on this occasion. He reminded them that, being at some distance from their home territory, they needed to be prudent in their approach. And he hinted that if they moved cautiously and cunningly, they might even be able to extend their plan so that it would include the destruction of all those they had reason to hate.

In short, he so blended the warlike with the artful, the obvious with the obscure, that all those in the council lodge believed his plan was built on their ideas. This in spite of the fact that none could say they clearly understood precisely what he intended to do. Each elder and warrior present understood that Magua meant more than he actually said. And each one believed that the hidden meaning was exactly what he had hoped would be the decision.

Magua's effectiveness and slyness as a speaker had served him well. The tribe consented to act with deliberation, as he had urged. And furthermore, they agreed with one voice to commit the entire oversight of the plan to him, as he had implied they should.

Magua had now attained one great object of all his cunning and effort. He was not the undisputed leader of the tribe. The humiliation of his youthful foolishness was behind him. The outcast had returned and become the ruler.

He assumed the grave air of authority and the proper dignity of his office. He immediately sent runners to collect intelligence. He ordered spies to go to the encampment of the Lenape and see what they could learn. He dismissed the warriors to their lodges, hinting that their services would soon be needed. He then dismissed the council.

As he passed through the village on the way to his own hut, he stopped here and there to have a flattering word with a few chosen individuals. In this way he managed to further secure the support of key members of the tribe. Finally, the Huron chief went to his own lodge. The wife he had abandoned when he was chased from his people had died in the years while he was away.

He sat alone in his hut, staring into the embers of the low fire and brooding sullenly. Had anyone seen him, it would have been possible to mistake him for the Prince of Darkness himself, thinking about the imagined wrongs done to him and plotting evil.

Long before the day dawned, warrior after warrior entered the solitary hut of Magua, until they had collected to the number of twenty. Each carried his rifle and all the other accouterments of war, but the paint on their skins was uniformly peaceful.

Once all twenty of the designated men had assembled, Magua arose and gave the signal to proceed. With Sly Fox in front, they followed their leader single file. They slipped from the camp silent and unobserved, like a band of gliding specters.

Magua led his party for some distance down the windings of the stream and along the little artificial lake of the beavers. The day began to dawn as they entered the clearing that had been formed by those industrious animals. One of the chiefs in the party had the beaver as his own particular symbol or totem. He, therefore, stopped for a moment by the pond and promised to continue his reverence for the animals; in exchange, he asked that the animals bestow their wisdom on this expedition to the Lenape village.

When Magua thought sufficient time had been lost in gratifying the family affection of the warrior, he again made the signal to proceed. The Indians moved away with a step that would have been inaudible to the ears of any common man. As they went, the head of Great Snake appeared from the entrance of an abandoned beaver lodge. Chingachgook watched the departing band until they disappeared into the forest.

CHAPTER 28

While Magua was leading his twenty selected warriors past the beaver pond and through the forest, the encampment of the Lenape was greeting the sunrise with a burst of activity. The women were running from lodge to lodge, preparing their morning's meal and engaging in hasty and whispered conversations. The men gathered in small groups exchanging a few carefully chosen words. Occasionally, the eyes of one group or another would turn toward a large and silent lodge in the center of the village.

On a platform of rock at the edge of the village, a man appeared. He made a gesture of friendship. He was welcomed by a low murmur of greeting from the Indians who were in the vicinity. He then made his way into the village and to the group of chiefs who were collected near the middle of the camp. As he approached they recognized he was the well-known Huron chief, Sly Fox.

His reception was grave, silent, and wary. The warriors in front stepped aside, opening the way to one of their most respected chiefs, Hard Heart.

"The wise Huron is welcome," said Hard Heart, in the language of the Maquas, "by his brothers of the lakes."

The chief extended his arm and taking the other by the wrist, they exchanged a friendly greeting. Then the Lenape invited his guest to enter his own lodge, and share his morning meal. Magua accepted the invitation; the two warriors, attended by three or four of the old men, entered Hard Heart's lodge.

During the short meal, the conversation centered on the events of the hunt that Magua had recently been on. The Lenape acted as if the visit by the Huron was purely a social one, but they well knew that their guest must have some secret aim in mind. Once the meal was over, Hard Heart and Sly Fox began to prepare themselves for a subtle contest of wits.

"Does the great Canada father look toward his Huron children with favor again?" Hard Heart asked.

"When was it ever otherwise?" returned Magua. "He calls my people 'most beloved.'"

The Lenape gravely bowed in agreement, although he knew Magua's statement was false. He continued, "The tomahawks of your young men have been very red."

"It is so; but they are now bright and dull; for the Yankees are dead, and the Lenape are our neighbors."

Hard Hart again nodded and remained silent.

After a moment Magua asked, "Does my prisoner that you hold give trouble to my brothers?"

"She is welcome."

"The path between the Hurons and the Lenape is short and it is open; let her be sent to my squaws, if she gives trouble to my brother."

"She is welcome," Hard Heart said again, more forcefully.

The baffled Magua continued silent several minutes. He did not show any reaction to this initial failure in his attempt to regain possession of Cora. After a few moments he continued, "Have there not been the footprints of white men in the woods?"

"Let my Canada father come," Hard Heart said evasively. "We, his children, are ready to see him."

"When our white Canada father comes," Magua said, "we Hurons also say he is welcome. But my young men believe they have seen the footprints of Yankees near the village of the Lenape."

"They will not find us asleep," replied Hard Heart.

"It is well. The warrior whose eye is open can see his enemy," Magua said. Then, unable to cut through the caution of the Lenape chief, Sly Fox tried a different approach. "I have brought gifts to my brother. Although your nation chose not to join with us and our French brothers to fight the Yankees, we remain friends."

Magua then spread his gifts before the dazzled eyes of his hosts. They were mostly trinkets of little value, plundered from the slaughtered females of Fort William Henry. However, he presented them with words of flattery. This well-judged and shrewd move achieved the results Sly Fox had hoped for. The Lenape replaced their grave looks with much more cordial expressions.

"My brother is a wise chief," Hard Heart said. "You are welcome in our village."

"The Hurons love their friends the Lenape," returned Magua. "Why should they not? They are of the same color skin. They should be friends and look with open eyes on the white men. Is my brother aware of spies in the woods?"

Hard Heart's face grew less stern and he was now willing to answer more directly, saying, "There have been strange footprints around the camp and they have entered my lodges."

"Did you drive out the dogs?" asked Magua.

"It would not do. The stranger is always welcome among the Lenape."

"The stranger, yes; but not the spy," Sly Fox replied.

"Would the Yankees send their women as spies?" asked the Lenape chief. "Did you not say you took women prisoners in the battle?"

"That is true," Magua answered. "But the Yankees have sent out their scouts. They came to the village of the Huron, but they were not welcomed. Now they have fled to the Lenape. They say the Lenape are their friends. They believe that the Lenape have turned their backs on the white Canada father."

This hint of an accusation struck home with Hard Heart. The Lenape had agreed to help the French in their fight against the British. But, at the moment when their support was most needed, they had withheld their assistance. The French general Montcalm, preferring that they remain a passive friend rather than become an open enemy, had accepted their decision not to fight. But the Lenape knew that their decision had brought them much criticism from their French allies. They now felt that their future actions would be viewed with distrust. Many of their distant villages and their hunting grounds actually lay within the limits of the French territory. To be seen as having turned against the French could prove highly dangerous to their future movements. Therefore, Magua's calculated words had their intended affect. Hard Heart was struck deeply by the hint.

"Let my white Canada father look in my face," said the Lenape chief defensively. "He will see no change. It is true, my young men did not go out on the warpath with him; their dreams told them not to. But they love and honor the great white Canada chief."

Sly Fox knew that he had Hard Heart worried. He pressed his advantage, saying, "Will he think so when he hears that his greatest enemy rests in the camp of the Lenape? When he is told that a Yankee sits by your fire? When he is told that the pale face who has slain so many of his friends is welcomed by your warriors? My great white Canada father is not a fool!"

"Where is the Yankee that the Lenape fear?" returned Hard Heart. "Who has slain these young men? Who is the mortal enemy of my Great Father?"

"Long Rifle!"

The small group of Lenape in the lodge started at the mention of the well-known name. They were amazed to learn that one so famous among the Indian allies of France was in their camp.

"What does my brother mean?" demanded Hard Heart, in a tone of astonishment.

"A Huron never lies!" returned Magua, coldly. "Let the Lenape count their prisoners; they will find one whose skin is neither red nor pale—the one called Long Rifle."

After a long pause, Hard Heart called his companions aside and consulted with them. Messengers were sent to bring some of the other distinguished warriors to the lodge.

Each who entered was told of the important information that Magua had just communicated and each reacted with great surprise. The news spread from mouth to mouth, until the whole encampment became powerfully agitated.

When the excitement had died down a little, the old men set themselves seriously to consider how to best handle this delicate and embarrassing situation in a way to protect the honor and safety of their tribe.

Throughout all of this, Magua remained seated. He secretly watched the actions that he had cunningly set in motion. But he acted as if he had no concern for how the matter ended.

The council of the Lenape was short. When it was ended, a general bustle announced that it was to be immediately followed by a solemn and formal assemblage of the nation. Such meetings were rare and called only on occasions of the greatest importance. Magua now knew that his plan was falling into place. He left the lodge and walked silently forth to the place where the warriors were already beginning to collect.

By the time the sun's rays came over the trees on the top of the mountain next to the Lenape village, more than a thousand men, women, and children were gathered for the unusual conference.

It was the responsibility of the oldest and most experienced of the men to present the subject of the gathering to the people. For a time, the aged warrior whose privilege it was to speak remained silent in his lodge, seemingly oppressed with the magnitude of his subject. Except for an occasional glance toward the lodge of the aged warrior, the crowd sat silent and unmoving.

At length a low murmur ran through the assembly, and the whole nation arose to their feet. At that instant the door of the lodge opened, and from it three men slowly approached the place of consultation. They were all aged; but one in the center, who leaned on his companions for support, had the weight and wisdom of more than a century on him. The elastic, light step of an Indian was gone; he toiled over the ground, inch by inch. His dark, wrinkled face was in sharp contrast with the long white locks that floated on his shoulders.

His robe was made of the finest skins. His chest was loaded with medals, some in massive silver and some in gold, which had been gifts of various Christian leaders during the long period of his life. His head was encircled by a sort of plated crown and glittered with ornaments. His tomahawk was nearly hidden in silver and the handle of his knife shown like a horn of solid gold.

As he slowly made his way, the name Tamenund was whispered from mouth to mouth in the crowd. Magua had often heard the fame of this wise and just Lenape; even among the Hurons it was said that this wise man held secret communion with the Great Spirit. Magua stepped forward to catch a glimpse of this man whose decision was likely to have a deep influence on his own fortunes.

The eyes of the old man were closed, as though weary with having so long witnessed the selfish workings of the human passions. A delicate maze of lines tattooed on his skin formed complicated and beautiful figures over his entire person. Leaning on his two honored supporters, he proceeded to the high place of the multitude, where he seated himself in the center of his nation, with the dignity of a monarch and the air of a father.

Nothing could surpass the reverence and affection with which this unexpected visit was received by his people. The entire nation gazed with joy on this beloved and honored being. After a suitable pause, the principal chiefs of the nation arose and approached him; they placed his hands on their heads, as if receiving a blessing. When these acts of affection and respect were performed, the chiefs drew back again to their places, and silence reigned in the whole encampment.

After a short delay, a few of the young men, receiving whispered instructions from one of the aged attendants of Tamenund, arose and left the crowd. They entered the large and silent lodge in the center of the village. In a few minutes they reappeared, escorting the four individuals who had caused all these solemn preparations. As they led them toward the seat of judgment, the crowd opened in a lane; and when they had passed, the crowd closed in again, forming a large and dense belt of human bodies, arranged in an open circle.

CHAPTER 29

Cora stood foremost among the prisoners, tenderly supporting her sister by the arm. She appeared not to notice the array of Indians on every side of her. She kept her eyes fastened on the pale and anxious features of the trembling Alice. Close at their side stood Heyward, prepared to do anything possible to protect the young women. Hawkeye stood slightly behind them. Uncas was not there.

After a silence, one of the two aged chiefs beside Tamenund rose and said, in English, "Which of my prisoners is Long Rifle?"

Neither Duncan nor the scout answered. Duncan glanced at the crowd around them. He pulled back slightly when his eyes fell on the malignant face of Magua. He realized immediately that the Huron was somehow connected with their having been brought before this meeting of the entire Lenape nation. At that moment, he determined to do anything he could to thwart Magua's sinister plans, whatever they might be. He knew, at the very least, that the Huron would not be satisfied until he had made Hawkeye pay with his life.

Again the aged chief demanded, "Which of my prisoners is Long Rifle?"

Duncan saw his chance to delay Magua's poisonous design. "Give us each a rifle," the young major replied haughtily, "and let us show you the one you seek. Our deeds will speak for us!"

"So this is the one whose name has filled our ears!" replied the chief, looking at Heyward. "What has brought the white man into the camp of the Lenape?"

"I come for food, shelter, and friends," Duncan answered.

"This cannot be," the chief said. "The woods are full of game and the hunter needs no shelter other than the open sky. And the Lenape are the enemies, not the friends, of the Yankees. You have not spoken the truth."

Duncan was at a loss as to what to say next when the scout spoke up: "I am called Hawkeye by the Lenape and Long Rifle by the Hurons. I am the man you seek."

It was important to the severe justice of the Lenape that there be no mistake about who was Long Rifle. Some of their old men briefly consulted together. Then, turning to Magua, one of them said, "My brother has said that a snake crept into my camp. Which of these men is it?"

Magua pointed to the scout.

Duncan was now more convinced than ever of the evil intentions of the Huron. "Will a wise Lenape believe the barking of a wolf?" he exclaimed. "A dog never lies, but when was a wolf known to speak the truth?"

The insult caused Magua's eyes to flash fire for an instant; then he regained control of himself and turned away in silent disdain.

The wary chiefs consulted again for a moment. Then one of them said, "My brother has been called a liar and his friends are angry. They will show that he has spoken the truth. Give the prisoners guns and let them prove which one is Long Rifle."

Magua knew that the Lenape did not completely trust him and therefore wanted proof. But he played the game and gave the appearance of accepting their words as a compliment.

The two prisoners were each given a rifle and told to shoot, over the heads of the seated crowd, at an earthen pot that sat on a stump some fifty yards away.

Heyward smiled to himself at the idea of competing with the scout. But he was determined to keep up the deception as long as possible in an attempt to hinder Magua's evil scheme. Raising his rifle slowly, he took careful aim and fired. The bullet cut the wood within a few inches of the clay pot. An exclamation from the crowd announced that the shot was considered proof of great skill.

"If the white man is the warrior he pretends," said the aged chief, "let him strike closer to the target."

The scout laughed aloud. Then dropping the rifle casually into his extended left hand, he fired, hardly seeming even to look. The fragments of the pot flew into the air and scattered on the ground. At almost the same instant, Hawkeye dropped the rifle contemptuously on the ground.

An increasing murmur ran through the crowd. Some of the spectators felt that this shot proved the scout's claim. However, many others believed that the success had just been an accident. Heyward took advantage of this second opinion.

"It was chance!" he exclaimed. "No one can shoot without aiming!"

"Chance!" echoed Hawkeye. "Does that lying Huron, too, think it was chance? Give the Huron dog a gun and place us face to face in the open! Then let Providence and our own skill decide the matter between us!"

"It is evident that the Huron is a liar," returned Heyward, coolly. "You yourself have heard him say that you are Long Rifle."

The aged Lenape interrupted this exchange by saying, "Give them the guns again. Let them shoot again to prove their skill."

"Now let it be proved, in the face of this tribe of Lenape, which is the better man," cried the scout, tapping his rifle. "You see that gourd hanging against that tree, major? If you are the marksman you claim to be, let me see you break its shell."

Duncan noted the gourd, which hung from a dead branch of a small pine a hundred yards away. Duncan took aim with deliberate care. He fired. Three or four young Indians sprang to the target and announced with a shout that the bullet was in the tree, only slightly to one side of the gourd.

"That may be good enough for the Royal Americans!" said Hawkeye, "but I'll make sure that gourd never holds water again!"

So saying, the scout slowly raised the muzzle of the rifle with a steady, uniform motion. When it was on a perfect level, it remained for a single moment, without tremor, as though both man and rifle were carved in stone. During that stationary instant, it poured forth its contents, in a bright, glancing sheet of flame. Again the young Indians bounded forward; but their disappointed looks announced that no traces of the bullet were to be seen.

"Enough!" said the old chief to the scout, in a tone of strong disgust. "You are a wolf in the skin of a dog." Then, turning to Heyward, he said, "I will talk to the true Long Rifle."

"Fools," Hawkeye replied. "If you are to find the bullet of a sharpshooter in these woods, you must look *in* the object, and not around it!"

The Indian youths, tearing the gourd from the tree, held it on high with an exulting shout, displaying a hole in its bottom. The bullet had passed through the opening in the top and exited through the bottom of the gourd. This decided the question, establishing to everyone's satisfaction that the scout was in fact Long Rifle.

"Why did you wish to cloud the matter?" the aged chief asked Duncan. "Do you wish to make fools of the Lenape?"

"The Lenape will yet find that it is the Huron who makes fools of them," replied Heyward.

"The Lenape know who would make a fool of them," replied the chief. Then, turning to Magua, he said, "Brother, we listen to you."

The Huron rose and walked with great dignity to the center of the circle. Before he spoke, he looked at each of the four prisoners. On Hawkeye he cast a glance of respectful enmity; on Duncan, a look of inextinguishable hatred; the shrinking figure of Alice he scarcely bothered to notice; but when his glance met the commanding and yet lovely form of Cora, his eye lingered a moment. Then, filled with his own dark intentions, he spoke in French, a language that he knew would be understood by most of those present.

"The Spirit that made men colored them differently," the cunning Huron began. "Those that are black have been forced to be slaves. You may hear them groan when the south wind blows. Those that He made with pale faces are traders; they are dogs to their women and wolves to their slaves. These are the ones who devour the earth and who speak with false tongues. These are the ones who pay the Indians to fight their battles. These are the ones who take all. Their gluttony makes them sick. God gave them enough, and yet they want all. Such are the pale faces."

Here Magua paused to let his words take their effect on those assembled. Then he continued, "Some the Great Spirit made with skins brighter and redder than the sun. These did He fashion to His own mind. He gave them this land covered with trees and filled with game. Some He placed in the lands of snow; some He placed near the setting sun; some he placed on the lands around the lakes of fresh water. But His greatest and most beloved he placed on the sands of the great ocean of salt water. Do my brothers know the name of this favored people?"

"It was the Lenape!" exclaimed twenty eager voices at once.

"It was the mighty Lenape," returned Magua. He had succeeded in making his listeners feel as if each one of them were able to correct the wrongs done to his race. "It was the tribes of the brave and just Lenape. From the time the sun rose from the great ocean of salt water and it set in the great fresh water river, it always shone on the mighty Lenape tribes. But why should I, a Huron, tell a wise people of their traditions? Why should I remind them of their injuries? of their ancient greatness? of their losses, their defeats, their misery? Everyone among you has seen these things and knows they are true. I have spoken enough. I will listen."

From the moment when Tamenund had first sat down, he had not spoken a word. At first, it had not seemed as if he were even aware of the events going on around him. But as Magua had been speaking, Tamenund gradually raised his head. When Magua spoke of his nation by name, the ancient wise man had opened his eyes. Finally, after the Huron had finished speaking, Tamenund struggled to his feet with the aid of the men on either side of him.

"Who calls upon the children of the Lenape?" he asked.

"A Huron," said Magua, stepping toward the ancient man. "A friend of Tamenund."

"A friend!" repeated the sage. "What brings a Huron here?"

"Justice," replied Magua. "My prisoners are with my Lenape brothers, and I come to take them back with me."

"Justice is the law of the Great Spirit," Tamenund said. "My children, give this stranger food. Then, Huron, take your prisoners and depart."

After delivering this solemn judgment, the patriarch seated himself, and closed his eyes again. The words were barely uttered when four or five of the younger warriors, stepping behind Heyward and the scout, bound their hands and arms. The scout was a little surprised at this. Because he did not speak French, he had understood very little of what had just been said.

Magua cast a look of triumph around the whole assembly. He then proceeded to collect what he had come for. He turned toward Cora. She met his gaze with an eye so calm and firm that his resolution wavered. Then, believing that she would not desert her younger sister, he took Alice by the arm. Motioning for Heyward to follow, he turned to lead Alice through the encircling crowd.

Cora, however, did not follow as he had expected. Instead she rushed to the feet of the patriarch and, raising her voice, exclaimed, "Just and honorable Lenape, on your wisdom and power we lean for mercy! Be deaf to that cunning and remorseless monster, that Huron who

poisons your ears with falsehoods to feed his thirst for blood. You who has seen evil in the world surely has lived long enough to know how to temper its effect on others."

The eyes of the old man opened heavily and settled in a steady gaze on the beautiful woman before him. Cora was on her knees, her hands clenched, looking up into his majestic face with reverence. Rising without assistance, he demanded, in a voice that startled its auditors by its firmness: "Who art thou?"

"One of a hated race—a Yankee. But one who has never harmed you, and who cannot harm your people. I am one who asks for assistance in a time of trouble. We did not seek to come here but were brought here against our wills. We now ask permission to depart on our own in peace. Are you not Tamenund—the father and wise man of this people?"

"I am the ancient one called Tamenund," he replied.

"It is now some seven years," Cora continued, "since one of your people was at the mercy of a white chief on the borders of this province. When he claimed to have your blood in his veins, the white chief said to him, 'Go. For your parent's sake you are free.' Do you remember that white English chief by the name of Munro?"

"I remember that only yesterday the children of the Lenape were masters of the world," said the ancient man sadly. "But then the white chiefs drove my children from their lands and rivers. Now we must dwell in the mountains of the Hurons."

Cora bowed her head in disappointment, disappointment that her attempts to sway Tamenund were unsuccessful, and disappointment that the white man had dealt so unfeelingly with the red man. Cora bowed her head and, for a bitter moment, struggled with her sorrow at misdeeds of the white man. Then, raising her beaming eyes, she continued, in tones scarcely less penetrating than the unearthly voice of the patriarch himself: "Tell me, is Tamenund a father?"

The old man looked down upon her with a benign smile on his timeworn face. Then, casting his eyes slowly over the whole assemblage, he answered: "Of a nation."

"For myself I ask nothing. Like you and your children, honored chief," she continued, "the curse of my ancestors has fallen heavily on their child. But over there is one who is the daughter of an old and failing man, whose days are near their end. She is too good, much too precious, to become the victim of that curse of her forefathers."

"I know that the pale faces are a proud and hungry race. I know that they claim not only to have the earth, but also that the least worthy among them is better than the wisest red man," said Tamenund. He did not look at Cora, whose head was nearly crushed to the earth in shame, as he continued, "But let them not boast too loudly before the face of the Great Spirit. The winds may change. Many times have I seen the locusts strip the leaves from the trees, but the season of blossoms has always come again."

"It is so," said Cora, drawing a long breath and raising her face. "But there is yet one of your own people who has not been brought to speak to you; before you let the Huron depart in triumph, hear him speak."

Tamenund looked about questioningly. Observing this, one of his companions said, "It is a snake—a red-skin in the pay of the Yankees. We keep him to be tortured."

"Let him come," returned the sage.

Then Tamenund once more sank into his seat, A young warrior went to get the prisoner that Cora had referred to. A silence so profound lay over the assembly that the leaves, fluttering in the morning breeze, were distinctly heard rustling in the surrounding forest.

CHAPTER 30

The silence continued unbroken by human sounds for many anxious minutes. Then the waving multitude opened and shut again, and Uncas stood in the living circle. He cast a deliberate look on every side of him, meeting the settled expressions of hostility of the chiefs with calmness. But when Tamenund came under his glance, his eye became fixed, as though all other objects were already forgotten. Advancing with a slow and noiseless step, he placed himself immediately before the sage.

The ancient man sat with his eyes closed. One of the chiefs told him that the Indian prisoner had been brought before him.

"With what tongue does the prisoner speak?" demanded the patriarch, without opening his eyes.

"Like his fathers," Uncas replied; "with the tongue of a Lenape."

An angry murmur ran through the crowd in

response to this statement. Then Tamenund spoke: "A Lenape! I have lived to see the tribes of the Lenape driven from their council-fires and scattered, like broken herds of deer, among the hills of the Hurons! And I have seen many other terrible wonders; but never before have I found a Lenape so vile as to creep, like a poisonous snake, into the camps of his nation."

"The Huron dog has spoken," returned Uncas softly, "and Tamenund has heard his words."

"The false Lenape trembles in fear of hearing the words of Tamenund," the sage said. "It is a hound that howls, when the Yankees show him a trail."

"And you," returned Uncas, looking sternly around him, "are dogs that whine, when the Frenchman tosses you the entrails of his deer."

Twenty knives gleamed in the air, and as many warriors sprang to their feet, at this biting statement. But they were silenced when Tamenund indicated that he was about to speak again.

"Lenape!" resumed the sage, "you are not worthy of that name. My people have been driven from their lands for many years. And the warrior who deserts his tribe when it has been cast out is doubly a traitor. The law of the Great Spirit is just. He is yours, my children. Deal with him as he deserves."

As soon as Tamenund had pronounced his verdict, a cry of vengeance burst forth from the assembled nation. In the midst of this, a chief proclaimed that the captive was condemned to endure the dreadful trial of torture by fire.

The circle broke its order and yells of delight mixed with the bustle of preparation to carry out the sentence. In the midst of this wildness Uncas remained serene. He looked on the preparations with a steady eye, and when the tormentors came to seize him, he met them with a firm and upright attitude. One of the warriors seized the hunting-shirt of Uncas and tore it from his body. Then, as he grabbed his victim in order to lead him to the stake, he froze in a look of amazement. He pointed, speechless, at the chest of the prisoner. As his companions crowded around, they too became frozen as they stared in wonder at the figure of a small tortoise, beautifully tattooed on the chest of Uncas in a bright blue tint.

For a single instant Uncas enjoyed his triumph, smiling calmly on the scene. Then motioning the crowd away with a sweep of his arm, he advanced in front of the nation with the air of a king. A murmur of admiration ran through the multitude. Then he spoke.

"Men of the Lenape nation," he said, "my race upholds the earth! Your feeble tribe stands on my shell! My race is the grandfather of nations!"

"Who are you?" demanded Tamenund, rising at the startling tones he heard.

"Uncas, the son of Chingachgook," answered the captive modestly, turning from the nation, and bending his head in reverence to the ancient man; "a son of the great Tortoise who holds up the earth."

"The hour of Tamenund is near!" exclaimed the sage; "the day is turned, at last, to the night! I thank the Great Spirit that one is here to fill my place at the council-fire. Uncas, the child of the Tortoise, is found!"

Uncas stepped proudly to the ancient man. Tamenund put his hands on the young chief's arms and gazed at him with unspeakable happiness. At length, the bewildered prophet exclaimed, "Am I a boy again? No, my arrow would no longer frighten a fawn; my arm is withered like the branch of a dead oak. And yet I see before me an image from my youth—the very image of one who was the wisest Sagamore of the Mohicans!"

Uncas looked into the patriarch's face with the fondness and admiration of a favored child. He replied, "Four generations of warriors have lived and died since the friend of Tamenund led his people in battle. The blood of the tortoise has been in many chiefs, but all have returned to the earth except Chingachgook and his son who now stands before you."

"Our wise men have often said that two warriors of Mohicans were in the hills of the Yankees. Why have their seats at the council-fires of the Lenape been so long empty?"

"Once we lived by the great ocean of salt water," Uncas said in answer to the old man's question. "Then the Mohicans were rulers and Sagamores over the land. But when the pale face came, we followed the deer back to the river. Then my fathers said, 'We will hunt here. We will stay here, near the rising sun, until the Great Spirit tells us to follow the river back to the sea. Then we will take our own lands back. That, my Lenape brothers, is the belief of the children of the Tortoise, the Mohicans. We did not follow you and sit at the council-fires of the Lenape. We wished to wait to return to our land."

The people of the Lenape nation listened with respect. In the silence that followed his explanation, Uncas cast his eyes about the assembly. His glance fell on Hawkeye, who stood, arms bound, at a short distance. Uncas walked to the side of his friend and cut the bonds with an angry stroke of his knife. He then led the scout back to the old man.

"Father," he said, "look at this pale face; he is a just man and a friend of the Lenape. He has earned the name Hawkeye, for his sight never fails. But the Mingoes call him Long Rifle, for they have often known his deadly aim."

"Long Rifle!" exclaimed Tamenund, opening his eyes and regarding the scout sternly. "My son has not done well to call him friend."

"I call him so because he has proven himself such," returned the young Mohican, with great calmness. "If Uncas is welcome among the Lenape, then Hawkeye and his friends are also welcome."

"The pale face has slain my young men; his name is known for the blows he has struck against the Lenape."

"If a Mingo has whispered that in the ear of the Lenape, he has only shown that he is a lying dog," said the scout, defending himself against such offensive charges. "It is true that I have slain the Maquas and I will not deny it. But my hand has never knowingly harmed a Lenape. I am a friend to them and all of their nation."

A low exclamation of applause passed among the warriors.

"Where is the Huron?" demanded Tamenund. "Has he deceived me?"

Magua had watched this triumph of Uncas with increasing uneasiness. He now stepped boldly in front of the patriarch and said, "The just Tamenund will not keep what a Huron has lent him."

The sage turned to Uncas and said, "Tell me, son of my brother, has the stranger a conqueror's right over you?"

"He has not."

"And Long Rifle?"

"Again, he has not a conqueror's right," Uncas answered.

"And the stranger and the pale maiden that came into my camp together?"

"He does not have the conqueror's right to them, either," replied Uncas.

"And what of the woman that the Huron brought to my camp earlier?" the sage asked.

Uncas made no reply.

"And the woman that the Mingo has brought into my camp?" repeated Tamenund, gravely.

"She is mine," cried Magua, shaking his hand in triumph at Uncas. "Mohican, you know that she is mine."

"My son is silent," said Tamenund, as the young Mohican turned from him in sorrow.

"It is so," was the low answer.

A short pause followed. It was apparent that the multitude reluctantly accepted the justice of the Mingo's claim.

At length the sage, on whom the final decision depended, said, in a firm voice, "Huron, depart."

"Taking with me nothing, wise Tamenund?" demanded the wily Magua. "The lodge of Sly Fox is empty. Let me take with me the woman who can give me children."

The aged man thought for a time; and then,

turning toward one of his companions, he asked, "Is this Mingo a chief?"

"The first in his nation."

"Woman, a great warrior takes thee as his wife. What do you wish?" the sage asked Cora.

"Better to die than to meet such a degradation!" exclaimed the horror-stricken Cora.

Turning back to Magua, the ancient man said, "Huron, her mind is with her fathers. An unwilling wife makes an unhappy lodge."

"She speaks with the tongue of her people," returned Magua. "Tamenund is just and wise. Magua should have what is his."

"Then depart with what is yours," the sage replied. "The Great Spirit forbids that a Lenape should be unjust."

Magua advanced and seized his captive strongly by the arm. The Lenape fell back in silence. Cora, aware that argument would be useless, prepared to submit to her fate without resistance.

"Wait!" cried Duncan, springing forward. "Huron, have mercy! Leave her here and you will have a ransom that will make you richer than any of your tribe has ever been. Gold, silver, gunpowder—all that a warrior needs you shall have; all that becomes the greatest chief."

"Sly Fox is strong," cried Magua, violently shaking the unresisting arm of Cora. "He has his revenge and that is enough!"

"Mighty ruler and wise chief!" Heyward said with force, turning toward the ancient man. "Can this be permitted? To you, just Tamenund, I appeal for mercy."

"The words of the Lenape are said," returned the sage, closing his eyes, and dropping back into his seat. "Men speak not twice."

"That a chief should not unsay what has been spoken is wise and reasonable," said Hawkeye, motioning to Duncan to be silent. "But it is also wise for a warrior to consider well before he makes his choice. Huron, you know that many of your people have met their fate because of me. If this war does not end soon, many more of your warriors will meet me in the woods. Consider, then, if you would not prefer to take me to your camp as a prisoner. Your people would rejoice at the sight."

"Will Long Rifle give his life for the woman?" demanded Magua, hesitating.

Seeing how eagerly the Huron responded to his proposal, the scout pulled back a little. "No, I have not said all that," Hawkeye replied. "It would be an unequal exchange, to give a warrior such as me in exchange for one who cannot fight. But, if you were to release the maiden, I would consent to go into winter quarters now and not fight again until the spring."

Magua shook his head, and made an impatient sign for the crowd to let him through.

"Well," said the scout, "I'd also be willing to give you Killdeer and to teach your warriors how to use it properly. Maybe that would make the offer more valuable to you."

Magua did not reply except to take another step through the crowd with Cora.

"What is ordered must sooner or later happen," continued Hawkeye, turning to Uncas with a sad look. "The Mingo knows his advantage and will keep it! God bless you, lad; you have found friends among your natural kin. As for me, sooner or later, I must die. A day or two will make no great difference in the everlasting reckoning of time. Tell Chingachgook I loved him well. And you, lad, you'll find the rifle in the place we hid it; take it, and keep it for my sake." Then, turning to Magua, he said, "Huron, I accept your offer; release the woman. I am your prisoner!"

Magua paused, and for an anxious moment, he seemed uncertain; then, casting his eyes on Cora, with an expression of ferocity and admiration, his purpose became fixed forever.

He showed his contempt of the offer with a backward motion of his head, and said, in a steady and settled voice, "Sly Fox is a great chief; he has but one mind." Then, laying his hand too familiarly on the shoulder of his captive to urge her forward, saying, "Come. A Huron does not waste time in idle chatter. We will go."

Cora, her dark eye kindling with contempt, said coldly to Magua, "I am your prisoner, and at a fitting time shall be ready to follow, even to my death. It will be unnecessary to drag me by the shoulder." Then, turning to Hawkeye, she said, "Generous hunter! From my soul I thank you for your kind offer. I only ask of you that you not abandon my dear sister until she and our dear father are safely back in civilization." Her voice became choked, and, for an instant, she was silent; then, advancing a step closer to Duncan, who was supporting the unconscious Alice, she continued, "I need not tell you to cherish the treasure you will possess. You love her, Heyward. Watch over her." Then Cora, brushing Alice's golden hair back, kissed her sister's forehead for a long moment. She then turned away and said to the Huron, "Now, sir, if it be your pleasure, I will follow."

As Magua turned to lead Cora away, the crowd began to part to let them through.

Duncan took a step as if to follow, but Hawkeye took his arm to stop him. "Don't follow," said the scout. "You know not the craft of the imp. He would lead you to an ambush and your death."

Before Magua and his captive had gone more than a few steps, Uncas said firmly, "Huron, the justice of the Lenape comes from the Great Spirit. Look at the sun. It is now in the upper branches of the hemlock. Your path is short and open. When the sun is seen above the trees, there will be men on your trail."

"I hear a crow!" exclaimed Magua, with a taunting laugh. "Where are the petticoats of the Lenape! Let them send their arrows and their guns to the Hurons! Dogs, rabbits, thieves—I spit on you!"

His parting insults were listened to in a dead, boding silence. With these biting words, the triumphant Magua passed unmolested into the forest, followed by his passive captive, and protected only by the sacred laws of Indian hospitality.

CHAPTER 31

Uncas kept his eyes on the disappearing form of Cora until the colors of her dress blended with the foliage of the forest. Once she was no longer in sight, he moved silently through the crowd and back to the lodge he had come from a short while before. A few warriors followed the young chief. The rest of the nation gradually dispersed.

At length, a young warrior appeared from the lodge and walked deliberately to a dwarf pine tree that grew from among some rocks in the village. He tore the bark from the trunk of the sapling. Then he removed all of the branches. Then a second warrior appeared who painted the stripped tree trunk with dark red stripes. Finally, Uncas himself appeared. Half of his face was hidden in threatening black paint.

Uncas moved with slow dignity toward the red-striped post. He slowly encircled the post and began a war chant and dance that called on the Great Spirit to aid them. Soon an admired chief of the Lenape nation followed the example of Uncas. Then, one by one, other warriors joined the chant and the dance. The spectacle became a wild frenzy as a hundred bodies swirled about the symbolic enemy. Just before the impassioned ecstasy reached its peak, Uncas plunged his tomahawk deep into the red-striped post and raised his voice in a shout that could be heard above all others. The act announced that he was the chief authority in the war party.

At that moment, a hundred warriors rushed in a frantic body onto the symbolic enemy and hacked it apart, splinter by splinter, until nothing remained but its roots in the earth.

The instant Uncas had struck the blow, he moved out of the circle and cast his eyes up to the sun. It was just rising above the branches of the hemlock, the point when the truce with Magua was to end. He announced this fact with a significant gesture and a piercing cry. Immediately the mass of warriors ended their symbolic warfare.

The whole face of the encampment was instantly changed. The warriors settled into quiet stillness, while all others in the village bustled about in energetic preparation. Tamenund held a short conversation with Uncas. When they had finished, the sage separated from the Mohican, like a reluctant parent leaving his child, and retired to his lodge. In the meantime,

Duncan saw Alice to a place of safety and then joined the scout.

Hawkeye had sent and Indian boy to get Killdeer and the rifle of Uncas. The two had hidden their guns in the woods before arriving at the Lenape encampment so that they would not be perceived as a threat when they first arrived. The scout knew that Magua would have Huron spies in the woods nearby watching the movements of their new enemies. He had therefore sent the boy, who the Hurons would not bother with. When Heyward joined the scout, the woodsman was waiting for the boy to return from his errand.

The boy had been well instructed and was crafty in carrying out his assignment. After casually crossing the clearing to the woods, he had disappeared into the foliage. Once there, he had glided like a snake to the location of the hidden weapons. In another moment he appeared flying with the velocity of an arrow across the narrow clearing that skirted the village. In each hand he proudly carried a rifle. As he crossed the clearing, a shot rang out from the woods. The boy answered it with a shout and immediately a second shot was fired at him. The next instant, he appeared before the scout with the two prizes.

As Hawkeye received the treasures from the boy, he asked if he was hurt. The youth looked up at him proudly but did not reply.

"Ah! I see, lad, the knaves have nicked your arm," said the scout, examining a deep flesh wound on the boy. "I will wrap it in a badge of wampum! You have done well, my brave boy, and are likely to bear plenty of honorable scars before you go to your grave." Then, having bound up the wound, he added, "There! Go show your friends your mark of honor. You will be a chief!"

The lad departed, proudly wearing his symbol of courage.

The shots from the forest had warned the Lenape of the position of their enemies. In response, a party was sent to dislodge the spies. The Hurons, however, had withdrawn once they had been discovered. The Lenape followed them until they were a safe distance from the camp. Both parties then hid themselves in the woods to await orders.

Meanwhile, the calm Uncas collected his chiefs and divided his power. He explained to the Lenape that Hawkeye and Duncan were each accomplished men in battle. He then put Hawkeye in charge of a group of twenty warriors. He offered Heyward a group of twenty to command as well, but the young major declined, in favor of serving as part of Hawkeye's party.

The Mohican then appointed various Indian chiefs to different positions of responsibility.

This done, he gave the word to march and was willingly obeyed by the more than two hundred warriors.

They entered the forest without incident and proceeded until they reached the line of their own scouts. Here a halt was ordered, and the chiefs were assembled to hold a "whispering council."

While they were discussing plans, a solitary individual was seen approaching hurriedly from the side of the enemy. When within a hundred yards of the cover behind which the Lenape council had assembled, the stranger halted. All eyes turned to Uncas for directions how to proceed.

"Hawkeye," said the young chief, in a low voice, "that stranger must never speak to the Hurons again."

"His time has come," said the scout, thrusting the long barrel of his rifle through the leaves, and taking fatal aim. But, instead of pulling the trigger, he lowered the muzzle again and laughed silently to himself. "Do you believe it, Uncas! It's the singer. He may be of some use to us. I'll go get him."

Hawkeye laid aside his rifle and crawled through the bushes until he was a few yards from the bewildered Gamut. He then imitated some of the singing sounds he had made when disguised as the bear. The poor fellow appeared relieved when he heard the familiar sounds. He followed the direction of the sound until he discovered the hidden scout.

"I wonder what the Hurons will think of my song!" said the scout, laughing, as he took his companion by the arm, and urged him toward the rear. "But here we are safe," he added, pointing to Uncas and his associates. "Now tell us what you know of the Mingoes' plans."

David gazed about him, at the fierce and wild-looking chiefs, in mute wonder. But he soon recovered enough to make an intelligent reply.

"The heathens are about in great numbers," said David, "and, I fear, with evil intent. There has been much howling and ungodly revelry, in their village within the past hour—so much so, in fact, that I have fled to the Lenape in search of peace."

"Where are the Hurons?" Hawkeye asked.

"The women and children have been sent to the cavern for safety. The warriors lie hidden in the forest, between this spot and their village. They are in such force, that it would be wise for you to go back."

Uncas looked at the singer and asked, "Where is Magua?"

"He is among them. He brought in the dark-haired maiden. After leaving her in the cave, he has put himself, like a raging wolf, at the head of his savages. I know not what has troubled his spirit so greatly."

"Now that we know where Cora is," interrupted Heyward, "we must try to help her."

Uncas looked at the scout and asked, "What says Hawkeye?"

"I will take my twenty men and slip around to the right, along the stream. We will go to the beaver pond where Chingachgook and the colonel are. Once we're there, I'll signal you with a whoop. Then, Uncas, you push in from this side with the rest of your warriors. Once you have driven them back to where we are, we'll surprise them from that side. That should take care of these knaves. Then we can take the village and get the woman from the cave."

After a short conference, the plan was refined. Signals for communicating were decided on and the chiefs separated, each to his appointed station.

CHAPTER 32

The woods were still. The eye could not detect anything that might disrupt the peaceful scenery of the apparently sleeping forest. A gentle breeze occasionally murmured in the green canopy overhead. Except for this, there was nothing but a deep silence. It seemed as if no human being had ever set foot in this wilderness. The vast stretch of forest that lay between the Lenape warriors and the village of the Hurons seemed an unbroken woodland fresh from the hands of the Almighty Creator.

But Hawkeye knew better than to trust the treacherous quiet of the forest. He understood his enemy too well for that. Silently, he led Duncan and the band of twenty Lenape through the trees a few hundred yards to the rear of where Uncas was dispersing his warriors. At the edge of a small brook he halted.

As the Indians gathered about him, he asked, "Do any of you men know where this stream goes?"

"A little below here, it joins a bigger stream, near the beaver pond," one of the warriors replied.

"I thought as much," the scout said. "Men, we will keep under the cover of its banks until we reach the Hurons."

As he turned to lead the party along the bed of the stream, he noticed that David Gamut had followed along with them.

"Do you know, friend," asked the scout gravely, "that we are on a dangerous mission to circle around the flank of the enemy. We will be engaged in battle within half an hour or less."

"I am aware," replied Gamut. "But I have traveled far with the young woman you are going to rescue. We have been through much evil. Although I am not a man of war, I would gladly strike a blow on her behalf."

"But you don't know how to use a gun or a knife," Hawkeye said, looking skeptically at the man.

"Even so," David replied, producing a sling from his pocket. "In my youth I practiced with this ancient instrument of war. It was good enough for the David in the Bible who killed Goliath, and it is good enough for me."

"Ay!" exclaimed Hawkeye, dubiously. "The stones from your sling won't do you much good against the rifles of the Hurons. But you may come along if you wish. We might find some use for your singing."

"I thank you, friend," returned David, supplying himself with a few small stones from the brook.

The scout pointed significantly to the still healing wound that Gamut had received on the forehead in the battle at the waterfall and said, "Remember we come to fight, not to sing. Make no noise before the fighting begins."

David nodded agreement. Hawkeye then gave the signal to proceed.

They traveled for a mile along the bed of the brook. The high banks and thick bushes along the edges protected them from being observed. But they still moved forward with great caution. Every few minutes they came to a halt and listened for hostile sounds. When they reached the larger stream, the scout stopped to take stock of the situation.

"Our cover ends here," he said to Heyward. "The beavers haven't left a tree standing in the area."

Duncan could see it for himself. Looking out over the acres of bottomland that surrounded the beaver pond, he observed only stumps and patches of moss—nothing that offered any protection from the keen eyes of their enemy.

Hawkeye was uneasy. He knew that the Huron encampment lay a short half-mile up the brook. Beyond that was the cavern where Cora was being held. He was greatly troubled at not finding the smallest trace of the presence of his enemy. As yet, there were no sounds to indicate that Uncas had engaged the Hurons at his location. There was only silence, except for the sighing of the wind that swept over the forest in gusts, threatening a coming storm. At length he determined that he had no choice other than to proceed cautiously up the stream, even though it meant leading his small band into the open. He had to risk leaving the protection of the forest if they were to reach Cora quickly.

The scout had been standing in a sheltered thicket, looking out at the treeless area in front of them. Having made his decision, he gave a low signal to his companions and pointed in the direction they must go. Silently, they fell into line behind him, like so many dark specters moving into the open ground along the beaver pond.

The party had barely cleared the cover of the thicket when a volley from a dozen rifles was heard behind them. One of the Lenape warriors leaped into the air like a wounded deer and then fell dead.

"Take cover and charge!" Hawkeye ordered.

The enemy had fallen back after their opening volley. The scout set the example of pressing on this retreat by firing his rifle and darting from tree to tree as the enemy slowly yielded ground.

The initial attack had apparently been made by a very small party of the Hurons. However, they were falling back into a larger band of warriors. The advancing Lenape found themselves facing an increasing number of foes. Before long, the contest became stationary. The combatants on both sides kept hidden behind trees, leaning out only momentarily to fire. Hawkeye saw that the situation was becoming less favorable by the minute. The Hurons were moving men out on his flank, making it more and more difficult for the Lenape to get any shots off. But retreating was even more dangerous than maintaining their ground, for it would put them back out in the open.

Just as the scout began to think the whole hostile tribe was gradually encircling them, he heard sounds of battle coming from the direction where Uncas was posted with his warriors. Immediately, the number of Hurons firing on them decreased as many of them rushed to assist their companions on the main battlefront. Clearly, they were needed, judging by the speed with which Uncas and his warriors were moving up from the valley toward the Huron village.

No longer pinned down, Hawkeye gave his men the signal to bear down on their foes. Quickly, the Lenape moved from cover to cover, closing in on the few of the enemy who remained on that front. The Hurons withdrew, moving through more open ground and into a thicket. This put the Lenape at a disadvantage, being in a more exposed position than their opponents. The contest once more became stationary.

As the exchange of shots continued, Hawkeye managed to make his way to the same tree that Heyward was using for cover.

"You are a young man, Major," the woodsman said. "What strategy would you suggest if you had a company of the Royal Americans here?"

"A bayonet charge," the soldier replied.

"There's reason in that plan," Hawkeye responded, "but you would lose some men. I don't relish a plan that will cost us a scalp or two. On the other hand, if we are to be of use to Uncas, we must get rid of these imps in the thicket in front of us."

Then, turning with an air of decision, he called aloud to his warriors. His words were answered by a shout. At a given signal, the Lenape leaped in long bounds toward the thicket. Hawkeye was in front, brandishing Killdeer and encouraging his followers by his example. Three of the Lenape fell from enemy fire. But the charge moved forward. As the Lenape swept into the thicket, there was a brief moment of hand to hand combat before the Hurons abandoned their position. They yielded ground rapidly, until they reached the opposite edge of the thicket.

Here they clung to the cover. The success of the struggle was again becoming doubtful. At this critical moment, the crack of a rifle was heard behind the Hurons. The sound came from among the beaver lodges in the clearing behind them. It was followed by the fierce yell of the war-whoop.

"Chingachgook! Now we have the imps caught between us!" Hawkeye said to himself. Then he answered the war-whoop with his own yell.

Instantly, the Hurons, knowing they could no longer hold their position in the thicket, scattered into the open as they attempted to escape. Many of them fell under the bullets and blows of the pursuing Lenape.

In a few hurried words, Hawkeye explained the situation to Chingachgook, while Duncan filled Colonel Munro in. The scout then pointed out the Sagamore to his band of Lenape warriors and gave authority over the group into the hands of the Mohican. Chingachgook led the party back through the thicket. The warriors scalped the fallen Hurons on their way.

They continued until they reached a bit of level ground that was sprinkled with enough trees to afford them cover. The ground sloped away steeply in the front. Beneath them, a narrow wooded valley stretched for several miles. It was through this dense and dark forest that

Uncas was still contending with the main body of the Hurons.

Chingachgook and his friends advanced to the brow of the hill and listened to the sounds of the raging battle hidden in the trees below.

"The fight is moving in this direction," observed Hawkeye, "but the Hurons will stay in the heavier cover of the forest below us. That will put us on their flank and in a perfect position to surprise them."

The Mohican chief nodded in agreement.

"Heyward, the colonel, the singing master, and I will drop back to the other edge of this level," the scout went on. "You can be sure, my friend, that no Huron will sneak past Killdeer to attack you and your warriors from the rear."

Hawkeye and his three companions dropped back and hid themselves, ready to stop any Huron who attempted to come around from behind. At a signal from Chingachgook, the small band of Lenape warriors hid themselves along the upper edge of the slope.

The sounds of the battle were moving rapidly closer, evidence that Uncas and his men were triumphing. It was not long before a Huron warrior appeared, here and there at the edge of the forest below. Soon they were joined by others until there was a long line of them. They were making their last stand, stubbornly clinging to the last bit of cover.

"It's time for Chingachgook's men to fire!" said the impatient Duncan.

"Not so," returned the scout. "When he knows his friends are near enough, then the Mohican will give the signal."

An instant later, the whoop was given. A dozen Hurons fell in the hale of bullets discharged by Chingachgook and his band. The cry was answered by a single war-cry from the forest and a yell passed through the air that sounded as if a thousand throats were united in a common effort. The Hurons staggered and the center of their line of men broke. Through that break, Uncas emerged from the forest with a hundred warriors close behind.

The war now divided, with both wings of the broken Hurons seeking protection in the woods again. Uncas directed his men in pursuit of the scattering enemy. Chingachgook and his warriors left their positions and descended to join in the chase. Within a minute the sounds were receding in different directions. Gradually, they lost their distinctness beneath the echoing arches of the forest.

One small knot of Hurons did not take to the forest. Instead, they were making their way sullenly up the steep slope. Magua could be clearly seen in this group. Uncas caught sight of Sly Fox. All else was forgotten. Leading the band of six or seven warriors who were still with him, he rushed toward his enemy. Sly Fox saw that Bounding Elk was headed for him. He paused with secret joy at the thought that the rashness of Uncas had put the young chief at his mercy. Just as he was savoring this moment, another shout arose. Long Rifle, followed by his three companions, was rushing to the rescue. Magua instantly turned and rapidly retreated up the hill.

Uncas, braving the dangerous gunfire from the group he pursued, continued to race up the hill moving like a bolt of lightening. Hawkeye and his companions joined in the chase. The Hurons were forced to fly. Shortly, the pursued entered the Huron village, closely followed by their pursuers.

The Hurons made a desperate stand in front of their council lodge. They fought in a fury of despair. Uncas, the half-dozen Lenape warriors, and their white companions fell on the Hurons like a whirlwind of destruction. In moments the enemy lay scattered about on the ground. Only Magua and two of his friends had managed to survive. The subtle chief raised a yell of anger and disappointment when he saw his comrades had fallen. He darted away from the place, accompanied by his two surviving friends.

Uncas bounded after him. Hawkeye, Heyward, and David followed close behind, leaving the Lenape warriors engaged in stripping the dead of the bloody trophies of their victory. Magua led the chase through a thicket of bushes and into the mouth of the cavern from which Alice had been rescued only the night before. Uncas and the others entered the long, narrow passage in time to see the retreating forms of the Hurons.

The pursuers raced through the rocky galleries and rooms, preceded by the shrieks and cries of hundreds of women and children. The place, seen by its dim and uncertain light, appeared like the depths of the infernal regions, across which unhappy ghosts and savage demons were flitting in multitudes.

Still Uncas kept his eye on Magua as he and the others chased after their enemy. But the way was becoming intricate, in those dark and gloomy passages. The glimpses of the fleeing warriors were becoming less distinct and frequent. For a moment the trace was believed to be lost, when a white robe was seen fluttering in the far end of a passage that seemed to lead up the mountain.

"It's Cora!" exclaimed Heyward, horror and delight wildly mingled in his voice.

"Cora! Cora!" echoed Uncas, bounding forward like a deer.

This glimpse of the captive encouraged them to continue the chase with renewed energy. But the way was rugged, broken, and in spots nearly impassable. Uncas abandoned his rifle and leaped forward with uncontrollable force. Heyward rashly imitated his example. A flash of light and a deafening explosion rolled down the passage in the rocks. The bullet slightly wounded the young Mohican chief.

"We must close in on them quickly before they have time to pick us off!" the scout said as he leaped past his two friends. "They are using Cora to shield themselves from Killdeer!"

They got close to see that Magua was leading the way while his two warriors dragged Cora along behind them. At this moment the forms of all four were strongly drawn against an opening onto the sky, and they disappeared. Nearly frantic with disappointment, Uncas and Heyward raced on toward the opening; a moment later they emerged from the cavern on the side of the mountain. They were in time to catch a glimpse of the pursued, who were continuing up the mountain by a hazardous and steep route.

His progress slowed by his rifle, Hawkeye emerged from the cave a few seconds later, in time to see his two companions continuing their impetuous pursuit. The two hurtled over rocks and crags that would have seemed insurmountable under ordinary circumstances. However, because Cora slowed the progress of the Hurons, the fugitives were losing ground in the race.

"Stop, you Huron dogs," called Uncas, shaking his bright tomahawk at Magua.

"I will go no further!" cried Cora, stopping unexpectedly. She was standing on a ledge of rock that overhung a deep chasm, near the summit of the mountain. "Kill me if you will, detestable Huron; I will go no further!"

The two Huron warriors raised their tomahawks with delight, but Magua wrested the weapons from their hands. The Huron chief, after casting the weapons over the edge of the cliff, drew his knife. He turned to his captive with a look filled with conflicting passions.

"Woman," he said, "choose; the lodge or the knife of Sly Fox!"

Cora did not look at him. Dropping on her knees, she raised her eyes toward the heavens and said, "I am yours. Do with me as you see best!"

"Woman," repeated Magua, hoarsely, and hopelessly attempting to catch a glance from her calm and shining eye, "choose!"

Cora did not respond. The form of the Huron trembled in every fiber. He raised his arm on high, but dropped it again with a bewildered air, like one who doubted. Once more he struggled with himself and lifted the shining weapon again. But just then a piercing cry was heard above them. Uncas appeared, leaping frantically, from a fearful height, down toward

the ledge. Magua took a step backwards. As he did, one of the Huron warriors took advantage of the moment and plunged his own knife into the heart of Cora.

Magua sprang like a savage beast after the retreating murderer. But the falling form of Uncas separated the unnatural combatants. Diverted by this interruption and maddened by the murder he had just witnessed, Magua buried his knife deep in the back of the Mohican chief who lay face down before him. At the same moment he uttered an unearthly shout.

But Uncas arose from the attack and, raising his tomahawk, struck a powerful blow on the head of the murderer of Cora. The Huron sank to the ground. The Mohican's effort took the last of his failing strength. With a stern and steady look, he turned to Sly Fox. The expression in his eye reflected all that he would do if his strength had not deserted him. Magua seized the arm of the unresisting Mohican and passed his knife into his chest. Three times he repeated this action before his victim, still keeping his gaze riveted on his enemy with a look of inextinguishable scorn, fell dead at his feet.

"Mercy! Mercy! Huron," cried Heyward, from above, in tones nearly choked by horror. "Give mercy, and you shall receive it!"

The victorious Magua whirled his bloody knife up at the imploring youth. As he did so, he uttered a cry so fierce, so wild, and yet so joyous, that it conveyed the sounds of savage triumph to the ears of those who fought in the valley, a thousand feet below. He was answered by a shout from the scout who was moving swiftly toward him. The woodsman raced across the dangerous crags with steps as bold and reckless as if he possessed the power to move in air. But when the hunter reached the scene of the ruthless massacre, the ledge contained only the dead.

He glanced at the victims. He then looked up at the difficulties of the climb in front of him. He saw a form on the brow of the mountain, at the very edge of the height above him. The figure stood with arms raised in a menacing manner. Without stopping to think, Hawkeye raised

Killdeer. Before the scout had time to shoot, the figure hurled a rock down onto the head of the remaining Huron warrior, killing him. Hawkeye could now see the indignant and glowing face of Gamut on the brow of the mountain; his sling hung from his hand.

Magua appeared from a gap in the rocks and stepped with calm indifference over the body of the last of his associates. He then leaped a wide fissure and ascended the rocks at a place where the arm of David could not reach him. He was at a point where a single bound would carry him to the brow of the cliff and assure his safety. Before taking the leap, however, the Huron paused, and shaking his hand at the scout, he shouted: "The pale faces are dogs! The Lenape women! Magua leaves them on the rocks for the crows to eat!"

Laughing hoarsely, he made a desperate leap. He fell short of his mark, but his hands grasped a shrub on the ledge. The form of Hawkeye had crouched like a beast about to take its spring, and his frame trembled so violently with eagerness that the muzzle of the half-raised rifle played like a leaf fluttering in the wind.

Magua, hanging onto the shrub, let his body stretch out full length. His feet found a small outcropping to rest on. Then, summoning all his powers, he renewed the attempt to pull himself to safety. He succeeded in drawing his knees up onto the edge of the mountain.

It was now, when the body of his enemy was most collected together, that the agitated weapon of the scout was drawn to his shoulder. The surrounding rocks themselves were not steadier than Killdeer became for the single instant that it poured out its contents.

The arms of the Huron relaxed, and his body fell back a little, while his knees still kept their position. Turning a relentless look on his enemy, he shook a hand in grim defiance. But his hold loosened. For a fleeting instant his body was seen plunging head downward. Then it glided past the fringe of shrubbery that clung to the mountain and its rapid flight to destruction was lost from sight.

CHAPTER 33

The sun rose the next morning on a mourning nation of Lenape. The battle was over. They had avenged their recent quarrel with the Hurons through the destruction of the whole community. The encampment was a black and murky ruin. Hundreds of ravens settled in noisy flocks across the wide ranges of the woods, grim and squawking reminders of the places where the fallen Huron warriors lay.

No shouts of success, no songs of triumph were heard. Pride and exultation were replaced by humility. Fierce passions of war were replaced by deep demonstrations of grief.

The lodges were deserted. Every living being in the community encircled a spot beside the village. This human wall stood united in silence. Every eye was riveted on the center of the circle. At that center were the objects that united them in their mourning.

Six Lenape girls stood around a litter of fragrant plants. From time to time, one or another of them would scatter sweet-scented herbs and forest flowers over the litter. Resting on the litter was the body of the once vibrant and generous Cora. She was wrapped completely in Indian robes, her face hidden forever from the gaze of living beings.

At her feet sat the desolate Munro. His head was bowed in sorrow but a hidden anguish struggled on his lined forehead. Gamut stood beside him, his wandering and concerned eyes looking now at the grieving father and now at his book in search of some consoling words to offer. On the other side of the aged man stood Heyward, striving to keep subdued those sudden waves of sorrow that threatened to sweep over him.

Also in the center of the circle, next to this sad and melancholy group was an even more touching picture. Seated, as in life, in serious composure, was Uncas. He was dressed in the most gorgeous ornaments that the wealth of the tribe could supply. Rich plumes nodded above his head; bracelets and medals adorned his neck and arms. But his dull eye and vacant expression contradicted the pride of these decorations of honor.

Directly in front of the corpse sat Chingachgook. He carried no weapons, he wore no paint, he bore no ornaments. The Mohican warrior kept a riveted and intense gaze on the cold and senseless face of his son. The two figures were so motionless that a stranger might not have told the living from the dead, except for the occasional glimmer of emotion in one of the faces. The scout stood nearby, leaning thoughtfully on his rifle as he studied the scene.

Tamenund, surrounded by the elders of the nation, sat on a raised spot, looking down on the silent and sorrowful assembly of his people.

At the edge of the circle stood a young French officer. Behind him was a small group of Canadian soldiers. They seemed prepared to take some distant journey. But at the moment, their errand of peace had to be deferred. He and those with him stood as silent and sad spectators of the outcome of contest they had arrived too late to prevent.

From dawn until the sun was a quarter of the way across the sky, the circle stood in silence. Except for an occasional offering to commemorate the dead, no one moved.

At length, the sage of the Lenape rose to his feet, supporting himself on the shoulders of his attendants. He seemed to have aged even more since his appearance before his nation the previous day.

"Men of the Lenape nation," he said, in low, hollow tones, "the face of the Great Spirit is behind a cloud! His eye is turned from you; His ears are shut; His tongue gives no answer. You see him not; yet His judgments are before you. Let your hearts be open and your spirits tell no lie."

A deep stillness filled with awe fell on the assembly. It was as if the simple yet powerful statement had been made by the Great Spirit Himself. Gradually, this stillness gave way to a low murmur of voices. The women began a sort of chant in honor of the dead. For a time there was only one voice; then another voice would pick up the lamentation and while the previous voice faded; then there would be an outburst of many voices, all giving sound to the sorrow that pervaded the scene. Some of the words mourned the loss of the young woman. Others spoke of the young Mohican as one whose eye was brighter than a star in the dark night, whose voice, in battle, was as loud as the thunder of the Great Spirit. Some spoke of the mother who bore him, saying that she was blessed to have had such a child.

Then the voices went on to remind the Mohican chief of the stranger maiden whose death had almost coincided with his. Surely, this was a sign from the Great Spirit and should not be ignored. They reminded him of her matchless beauty and her noble resolution and asked him to be kind to her in the spirit world.

Next the voices sang to the maiden herself in the soft language of tenderness and love. They urged her to be of cheerful mind and to fear nothing for her future welfare. A hunter and warrior would be her companion and protector.

They promised that her path should be pleasant, and her burden light. They assured her that the blessed hunting grounds of the Lenape were as pleasant and pure and sweet as the heaven of the pale faces. They asked that she be attentive to the wants of the companion that the Great Spirit had linked her to. They reminded her that her companion was noble and generous and all that a maid might love. They said she was of a blood purer and richer than the rest of her nation; that she had proved herself equal to the dangers of life in the wilderness; and that now she was in a place where she and her warrior could be forever happy.

The voices then made a transition and sang of the maiden who wept in the nearby lodge. They spoke of her golden hair and compared her eye to the blue of the heavens. They urged her to be strong in sorrow.

As the voices of the women sang these prayer-like chants, the Lenape warriors listened like charmed men. Their responses to the music made the true depth of their sympathy evident. Even David, though he could not understand the words, was enthralled by this strange and haunting music.

The scout was the only one of the white men who understood the words. He turned his head a little to catch the meaning. But when the voices sang of the future of Cora and Uncas together, he shook his head a little, as if registering the error of this simple creed.

Only Chingachgook seemed unchanged by the song. He did not move a muscle. It was as if all his senses except for his sight were frozen. For him, only the cold and senseless remains of his son existed. His eyes were taking their final gaze at those features he had so long loved and which were now about to be hidden forever from his view.

When the song was concluded, silence again fell over the assembly. Then, one by one, each of the most respected and most honored warriors of the nation stepped forward. Each addressed the unhearing Uncas directly in speech or song. All praised his honor and glory and valor. And all spoke of the sorrow that his death cast into their hearts. After the last of these men spoke, another deep silence fell on the place.

Out of this silence a low, deep sound was heard. The sound grew and captured the ear of every living being in the circle. It was Chingachgook's song of mourning. The sounds then became fainter and more trembling, as if borne away by a passing breath of wind. The lips of the Sagamore closed, and he remained silent and motionless in his seat, his eye riveted his son.

One of the elder chiefs gave a signal to the women who crowded that part of the circle near the body of Cora. The six girls raised the bier to the elevation of their heads. Then they moved forward with slow and regulated steps, chanting a song of mourning.

Gamut bent his head over the shoulder of Munro, who remained seated as one in a trance. The singing master whispered gently, "They move with the remains of thy child; shall we not follow, and see them interred with Christian burial?"

Munro started and glanced anxiously around him. He then arose and followed with the dignity of a soldier but also with the suffering of a parent. His friends gathered close and walked with him, sharing his sorrow. Even the young French soldier joined the procession with the air of a man who was moved by this death. Once the last women had left in the procession, the men of the Lenape nation closed the circle again around the body of Uncas.

The place that had been chosen for the grave of Cora was a small hill. There a cluster of young pines had taken root, forming a melancholy shade over the spot. On reaching the place, the girls set down their burden. They waited for an indication that the arrangements were satisfactory to the father.

At length the scout, understanding their customs, said, in their own language, "My daughters have done well; the white men thank them."

The girls proceeded to deposit the body in a shell made of the bark of the birch; then they lowered it into its dark and final abode. They covered the remains and concealed the signs of the fresh earth with leaves.

Once this part of the ceremony was completed, the scout said to them, "My young women have done enough. The spirit of the pale face has no need of food or clothing, as is your custom." Then glancing at David, who was preparing to sing a hymn, he continued, "I see that one who better knows the Christian customs is about to speak."

The six young women stepped aside. As David poured out his pious feelings in the song, they listened respectfully. It seemed almost as if they understood the meaning of the strange words and the feelings of sorrow and hope that the words were intended to convey.

When the song ended, silence fell over the group once more. Munro understood that he was now expected to speak to the assembly. Turning to the scout, he said, "Say to these kind and gentle women that a heartbroken and failing man gives them his thanks. Tell them that the Being we all worship, under different names, will recognize their kindness; and that the time shall not be distant when we may assemble around His throne without distinction of sex, or rank, or color."

The scout listened to the trembling voice in which the veteran delivered these words. Then he shook his head slowly, as one who doubted their effectiveness.

"To tell them this" he said, "would be to tell them that the snows do not come in the winter." He turned to the women and told them of the father's gratitude for what they had done.

Munro was sinking again into melancholy when the young French officer touched him lightly on the elbow. He directed the old man's attention to a group of young Indians. They were approaching and they were carrying a covered litter. Then the young officer pointed toward the sun.

"Yes, I understand you, sir. It is time to go," said Munro, with forced firmness. "It is the will of Heaven, and I submit to it. Cora, my child! If the prayers of a heartbroken father could help you now, how blessed you would be!" Then, looking about with an air of composure that ill concealed his anguish, he said, "Come, gentlemen. Our duty here is ended; let us depart."

Heyward gladly obeyed the call. He was ready to leave this spot where, every moment, he felt as if his self-control was about to desert him. As the others were mounting their horses, he grasped the hand of the scout. He asked for and received the promise that they would soon meet again within the posts of the British army. Throwing himself into the saddle, he spurred his horse to the side of the litter. From within it he heard the low and stifled sobs of Alice.

Munro, followed by Heyward and David and attended by the French officer with his guard, turned his horse south and rode slowly away. In a few moments, all of the white men except for Hawkeye disappeared from before the eyes of the Lenape and were buried in the vast forests of that wilderness.

But the bond of the common calamity shared with these white visitors was so strong that it was not easily broken. For years to come the tale of the white maiden and the young warrior of the Mohicans was told around the night fires. And news of what became of the visitors was carried to them by the scout. They learned that the "Gray Head" was soon gathered to his fathers, borne down by his sorrow. And the young major took the surviving daughter far into the settlements of the pale faces. There, she eventually overcame her tears and replaced them with bright smiles that suited her joyous nature.

But these events were in the future. Once the procession was lost from sight in the forest, Hawkeye returned to the ceremonies surrounding his young friend. He was just in time to catch a parting look at the features of Uncas. The Lenape were enclosing the body in its last clothing of skins. They paused to permit the woodsman to gaze once more upon young chief's face. When he had done so, the body was wrapped, never to be uncovered again.

A solemn procession of the whole nation moved silently to the temporary grave of the chief—temporary because at some future day, his bones should rest among those of his own people.

The body was laid to rest in the grave. It was positioned to face the rising sun. The implements of war and of the chase placed beside it, in readiness for the final journey. The remains were covered and the fresh dirt concealed to protect the site from the ravages of the beasts of prey.

In the silence that followed, it was time for Chingachgook to speak. The stern and self-restrained warrior raised his face and looked about him with a steady eye.

"Why do my brothers mourn?" he said. "Why do my daughters weep? Because a young man has gone to the happy hunting grounds? Because a chief has filled his time with honor? He was good; he was dutiful; he was brave. Who can deny it? The Great Spirit had need of such a warrior, and He has called him away. As for me, the son and the father of great chiefs, I continue to stand like a lone pine tree in a clearing of the pale faces. My race has gone from the shores of the great salt water and the hills of the Lenape. But who can say that the serpent of his tribe has forgotten his wisdom? I am alone—"

"No," cried Hawkeye, who had been gazing at his friend, "no, Sagamore, not alone. The gifts of our colors may be different, but God has so placed us as to journey in the same path. I have no kin, and, like you, no people. He was your son. But I can never forget the lad who has so often fought at my side in war and slept at my side in peace. And if I do, may He who made us all, whatever our color or our gifts, forget me! The boy has left us for a time; but, Sagamore, you are not alone."

Chingachgook grasped the hand that the scout had stretched across the fresh earth. In an attitude of friendship these two sturdy and intrepid woodsmen bowed their heads together. Scalding tears fell to their feet, watering the grave of Uncas like drops of falling rain.

This burst of feeling from the two most renowned warriors of that region was followed by an awed silence. Out of this silence, Tamenund lifted his voice to disperse the multitude.

"It is enough," he said. "Go, children of the Lenape, the anger of the Great Spirit is not done. Why should Tamenund stay? The pale faces are masters of the earth, and the time of the red men has not yet come again. My day has been too long. In the morning I saw the sons of the Tortoise happy and strong; and yet, before the night has come, have I lived to see the last warrior of the wise race of the Mohicans."

AFTERWORD

ABOUT THE AUTHOR

You never know where the twists and turns in life's path will lead. James Fenimore Cooper did not write his first book until he was thirty years old. Before that, he apparently did not like to write—not even letters to friends and family, let alone books. But by the time he died at the age of sixty-two, he had written approximately four *dozen* books, most of them novels. In addition, he had earned an international reputation as America's "national novelist." No one who knew him before he began writing could have guessed how his life would turn out.

Not a lot is known about Cooper's life. In part, Cooper himself is responsible for this. When he was on his deathbed, he made his family promise that they would not authorize anyone to write the story of his life. Therefore, no complete biography about this famous author was written, even though he had been a very popular writer.

Cooper was born on September 15, 1789 in Burlington, New Jersey. His family moved to upstate New York when he was a year old. His father purchased a large tract of land near Otsego Lake, moved the family there, and founded the village of Cooperstown.

It is hard to imagine that this present day home of the Baseball Hall of Fame was once a frontier village in the wilderness. It may help if we think about how young the United States was at this time. The Declaration of Independence was written only fourteen years before the family moved. The Revolutionary War that freed the country from England had ended only six years before Cooper's birth. We can guess that Cooper spent some of his youth playing in and exploring the wilderness around Cooperstown. Cooper's experience growing up in a frontier town gave him many of the ideas for the settings and events in the novels he wrote years later.

At the age of eleven he was sent to a small boarding school in Albany, New York. Two years later, at the age of thirteen, he went on to Yale College (now Yale University). Apparently, he enjoyed playing pranks but sometimes went too far. He never graduated from Yale; he was expelled in his third year for one of his pranks.

There is some evidence that it may have involved blowing up the door to another student's room in the dormitory. Or, he may have been expelled because he trained a donkey to sit in the chair of one of his professors. In any case, he was asked to leave in his third year.

So at the age of sixteen he ran away to sea. His experiences as a sailor gave him additional material to eventually write about. Several of his novels are sea stories. A year or so later, his father caught up with him and got him a commission in the United States Navy. For part of the time he was in the Navy, he was stationed at a frontier outpost on Lake Ontario. This experience added to his store of material for his novels about the American frontier. His time in the Navy may also have been the inspiration for a book he wrote twenty years later entitled *History of the Navy of the United States of America*. But, at the time, he probably did not imagine that he would someday use these experiences in books that would make him the most popular author of his time. That part of his life was still more than ten years in the future.

During his last year in the Navy, he worked as a recruiter in New York City. While he was there, he met Susan De Lancey. Late in 1810, he resigned his commission and, on New Year's Day of 1811, he married Susan. The marriage seems to have been a happy one. Ultimately, he and Susan had four daughters and a son. Two other children died before the age of two.

Cooper had a good bit of experience dealing with the death of loved ones by the time he became a writer. He was the eleventh of twelve children. Five of his brothers and sisters died in infancy. A beloved older sister, Hannah, lived to the age of twenty-three, when she died in a fall from a horse. Cooper was eleven at the time. When Cooper was twenty, his father unexpectedly died. Over the next ten years, his four older brothers and his mother died. So, by the time he was thirty years old, he had lost both parents and all but one of his eleven brothers and sisters. Only his sister Anne, who was five years older than he was, outlived him.

When his father died, he left a fairly large estate. It seems as if Cooper lived as a gentleman farmer over the next ten years. But apparently, he ran into financial difficulties. The country's economy fell apart after the War of 1812 and there was a depression. As a result, the value of the estate left by his father was significantly reduced. In addition, the deaths of Cooper's four brothers during that decade left him with many debts and many family responsibilities. He needed to find a way to earn money, but he was not well prepared to do so. He had been raised as the son of a wealthy man and did not know how to be anything more than a country gentleman.

We do not know for certain what made him turn to writing, but it is clear that becoming a writer solved his financial problems. It is possible that he wrote his first novel on a sort of dare. There is a family story, reported by his eldest daughter, that suggests this. According to the story, the family would sit around reading aloud in the evenings. One evening, he was reading a new English novel to his wife, who was not feeling well. After a couple of chapters, he threw the book aside, stating that he could write a better book than that. His wife, Susan, laughed at the idea. It seemed absurd to her that he would ever write a book since he didn't even like to write letters to friends and family. Supposedly, Cooper took up the challenge. For whatever reason, he wrote his first novel, *Precaution*, in 1820.

Precaution was modeled on the popular English novels of the period. It is set in England and the characters are British. Although the book was not a great success, it was well enough received that he tried writing a second novel. This book, called *The Spy*, came out in 1821. It is a much more important book in two ways. First, it is set during the American Revolution; it was one of the first pieces of fiction by an American author to use a uniquely American setting and to begin to establish a truly American literature. Second, it quickly became a very popular book and in this way helped establish

Cooper as one of the important writers—and the most important novelist—of his time. Over the next thirty years, he wrote thirty-one more novels, as well as more than a dozen works of non-fiction.

Cooper seems to have been bursting with ideas. Some of his books were travel books, based on the seven years he spent in Europe with his family between 1826 and 1833. Others were historical books. Still others were commentaries on American democracy and American society. But the majority of the books, like *The Last of the Mohicans,* were novels. And it is these novels that made him an immensely popular writer in the United States and in Europe.

But it was not Cooper's international popularity that made people consider him America's "national novelist." It was the things he wrote about and the characters he created that won him this distinction. In part it was his use of the American frontier as settings for many of his novels. He also used many uniquely American events such as the French and Indian War and the American Revolution as the background for his books. And he frequently included Native American characters in his stories.

Especially important in earning Cooper his reputation was his invention of the mythic frontier character of Natty Bumppo. Natty is a frontiersman who exists between the world of the white European settlers and the world of the Native Americans. He disapproves of the selfish exploitation of nature that the white man practices. He prefers the appreciation for nature shown by the Native Americans. He is loyal and courageous and his skill as a marksman is legendary.

In *The Last of the Mohicans* Natty is usually referred to as Hawkeye or Long Rifle and is presented as a man a little under forty years of age. But Cooper had first introduced this character in a novel he wrote three years earlier called *The Pioneers*. In *The Pioneers*, Natty is a man in his early seventies. His close friend Chingachgook also appears (and dies) in that novel. When Cooper first created the character, he had not planned to use him in other books. But, over a period of eighteen years, he ended up writing five novels about Natty. Together, these five books are known as the *Leatherstocking Tales*. They cover various parts of Natty Bumppo's life from the age of about twenty-three until his death at the age of about eighty-three.

Cooper was raised to be a country gentleman. But he ended up inventing a legendary frontiersman and writing stirring tales of adventure set in the wilderness and on the sea. He was also a man who didn't even like to write letters during the first thirty years of his life. But he ended up writing almost fifty books during the last thirty-two years of his life. That is about one book every eight months. You never know where life's path will lead you. And you never know how the experiences you have today will fit into your life tomorrow.

ABOUT THE BOOK

The Last of the Mohicans was written in 1826. Even though the book is more than 175 years old, it still works today as an exciting adventure story. Look at the ingredients. The setting is the dangerous wilderness forests of frontier America. The French army is invading. There are rumors of savage attacks on settlers by the Hurons. Enemies are lurking everywhere. Every major character—Hawkeye, Chingachgook, Heyward, Uncas, Alice, Cora, Magua, and even David Gamut—narrowly escapes death at least once during the novel. Many of them have more than one close call. There is a frontier super-hero—the honest and courageous Long Rifle, the legendary marksman who is honored by his friends and feared by his enemies. There is a wilderness super-villain—the evil and deceptive Magua, the outcast who will stop at nothing to get revenge on his enemies. There are kidnappings, desperate escapes, wild chases, and violent battles. There are characters who disguise themselves and deceptions at every turn. There is the love interest between Duncan and Alice, destined to end in happiness. And there is the love interest between Uncas and Cora, destined to end in tragedy. In short, there are plenty of elements to keep a reader involved in the plot.

But James Fenimore Cooper was a man of many ideas. He wanted to do more than write a story that would just hold the reader's attention with its hair-raising adventures. And many of Cooper's ideas are still important today, more than 150 years after his death. What are some of those ideas? And how does Cooper communicate them to us?

These days, we often hear that the white European settlers who first came to America mistreated and deceived the Native Americans. But this is not a new concept. It is one of the ideas that Cooper presents throughout *The Last of the Mohicans*. It first shows up in Chapter 3, when Hawkeye asks Chingachgook to explain the story of his people. The Sagamore seems saddened by the way his people have been ruined and driven from their land. Chingachgook tells his white friend:

> My fathers had made peace with the red men around them. Then . . . we were one people, and we were happy. The great salt water gave us its fish, the wood its deer, and the air its birds. . . . The first pale faces who came among us spoke no

English. The Dutch landed and gave my people the firewater; they drank until the heavens and the earth seemed to meet, and they foolishly thought they had found the Great Spirit. Then my people parted with their land. Foot by foot, they were driven back from the shores.

Later in the book, the ancient and wise Tamenund not only describes the mistreatment at the hands of the Europeans but also emphasizes how much the white settlers look down on the Native Americans. Even the worst white man, he says, is thought to be better than the best Native American. In Chapter 29 he says, "I know that the pale faces are a proud and hungry race. I know that they claim not only to have the earth, but also that the least worthy among them is better than the wisest red man."

But Cooper does not just leave it up to the Native American characters to point out these injustices. Early in Chapter 3 Hawkeye tells Chingachgook that he disagrees with many of the things that the European settlers do. He then goes on to condemn the manner in which they attempt to hide the past so that it will be forgotten. He says:

My people have many ways which, as an honest man, I can't approve of. It is one of their customs to write in books what they have done and seen. In books, it is possible to hide the truth and to ignore misdeeds that occurred in the past. As a result, a man may never hear of the wrongs done by his fathers, nor feel a pride in working to make up for them.

Later in the book, Cora, when arguing with Magua, acknowledges that wrongs have occurred when she talks about the "thoughtless and unprincipled men" who did these things. And near the end of the novel, when she is urging Tamenund not to execute Hawkeye and Heyward, we are told that she feels great "sorrow at misdeeds of the white man."

Cooper has characters comment on the problem several times throughout the book. And at no point does he present a character who defends the encroachment of the Europeans on the wilderness of the Native Americans. In these ways, Cooper shows us where he stands on this matter. This is an issue that is still discussed 175 years after Cooper talked about it.

But Cooper does not just point out the problem of people mistreating one another. He also suggests a way that two races might be able to appreciate one another and live in harmony. He does this by showing us a response that he says will *not* work and a response that he believes *will* work.

The response that Cooper feels does not work is presented through Colonel Munro. The view he presents is that we are all equal in the eyes of God. After Cora's funeral, Munro asks

Hawkeye to tell the Lenape women "that the Being we all worship, under different names, will recognize their kindness; and that the time shall not be distant when we may assemble around His throne without distinction of sex, or rank, or color." Munro suggests that God is colorblind. But there is a problem in this view. Munro believes that they will all gather around the throne of *his* God and that *his* God will not notice their color, rank, or sex. The Colonel's view is one-sided. It does not take into account what the Lenape may believe.

Hawkeye seems to recognize the problem. He protects the Lenape women from Munro's one-sided views. In response to the Colonel's comment about them all gathering around the throne of God together, Hawkeye says that he might as well tell the Lenape women "that the snows do not come in the winter." He then merely thanks the women for their kindness, skipping the rest of Munro's comments.

Cooper does suggest, however, that there is another way that people can live in harmony. He presents this idea through the words and actions of Hawkeye. The first hint comes in Chapter 5, when the scout is talking with David Gamut. In that conversation, he learns that David is a singing master and that he cannot do any of the things that Hawkeye values (such as shooting, or mapping the wilderness or carrying messages for the army). He thinks David's occupation is a "strange" one, but goes on to say, "Well, my friend, I suppose it is your gift and mustn't be denied any more than if it were shooting or something else." He suggests the importance of respecting each person for his or her own qualities, even if the qualities are out of keeping with one's own ways.

Later in the book Hawkeye makes an even stronger statement of his belief in recognizing the gifts of others. This statement comes when David says he will take the place of Uncas so that the Mohican can escape from the Huron village. At this point Hawkeye truly begins to appreciate David's strengths. Then David says that, if he is killed, the scout should forgive the killers and not seek revenge. Hawkeye genuinely acknowledges the singing master's gifts as he says, "I do not believe your way of life is wrong, when all is considered. Much depends on the natural gifts of a man. Each must take the path that life leads him down."

At the very end of the novel, Cooper shows us how acknowledging and respecting the gifts of others can create a true bond between people. Chingachgook, standing over the grave of his son, says that he is now alone. Hawkeye interrupts him, crying out,

> No, Sagamore, not alone. The gifts of our colors may be different, but God has so placed

us as to journey in the same path. I have no kin, and, like you, no people. He was your son. But I can never forget the lad who has so often fought at my side in war and slept at my side in peace. And if I do, may He who made us all, whatever our color or our gifts, forget me! The boy has left us for a time; but, Sagamore, you are not alone.

Hawkeye does not see God as one who is colorblind or one who sees all people as the same. That is Munro's God. Hawkeye believes in a God who gave people *different* colors and *different* gifts. In order for people to live in harmony and brotherhood, they must recognize and appreciate the differences between people and between races. Only then can a bond of true friendship be created.

Cooper's point raises questions that we still must ask ourselves today. What is the best way for people to live with one another? Should we try to have everyone fit into our image? Should we appreciate the gifts of everyone else and honor those gifts? And how should others treat us? Should they try to make us fit into their image? Or should they honor us for our gifts? In *The Last of the Mohicans* Cooper gives us his answer to these questions.